RULES FOR PROPER PRINCESS IMPERSONATION

1) When approached by a perfect stranger offering you the opportunity to live in a castle and act like a princess, be sure your best friend can accompany you…so you don't have to sit through all those state dinners alone.

2) Remember, Prince Charmings don't marry commoners. Agree to stand in for the princess during her engagement to the prince-next-door *only* if you're guaranteed not to fall in love with him.…

3) Don't be kind, considerate and gentle if the princess you're impersonating is known to be none of these things. It will make your intended think that he's getting the woman of his dreams.…

4) When your prince discovers that you're not the princess he thought you were, make sure he realizes that you *are* the princess he wants!

Dear Reader,

Fall is to be savored for all its breathtaking glory—and a spectacular October lineup awaits at Special Edition!

For years, readers have treasured Tracy Sinclair's captivating romances…and October commemorates her fiftieth Silhouette book! To help celebrate this wonderful author's crowning achievement, be sure to check out *The Princess Gets Engaged*— an enthralling romance that finds American tourist Megan Delaney in a royal mess when she masquerades as a princess and falls hopelessly in love with the charming Prince Nicholas.

This month's THAT'S MY BABY! title is by Lois Faye Dyer. *He's Got His Daddy's Eyes* is a poignant reunion story about hope, the enduring power of love and how one little boy works wonders on two broken hearts.

Nonstop romance continues as three veteran authors deliver enchanting stories. Check out award-winning author Marie Ferrarella's adorable tale about mismatched lovers when a blue-blooded heroine hastily marries a blue-collar carpenter in *Wanted: Husband, Will Train.* And what's an amnesiac triplet to do when she washes up on shore and right into the arms of a brooding billionaire? Find out in *The Mysterious Stranger,* when Susan Mallery's engaging TRIPLE TROUBLE series splashes to a finish! Reader favorite Arlene James serves up a tender story about unexpected love in *The Knight, The Waitress and the Toddler*— book four in our FROM BUD TO BLOSSOM promo series.

Finally, October's WOMAN TO WATCH is debut author Lisette Belisle, who unfolds an endearing romance between an innocent country girl and a gruff drifter in *Just Jessie.*

I hope you enjoy these books, and all of the stories to come!

Sincerely,

Tara Gavin, Senior Editor

Please address questions and book requests to:
Silhouette Reader Service
U.S.: 3010 Walden Ave., P.O. Box 1325, Buffalo, NY 14269
Canadian: P.O. Box 609, Fort Erie, Ont. L2A 5X3

TRACY SINCLAIR
THE PRINCESS GETS ENGAGED

SPECIAL EDITION®

Published by Silhouette Books
America's Publisher of Contemporary Romance

SILHOUETTE BOOKS

ISBN 0-373-24133-X

THE PRINCESS GETS ENGAGED

Books by Tracy Sinclair

TRACY SINCLAIR

began her career as a photojournalist for national magazines and newspapers. Extensive travel all over the world has provided this California resident with countless fascinating experiences, settings and acquaintances to draw on in plotting her romances. After writing fifty novels for Silhouette, she still has stories she can't wait to tell.

A NOTE FROM THE AUTHOR

Dear Readers,

This is a very special book for me, and I hope it will be for you, too. It's my fiftieth romantic novel for Silhouette, marking a golden anniversary that I invite everyone to share with me. There wouldn't be anything to celebrate without all of you.

I want to take this opportunity to thank the many readers from all over the world who have written to tell me they enjoyed my books. The language of love is truly universal.

I'm sure I won't ever lose my enthusiasm for romance novels and I hope you won't, either, because I have so many more stories to tell. I sincerely hope they'll continue to please you.

With all best wishes,

Tracy Sinclair

Chapter One

"Can you believe it? Tomorrow at this time we'll be sunning ourselves on the Riviera!" Megan Delaney's blue eyes sparkled with anticipation as she closed her suitcase. "This is going to be our best vacation ever. The whole country of Beaumarre will be celebrating the engagement of Princess Gabrielle, and we'll be there to see all the excitement."

"I hope we catch a glimpse of her," Megan's friend and roommate, Carrie Tolliver, remarked. "They say the royals drive themselves around town and shop in local stores like normal citizens."

"I guess that's because Beaumarre is such a small country. The people feel they really know their royal family."

"The rest of the world does, too, thanks to Gabrielle." Carrie grinned. "What will the tabloids do without her? They have her involved with a new celebrity every week. I wonder if she'll be satisfied with just one man."

"Are you kidding? Prince Nicholas is gorgeous! I was always partial to that lean, dangerous-looking type."

"I don't know about dangerous, but he's certainly athletic—if he's hopped in and out of as many beds as the tabloids say. The prince has had his share of publicity, too."

"Those scruffy papers always exaggerate things. I doubt that he's as promiscuous as their stories make out," Megan said dismissively. "Naturally he dates a lot, and it's easy to see why all the women are wild about him. Who wouldn't be? He's dreamy looking—in addition to being the heir apparent to the throne of Grandalia. Prince Nicholas is the most eligible bachelor in Europe."

"He and Princess Gabrielle will make a stunning couple," Carrie admitted.

"I can't wait to see them together." Megan sighed happily. "Wasn't it nice of Ambassador Hayes to get us tickets to the engagement ball? They must be awfully hard to come by."

Megan and Carrie were translators at the United Nations in New York City. It was stimulating work, and since both women were fluent in several languages, they got to meet interesting people from all over the world. When either of them traveled to foreign countries, they were often given extra little courtesies without even asking for them.

"I suppose the ambassador and his wife will be at the engagement party, too," Carrie remarked. "Maybe he'll introduce us to the princess. Do Americans have to curtsy?"

"I don't know," Megan answered. "But I'm more interested in meeting the prince."

"What good will it do you? He won't have eyes for anyone but the princess. She's pretty spectacular, too."

"Big deal. Take away that long, silky blond hair, big blue eyes and gorgeous figure, and what do you have?" Megan joked.

"Us!" Carrie laughed.

"We might not be princesses, but we get our share of guys," Megan protested.

That was an understatement. Both women had more dates than they could handle. Megan was the more classically beautiful of the two. Her features were delicate, even patrician, but she radiated warmth and friendliness. A mass of sun-streaked, light brown curls framed a heart-shaped face notable for thickly fringed blue eyes and flawless skin. Even without her smashing figure, Megan would have been outstanding.

The two best friends made good foils for each other. Carrie was a green-eyed natural redhead with a sprinkling of freckles across her upturned nose. She was pretty rather than beautiful, with an outgoing personality that drew people to her.

"I'm not complaining," Carrie said. "I'll admit we have quantity, but so far we haven't attracted a prince."

"Well, if we can't have him, I'm glad he picked somebody like the princess. They were made for each other."

Beaumarre was everything Megan and Carrie had hoped for. From the airplane, they could see verdant trees and shrubbery covering the landscape. The hills above the harbor were also dotted with pastel villas that overlooked white sand beaches and blue water topped with little whitecaps.

The palace was set among spacious grounds in the middle of Bienville, the capital city. The pink rococo building was impressive when they got a better look at it during the plane's descent. The palace was surrounded by lush green lawns and brilliant flower beds. Guarding the front portals were sentries in colorful uniforms. From the air they looked like toy soldiers.

"I could get used to living in a place like that," Carrie

remarked, peering out the window. "Just think of having all that closet space!"

"I wonder how many bedrooms there are," Megan said. "If the Montrechets are ever strapped for cash, they could turn the palace into a posh hotel."

"Money isn't one of their problems. Some of these small kingdoms are all show and no dough, but not this one. They're rolling in it, and so is the royal family of Grandalia," Carrie said as the plane touched down. "Gabrielle doesn't have to worry that Prince Nicholas is marrying her for her money."

"It's nice that they can afford to marry for love." Slinging her tote bag over her shoulder, Megan followed her friend down the aisle to the exit.

They had chosen to stay at a small pension—roughly the equivalent of an American bed-and-breakfast. Bienville had several large, glitzy hotels, but those were the same all over the world. Megan and Carrie wanted to get more of a feel for the country and its people.

Maison de Soleil was exactly what they were looking for. There were only eight rooms, each furnished with a haphazard assortment of things, as if from an old aunt's attic—one who hated to throw anything away. There were real and faux antiques mixed with mismatched lamps and overstuffed chairs covered in splashy prints.

The two young women were charmed by the funky atmosphere, and by the proprietress. Madame Fouchard looked like something out of a Toulouse-Lautrec painting. She was probably middle-aged, but her face was heavily made-up and her black hair was pulled back in a complicated arrangement of coils and curls.

When they checked in she asked them to have coffee with her in the parlor after they unpacked.

"Isn't she marvelous?" Carrie asked as they swiftly

hung up their clothes in a closet with a curtain instead of a door.

"A real character," Megan agreed. "We certainly lucked out. I'll bet she knows every place of interest in Bienville. Bring a pad and pencil so we can make notes."

Madame Fouchard was waiting impatiently for them in the parlor, but it soon became apparent that she was more interested in talking about the other guests than the places to see in Bienville. They were forced to hear about the older couple who were very affable, and the young honeymooners who weren't.

"Most of my guests like to gather for breakfast in the morning, or a glass of wine at the end of the day, but not the Cavanaughs. I ask you, what is the point of traveling if you keep to yourselves all the time?" Madame sniffed.

Megan and Carrie exchanged an amused glance. "I guess that's the purpose of a honeymoon," Megan murmured.

"Nonsense! They can carry on when they get home."

"Yes, well, maybe you can tell us what we should do while we're here," Carrie suggested, changing the subject.

"All of the best shops are along the Rue de Le Havre, but the prices!" Madame rolled her eyes. "Be prepared to pay dearly."

"We weren't really interested in shopping," Megan said. "What we had in mind was sight-seeing. Do you have any suggestions?"

"I suppose you could go to the historical museum and the aquarium. They attract a lot of tourists. But do at least stop in at Céleste's. She has the most gorgeous gowns! The Princess Gabrielle is a steady customer."

"We heard that the royal family patronizes local shops," Carrie said. "Have you ever seen the princess?"

"Oh, my, yes. Many times. She drives around town constantly. If you see a little red convertible parked illegally, it's a safe bet Her Highness is somewhere in the vicinity." Madame chuckled.

"Doesn't she have a chauffeur and a bodyguard?"

"Heavens, no! Gabrielle doesn't like to have anybody keeping tabs on her. Her older brother, Prince Louis, is the same way, although I must say, he's more discreet about his carryings-on. Of course he has to be, since he's heir to the throne. Those two have given their father more than a few gray hairs."

"I hope we catch a glimpse of them while we're here," Megan remarked.

"You won't see Louis," Madame Fouchard told her. "He's in America at an international trade conference."

"He can't be too much of a playboy if the king trusts him with an important mission like that."

"Louis takes his responsibilities seriously, contrary to what the foreign press would have you believe. He's young yet, so it's natural for him to sow a few wild oats. But he'll settle down when the time comes. Gabrielle, though. Now there's a different matter. Prince Nicholas will have a hard time keeping that one in the castle."

"I don't imagine it will be a problem," Carrie said. "He's gorgeous!"

"Gabrielle has had her pick of handsome men—film stars, dukes and earls, movie producers." The older woman enumerated them proudly. "Her last one was Jacques Duvalle, the famous tennis star."

"Wasn't that the affair that ended with a big argument in a nightclub?" Carrie was an avid reader of celebrity magazines.

Madame shrugged. "It ended several times. They fought, they made up. They're two of a kind, both with a temper."

"That's a recipe for disaster," Megan commented. "Two people who are both used to adulation. Can you imagine what would have happened if they'd gotten married?"

"It wouldn't have worked, but I can see why they were attracted to each other—besides the obvious," Carrie said.

"I'll bet Gabrielle's other boyfriends let her walk all over them. And Jacques is always surrounded by adoring groupies. He and Gabrielle must have found it refreshing to finally meet somebody who would stand up to them."

"Prince Nicholas won't be any pushover, either," Megan declared. "He has that strong jawline and no-nonsense way of looking straight at the camera. Gabrielle probably fell in love with him because he's as macho as Jacques, but with more stability."

"It's going to be a beautiful wedding." Carrie sighed happily. "Maybe we'll see the princess around town, shopping for her trousseau."

"I don't think she's in Bienville at the moment," Madame said. "Gabrielle was supposed to award the trophy to the winner of the Beaumarre Yacht Races at their annual award dinner last night. But according to this morning's newspaper, they had to get somebody else to substitute for her."

"Even if she were here, she'd scarcely buy her trousseau in a store like other people," Megan told Carrie. "I'm sure everything is being specially made for her."

"That's true, but you can see the king and his daughter before the private engagement party at the end of the week," Madame said. "King Claude will appear on the balcony of the palace with Gabrielle and Prince Nicholas. He will greet the people and make the formal announcement. Then champagne will be served and everybody will be free to stroll around the palace grounds until five o'clock. I have been there on many state occasions and I never tire of the spectacle. You girls are in for a rare treat."

Megan and Carrie murmured something appropriate. They didn't want to tell the older woman that they were invited to the engagement ball, since she—a native of Beaumarre—obviously wasn't.

"You are so fortunate to be in Bienville at this historic moment in our history," Madame continued.

"Well, actually, we planned it that way," Megan said. "We heard rumors of the engagement even before it was confirmed, so we had time to schedule our vacation to coincide with the announcement."

"How could you know ahead of time?"

"We work at the United Nations as translators," Carrie explained. "We hear all kinds of inside stuff."

"Ah, so that is why your accent is so perfect! If you had not told me differently, I would have thought you were both French."

"Thank you." Megan smiled. "That's a nice compliment."

"It is the truth. You could tell anyone you were born here and nobody would question it. Are your parents French? Perhaps you speak the language at home."

"Unfortunately my parents both died in an accident several years ago," Megan said. "But they and my grandparents were all born in the United States."

"Mine, too," Carrie said.

"Do you speak any other languages as fluently as French?" Madame persisted.

She questioned them minutely about their backgrounds, their positions with the United Nations, even their personal lives.

"Girls as pretty as you two should have husbands. You must have had many proposals, yes?"

"I guess we've had our share, but we're in no hurry," Carrie told her. "Women today have lots more options than marriage."

"What foolishness! There is nothing like a man to warm your bed at night."

Megan grinned. "A flannel nightie will do the same thing, and you can use it to wash the car when you get tired of it."

"Joke if you like, but you'll change your tune when the

right man comes along," the older woman said complacently.

After they'd left to go sight-seeing, Carrie said, "The sad thing is, she really believes a man is the solution to everything."

"If there's a man out there like that, I'd be interested in meeting him," Megan said.

"If you do, see if he has a friend for me." Carrie laughed.

Prince Nicholas didn't share the general euphoria over his imminent engagement. He'd rejected the idea violently when his father first proposed it, and he hadn't become any more reconciled as time went by. Now, just days before he was to leave for Beaumarre, the prince made a last, desperate effort.

"I'm pleading with you to reconsider, Father. This is the twentieth century, not the Middle Ages. How could you arrange my marriage without even discussing it with me first?" Nicholas raked his fingers through his thick dark hair as he strode up and down the luxurious library of the family castle in Grandalia.

"You've always had a strong aversion to the subject," the older man answered dryly.

King Damien de Valmontine was a distinguished-looking man. He had strong features and an air of authority befitting a king, but there were laughter lines in his face. His dark eyes could be cold and piercing, yet they could also brim with amusement. They held a mixture of compassion and impatience now as he gazed at his son.

"I don't understand what this frantic rush is to get me married," Nicholas said resentfully. "It isn't as though I'll be ascending the throne anytime soon. You're going to reign for years."

"God willing, but you never know. It's time for you to settle down and start a family."

Nicholas's gray eyes were stormy. "I'm not ready to get married."

"You're twenty-nine. You're as ready as you'll ever be."

"Isn't that something for me to decide?" his son challenged.

"That's what I've been waiting patiently for, without any result. You've had your pick of the most beautiful women on the Continent, but you've never been serious about any of them for more than a few months. What are you looking for?"

"I don't know." Nicholas sighed. "Somebody special, I guess."

"They've all been special," Damien said with a hint of irritation. "The actress, the high-fashion model, the dancer."

"Would you have been happy if I'd married one of them?"

"Did you love any of them?" Damien countered. When Nicholas didn't answer, his father said, "I thought not. If you had, you wouldn't have cared what I thought. We would be having a different kind of argument."

"All right, so I've never been in love." Nicholas flung himself into a chair, but his long body remained tense. "It's something that simply happens. You can't just go out and look for it."

"I thought that's what you were doing," Damien remarked ironically.

"What else do I have to do with my time? Besides things like cutting a ribbon at the opening of the National Flower Show."

"Ceremonial functions aren't always stimulating, but they're a necessity for someone in your position."

"That's the whole trouble—I don't have a position," Nicholas said morosely. "I graduated from a distinguished university with an engineering degree, but my 'position'—

as you so euphemistically put it—doesn't allow me to pursue a career. I'm a cardboard cutout, something to be displayed to the populace as a coming attraction.''

The king regarded his son with sympathy. ''I realize your job isn't stimulating. I can understand your frustration.''

''That's nice, but it doesn't change anything.''

''There might be a solution. King Claude and I have been discussing the possibility of building a more modern bridge over the river that separates our two countries, with a superhighway connecting it on both sides. As you know, the present roads are hopelessly inadequate.''

Nicholas's face came alive with interest. ''It would take hours off the trip and cut down on the present high accident rate. You've talked about this for years, but our two countries could never agree on the details.''

''We've moved a lot closer. There are still a few matters to be ironed out, but I think I can safely say the project will go forward.''

''Are you telling me I can work on it?'' Nicholas asked eagerly.

''I'm saying, perhaps you can help in some sort of advisory capacity,'' Damien answered cautiously.

Nicholas's high cheekbones sharpened. ''What you really mean is, I'm graduating from cutting ribbons to digging the first shovelful of dirt for a camera crew. I don't consider that much of an improvement.''

''You're being unreasonable. You have to consider your image, my boy. As the heir apparent to the throne of Grandalia, you can scarcely work on a construction site in jeans and a hard hat.''

''The world is changing, Father. Royalty is no longer merely ornamental. They work to make the world a better place to live. That's what I want to do—meaningful work. Surely that's not too much to ask?''

''No, I suppose not. I can see your point and you've definitely given me something to think about,'' Damien replied slowly. "We'll explore the possibilities when you return from your honeymoon."

"For a moment I thought you were actually listening to me!" Nicholas exclaimed. "I should have guessed this bridge idea was just a fantasy to keep me in line. Like promising a child an ice-cream cone if he'll stop whining."

"I'd appreciate that," his father said dryly. "But I can assure you the bridge has nothing to do with keeping you happy. It's taken so long to come to fruition because King Claude and I had different opinions on many things. But we each made concessions and finally came to an agreement."

"Was I one of the concessions?" Nicholas asked tautly. "I'm beginning to understand this sudden urgency to get me married—and your choice of brides."

"You're being ridiculous! Gabrielle is a beautiful girl. She doesn't need her father to arrange a marriage. She could have her pick of men."

"Yes, I've read about the ones she's picked," Nicholas drawled.

"You're in no position to criticize. Your own exploits have gotten far too much of the wrong type of coverage. Both of you need to settle down and assume your responsibilities."

"That may be true, but why did you have to choose Gabrielle? We detest each other."

"Nonsense! You've never spent any real time together."

"Why would anyone want to? She's spoiled, tempermental, and she makes a scene whenever she doesn't get her own way."

"I'm sure you're exaggerating. Perhaps Claude has overindulged her to some extent, but that's understandable. The poor child lost her mother while still in her formative years."

"Gabrielle has been fully formed for a long time," Nicholas observed derisively. "Unfortunately her behavior is still around the kindergarten level."

"This isn't getting us anywhere." Damien's impatience showed once more. "I can understand your reluctance to give up your carefree life-style. Whether you believe it or not, I was young once, too. But none of us can escape our responsibilities."

"I'm aware of that, and if you'll just reconsider, I promise I'll change my life-style."

"We've had this conversation before and nothing changes."

"It will. I suppose I didn't realize you felt this strongly about it."

"I'm not simply being arbitrary, son. I want you to live a productive life. You'll understand when you have children of your own."

Nicholas's trapped feeling vanished when his father's attitude softened. The two had a very special relationship. They'd argued in the past, but they'd always been able to work things out.

"I want children as much as you want grandchildren. Finding the right wife is the tricky part." He grinned.

"I've already found one for you."

Nicholas's amusement fled. "How can you expect me to marry Gabrielle after I told you how I feel about her?"

"I think you resent the idea of marriage, not Gabrielle," Damien said calmly. "You'll get used to both of them when the first shock wears off."

Nicholas's jaw set ominously. "I've agreed to look for a wife. I will *never* agree to marry Gabrielle."

Damien's temper flared at his son's open defiance. He didn't raise his voice, but there was no mistaking the implacable determination in it. "You don't understand. I'm not offering you a choice. As the sovereign ruler of Grandalia, I am giving you an order. You and your delegation will travel to Beaumarre to meet with Princess Gabrielle as

scheduled. The arrangements have all been made and festivities planned. At the end of the week a formal announcement of your engagement will be made by King Claude,
after which a date will be set for your wedding. Do I make
myself clear?''

"Perfectly clear, sire." Nicholas's rigid profile might
have been carved out of granite. "May I have your permission to leave the room, Your Majesty?''

Damien's eyes were somber as they watched his son go
through the door, the younger man's taut body radiating
fury.

Damien's wife joined him, looking quizzically at her
husband's grim expression. Queen Rosamund de Valmontine was a tall, regal woman with dark hair parted in the
middle and drawn back from her patrician face. She looked
unapproachable, but to the people who knew her well, she
was warm and witty.

"I gather that Nick is still resisting the idea of marriage," she remarked.

"That's the understatement of the year," Damien answered wryly. "He refused adamantly."

"So you lost your temper and gave him a direct order."
She made a clicking sound with her tongue. "Honestly,
Damien, you should know how to handle him better than
that. Nick isn't a child."

"All the more reason for him to act his age. He's known
since childhood that he's obligated to marry and start a
family. Heaven knows I gave him enough time to make his
own choice. And he has certainly had his pick of beautiful
women. I don't know what he's looking for."

Rosamund smiled. "True love."

"Since there are no other candidates on the horizon, he
can fall in love with Gabrielle. She's beautiful and she has
a smashing figure."

"I'm glad to hear you still notice such things." Rosamund laughed.

"You know the old saying, my dear—I'm married, not dead." Damien's brief smile faded. "Nick and I used to be so close. We could always discuss any problems that arose. He has never blatantly rejected my authority."

"I wouldn't worry about it. You both have hot tempers. When he cools off he'll realize you're only acting out of concern for him."

"I thought I was, but now I'm beginning to wonder if I'm doing the right thing," Damien said slowly.

"It's a little late to start having second thoughts. Perhaps you should have convinced Nick before you spoke to Claude, but everything has been finalized."

"If Nick is really that unhappy, though," Damien said hesitantly.

"He's your son. He doesn't like to be told what to do."

Damien looked at his wife sharply. "You agreed with me when I discussed the matter with you."

"You had already made up your mind," she answered evasively.

The king's jaw firmed. "Somebody has to make the hard decisions, whether they're popular or not."

Since there was nothing she could do about it, Rosamund hid her trepidation. "I'm sure everything will turn out fine," she said soothingly.

The queen's prediction seemed unlikely. Nicholas's black mood persisted all that night and into the next day. He remained withdrawn, taking long, solitary walks around the extensive grounds to avoid everyone, even his equerry and best friend, Michel Charbet.

An equerry was a member of the court who provided a variety of services to one of the highly placed nobles, like Nicholas. In some royal houses the position carried no responsibility beyond agreeing with the prince and seeing that everyone else did, too. But Michel kept Nicholas grounded in reality. He didn't hesitate to voice his opinion when he felt the prince was on the wrong course.

It often led to arguments, but the two men were closer than brothers, although their temperaments were directly opposite. Nicholas was volatile and impatient, while Michel was even-tempered and unflappable. He'd usually been able to smooth over any crisis that arose—until now.

After watching in concern as Nicholas retreated into his private hell, Michel finally said with determined enthusiasm, "Why don't we go out tonight and party hearty?"

Nicholas smiled mirthlessly. "A last fling for the condemned man?"

"Why not? It's better than sitting around here feeling sorry for yourself."

The prince's expression hardened. "I'm sorry I'm not a barrel of laughs," he said coldly.

"You know that isn't what I meant. I just thought it might make you feel better to get out and be with people instead of hanging around here alone. You're even shutting *me* out."

Nicholas's expression softened as he looked at his friend's concerned face. The two men were the same age, but their appearance was as different as their temperament. Michel was boyish looking and easygoing, with an infectious smile that was very appealing.

"This is no reflection on you," Nicholas told him gently. "I'm simply not fit to be around anyone right now."

"I'm not just anybody," Michel protested. "We've been through good times and bad together. This is one of the bad times and I want to share it with you."

"Unfortunately you can't. But you're right about sitting around." Nicholas paced the floor restlessly. "I have to get out of here. Call down and have the Porsche brought around. And inform my parents that I won't be dining with them." He smiled sardonically. "That ought to be a relief."

Michel slanted an oblique look at him. "Where are you going?"

"I don't know. I'll decide when I get in the car. Maybe I'll drive to Bienville and scope out the enemy."

"You'll be there in two days."

"As if I could forget!" Nicholas's mouth twisted bitterly. "Don't worry, I'll show up in my royal finery, like the obedient little prince that I am. Do you think Father will consider that a sign of maturity?"

"Come on, Nick, lighten up."

"That's what I intend to do." Nicholas exchanged his silk shirt and tailored slacks for a pair of jeans and a T-shirt. "See you around, buddy."

Michel sighed. "I can think of better ways to spend the evening, but if that's what you want to do, I'll come with you."

"Not this time."

"Be reasonable, Nick. You can't go running around alone. Your father would have my head on a stick if anything happened to you."

Nick grinned, almost naturally for the first time. "Not to worry. I've already used up all my bad luck."

During the first few days of their visit, Megan and Carrie explored Bienville thoroughly, from the picturesque harbor to the extensive green parks. They visited museums, took off their shoes and walked along white sand beaches, and admired the statues in numerous small squares around the city.

At night they avoided the glitzy restaurants catering to tourists, and ate instead in one of the many little cafés dotting the waterfront or tucked into quaint winding streets.

After dinner they often dropped in at some of the small clubs where the natives went. Le Carnaval was their favorite bistro. It had nightly entertainment by different local artists. Megan and Carrie had enjoyed a jazz combo there so much that they planned to return the next evening to hear the folksinger who was scheduled to appear.

Unfortunately, Carrie ate something at lunch the following day that didn't agree with her. By evening her stomach was queasy and she felt rotten, but she was determined not to let it slow her down.

"I'll feel a lot better after I take a shower and change clothes," she insisted when Megan advised her to go to bed.

"It's silly to drag yourself around when you feel this way. If you stay in and get a good night's sleep you'll have a better chance of feeling fine in the morning."

Carrie wavered. "I was looking forward to hearing that folksinger," she said tentatively. "She might not be there again while we're here."

"Then somebody equally good will be. Get into bed and I'll go out and bring you back some soup."

Carrie made a face. "I don't want anything to eat. Go ahead and have a good time at the bistro. If I'm asleep when you come back you can tell me all about it in the morning."

"I'm not going without you," Megan protested.

"Why not? I'm the one with the upset stomach. There's no reason for you to give up *your* evening."

"It's no big deal. We were out all day. I could use a restful night myself."

"That's just plain silly," Carrie insisted. "What would you do here, watch me sleep?"

They argued back and forth before Carrie prevailed on her friend to go out for dinner, at least.

Although Megan allowed herself to be convinced, she intended to return as soon as she'd eaten. After lingering over coffee, however, it was still only eight-thirty. Much too early to go to bed, but Carrie was undoubtedly asleep. Turning on a lamp might wake her, so it was pointless to go back to the room. Megan decided to stop in at Le Carnaval for just a short time.

The show had already started and every table was taken, but the owner found a place for her at the long bar that spanned one wall of the room.

The singer had a hauntingly beautiful voice. The crowded room was hushed as everyone listened, entranced. The show ended with enthusiastic applause, after many encores.

Megan turned impulsively to the man next to her. "Wasn't she fantastic?" It was more a comment than a question.

"I suppose so," he answered indifferently.

"That sounds as if you didn't like her."

She had only glanced at him before. Now she took a closer look, noticing that he was darkly handsome, although the days' growth of stubble on his face gave him a dangerous appearance. A striped cotton T-shirt clung to his broad chest and wide shoulders, and tight jeans molded his narrow hips. Quite an impressive specimen of manhood. He also looked faintly familiar, although that was unlikely. What movie star did he resemble? she wondered idly.

Nicholas was taking a comprehensive look at Megan, as well. A real beauty, he concluded. A woman who didn't need glamorous makeup to attract attention. Those thick lashes looked like her own, and her mouth was naturally seductive, not drawn with a brush into an exaggerated pout that was supposed to be sexy but turned him off.

She was definitely the kind of woman who would have interested him under different circumstances. But he no longer had freedom of choice, Nick reminded himself bleakly.

Megan was puzzled by the austere look on his face. "You're entitled to your opinion, of course, but everybody else seemed to like her. You must be very hard to please."

A sardonic smile curved Nick's mobile mouth. "That's what my father tells me."

"Well, he should know." She was sorry she'd started a

conversation. The man might be a real hunk, but he wasn't very pleasant.

As she started to slide off the bar stool he stopped her. "I'm sorry if I sounded abrupt. My life fell apart recently, but that's no reason to take it out on you. Please stay and let me buy you a drink to make amends."

"You don't have to be polite. I've been in those moods where I just wanted to be left alone."

"I thought I did, but I've discovered I'm not very good company." He gave her an appealing smile. "Won't you stay and talk to me?"

"If you really want me to. I'm a good listener if you'd like to talk about whatever is bothering you. Sometimes the problem doesn't seem as insurmountable after all, and it's easier to talk to a stranger, someone you know you won't ever see again."

"You're very kind, but a man would be a fool to waste time on introspection when he's with such a beautiful lady." Nick's expression changed as he gazed at her lovely face. "Tonight I'm just a fellow named Philippe who doesn't have a care in the world."

"That was a quick transition," Megan commented.

"I don't have much time left." His gray eyes were momentarily somber. Then they lightened. "But enough about me. Tell me about yourself."

"I have a feeling your story is more interesting." She provided the opening, but hesitated to question him further. Did Philippe have an incurable disease? He looked to be in perfect shape, but that remark about the shortage of time sounded ominous.

Nicholas didn't take the bait. "Everybody thinks his or her story would make a fascinating book," he said smoothly. "But in reality, most of them would be quite dull. The things people would do with their lives if they had the chance are a lot more interesting."

"What would you do with yours?"

He gazed at the bottles behind the bar without really seeing them. "I'd like to build a bridge over a canyon in South America, so people in remote areas aren't so isolated. Or a dam in Africa that would reclaim part of the desert for crops to feed starving people."

"Have you ever done that kind of work?" Megan asked. "Perhaps you could get a job with a construction company that handles those big projects."

His mouth twisted derisively. "We're talking about our private fantasies, remember? Acting them out would take away the glamour. I'd have to get up at dawn and do back-breaking labor."

She looked at him disapprovingly. "There's no free lunch. If you want something, you have to work for it. Nothing is handed to us on a silver platter."

"It is in a make-believe world. What would your life be like if you could do anything you wanted?"

"Actually, I wouldn't change much. Oh, I suppose I could use more money—everyone could. But I have a stimulating job, good friends and a wide variety of interests. I'm fairly satisfied with my life."

"You're remarkably wholesome." Nicholas smiled.

Megan wrinkled her nose in distaste. "That makes me about as stimulating as a bowl of Jell-O."

"What's wrong with being sweet and well-adjusted?"

"Nothing if you would just add glamorous and exciting." She grinned.

He gazed at her with a distinctly male expression. "I'm sure you could excite a man beyond his wildest dreams," he said in a deepened voice.

His husky tone evoked an image of just how exciting *he* could be. Suddenly Megan could imagine his firm mouth moving over hers, teasing her lips apart while he molded her body to his hard frame.

She gave a breathless little laugh. "That's very nice, but I notice you omitted any reference to glamour."

"You don't need me to tell you how beautiful you are. I'm sure great numbers of men have told you that."

"It's not something you ever get tired of hearing," she said lightly.

"In that case, I'll be happy to oblige." He took her hand and kissed the palm. "You have the face of an angel and the body of a siren. I'd like to hold you in my arms and make love to you all night long. I want to kiss every single spot that gives you pleasure, and hear you call my name as you reach fulfillment."

Megan was mesmerized by his seductive voice and the desire evident on his handsome face. She could almost feel his hands and mouth moving over her body.

With a conscious effort, she banished the erotic vision. Drawing her hand away she said coolly, "I didn't mean for you to be that graphic."

His eyes sparkled with amusement. As though he knew the effect he'd had on her, Megan thought crossly. No wonder. With his charisma and sexual potency, the man could make a mummy wake up and want to tango!

"I'm sorry," he said with a transparent attempt at penitence. "I was merely being honest. You have no cause for alarm, however. I'd like very much to make love to you, but I can't."

"Oh?"

Nicholas laughed at the startled expression on her face. "I didn't mean that the way it sounds. I'd bring great enthusiasm to the opportunity, but I can't because you are what's called 'a nice girl' and I'm an honorable man." Before she could question him, a small combo started to play and he stood and extended his hand. "Come, dance with me."

As Megan slid off the stool her purse fell to the floor. When Nick stooped to pick it up, a small gold disk he was wearing on a thin gold chain around his neck swung free. It had been concealed under his T-shirt.

He quickly replaced it, but not before she'd caught a glimpse of intricate workmanship. The little gold circle appeared to have a jeweled crest of some sort.

"That looked lovely," she remarked. "What is it?"

"Just something my parents gave me long ago," he answered dismissively.

She wanted to know more, but when he took her in his arms it didn't seem important. The chemistry between them was awesome. She'd been acutely aware of his masculinity at the bar, but nothing like this. Her body conformed to his as though it were made for that purpose.

He seemed to feel the magic, too. "Sweet stranger," he said huskily, curling his hand around the nape of her neck underneath the bright curls. "You're utterly bewitching."

Their faces were so close that she could see each spiky black lash fringing his gray eyes. "You don't even know my name," she murmured.

"It must be Angélique." His arm tightened around her waist, making her even more aware of him. "You look like an angel."

Megan gave a little laugh, seeking to break the dangerous spell he was weaving around her. "Appearances can be deceiving. You don't really know me. I could be like all the other women in your life—the ones you came here to get away from. Or should I say, the one." It suddenly occurred to Megan that Philippe might have been moody in the beginning because he'd just broken up with his girlfriend.

"You're the only woman in my life tonight." His lips brushed across her temple in a feathery caress. "This evening is more special to me than you know. I wish it didn't have to end."

Megan found herself wishing the same thing. She would never see Philippe again after tonight, but he would be a lasting memory of this romantic trip. She sighed happily and nestled her head in the curve of his shoulder.

When the music stopped they sat at a table and drank white wine and talked. They avoided any personal details; it was part of the piquancy of this strange encounter. But they still found a lot to talk about—everything from politics to modern art. Their discussions were lively because they were both well-informed, but they didn't always agree. That was also part of the stimulation.

The time flew by. They didn't realize how late it had gotten until the waiter told them the bistro was closing.

"We've been sitting for hours. Let's take a walk," Nicholas suggested.

"That's a good idea." Megan was as reluctant as he to see the evening end. "We can go down to the beach and stroll along the sand."

The deserted beach was beautiful in the moonlight. Little wavelets rushed in to foam along the shoreline before skittering back to sea. Fringing the sand were tall palm trees that bowed and whispered to each other in the flower-scented breeze. The only signs of life came from the lights on the sleek yachts anchored in the harbor.

"It's so quiet, no traffic noise or boom boxes," Megan commented. "We could be on a deserted island."

Nicholas squeezed her hand. "I can't think of anyone I'd rather be marooned with."

"It sounds romantic, but we'd need to chop wood and cook over an open fire. No supermarkets, either. We'd have to hunt and fish for our dinner. You're allergic to work," she teased.

"The rewards would be worth it. There wouldn't be anything to do at night except make love."

"That sounds romantic, too, but after a few days you'd miss your morning newspaper and the soccer games on television. You'd get very grumpy."

He grinned mischievously. "Not if you cooperated."

"Oh, I see!" she exclaimed in mock indignation. "I'm supposed to make all the effort."

He stopped walking and turned to frame her face in his palms. "It would be a privilege just to have the opportunity to bring you pleasure."

Their faces were so close that she could feel his warm breath feathering her skin. Megan gazed into the fathomless dark pools of his eyes and parted her lips, knowing he was going to kiss her.

Nick's mouth was cool and firm, moving gently against hers in savoring enjoyment. When she responded automatically, his arms closed around her and he deepened the kiss.

It was incredibly arousing. His mouth promised untold ecstasy, and his caressing hands reinforced the promise. She clasped her arms around his neck in an instinctive effort to get closer.

He reacted instantly, folding her so close that she was aware of every hard muscle in his lean body. Then his mouth claimed hers again and her satisfaction was complete.

"Lovely Angélique," he said huskily, when he finally dragged his mouth away. "You're irresistible."

Megan knew she was playing with fire. Philippe's desire was unmistakable, and her own was threatening to flame out of control. Still, it was difficult to move out of his seductive embrace.

He made the decision for her. Clasping her shoulders, he reluctantly put a small distance between them. Giving her a crooked smile, he said, "You're very potent medicine, little angel. If I don't stop now, I might not be able to."

Megan glanced up at the stars, hoping he didn't realize that for one impulsive moment she hadn't wanted him to stop. "It must be awfully late," she murmured. "I should go."

"I'll get you a taxi." He didn't try to persuade her to stay, or offer to take her home.

The taxi stand on the promenade was deserted at this late hour, but there was a telephone to summon a cab. The mood between them changed while they were waiting. Megan felt awkward suddenly, and Nicholas seemed withdrawn.

"It's been a lovely evening," she said, trying to make small talk to fill the silence. "I'm glad I decided to come tonight. I wasn't going to at first."

"It appears we were destined to meet," he said lightly. "I only dropped in there on a whim."

"Lucky for you," she joked. "You were really grouchy at first, but then I solved all your problems."

He touched her cheek gently. "Unfortunately they don't have a solution. I don't know if meeting you made them better or worse, but I'll always remember your generosity."

As she gazed at him uncertainly, wishing she could think of something that would revive his earlier high spirits, the taxi arrived. Nicholas leaned forward and kissed her cheek before stepping back.

She stared through the cab window at his tall, lean silhouette for as long as it was visible, feeling a curious sense of loss.

Chapter Two

Dawn was breaking as Megan paid the taxi driver and tiptoed into the pension. She felt guilty about having left her ailing friend alone for so long—although Carrie was merely under the weather, not really sick. What made her feel even guiltier was the realization that she hadn't given a thought to her friend all evening.

Megan tried to get undressed quietly, but Carrie woke before she'd gotten into her nightgown.

"What are you doing up so early?" Carrie yawned and looked at her traveling clock. "It's only five-thirty, for heaven's sake!"

"Go back to sleep," Megan murmured. "It's too early to get up."

"I've been asleep since nine o'clock last night." Carrie sat up and looked more closely at her friend. Then she glanced over at the other twin bed. "Are you just getting in? Your bed hasn't been slept in."

"Well, I... I'll tell you all about it in the morning."

"It *is* morning." Carrie grinned suddenly. "When I told you to go out and have fun, I didn't expect you to forget everything your mother taught you. Do I have to watch you every minute?"

"Don't worry, it was nothing like that."

"Then what were you doing all night?"

"I had dinner and since it was still early, I decided to stop in and catch that folksinger's act. She was fabulous. I'm sorry you had to miss her."

"Never mind the folksinger. Get to the good part. Who were you with all this time?"

"Well, I did meet a man at the bar. He was wildly handsome and he reminded me of someone—a movie star or somebody like that." Megan frowned. "I still can't quite put my finger on who he looks like."

"What did you and this Adonis do all night?"

"We talked for hours. He's very intelligent—but not in a stuffy way. He has a great sense of humor."

"Lucky you. I can see I'll be doing a lot of sight-seeing alone from now on."

"No, I won't be seeing him again."

"Why not? He sounds fantastic—looks, brains and a sense of humor. What more could you ask?"

"It was his decision, not mine."

"You spent the night with the guy and you don't expect to hear from him again?"

"You're making it sound more suggestive than it actually was," Megan protested. "We just happened to hit it off—although not right away. I made a chance remark after the show ended and we started to talk. He turned me off at first by his attitude, then I discovered he was just troubled about something."

"That sounds like a bummer," Carrie commented. "Don't tell me you spent all night listening to his problems."

"No, I never found out what they were. It might have

been a fight with his girlfriend, although I got the impression there was more to it than that.''

"Either way, you're well rid of him.''

"I suppose so,'' Megan answered slowly.

"You couldn't have fallen for somebody you merely had a conversation with.'' Carrie looked at her more closely. "Unless you left out a few details. Was there more to it?''

"He kissed me,'' Megan admitted.

"That's scarcely earth shattering.''

"You've never been kissed by Philippe.'' Megan sighed reminiscently. "I consider myself fairly knowledgeable in that department and I've never met a man with more expertise. He was positively awesome!''

"It was probably all the romance in the air over the royal engagement,'' Carrie said dismissively. "It's catching.''

Megan snapped her fingers suddenly. "*That's* who Philippe reminded me of! I thought it was somebody in the entertainment field, but he could double for Nicholas—if the prince wore jeans and a T-shirt and hung around bars alone.''

"No wonder you're so starry-eyed! I wouldn't mind meeting a guy like that, myself. Maybe he'll call you. Did you give him this number?''

"He didn't ask for it.'' Megan finished getting undressed. "It's just as well. This way I can remember him as the perfect male. If I saw him again I'd find out he isn't.''

"That's the spirit! Get some sleep. I'm going to get up and go wander, but I'll come back later this afternoon and we'll do something.''

"I don't intend to waste the day in bed, but it's too early to go anyplace yet. Give me a couple of hours and we'll take in some of the museums.''

* * *

After a few hours' sleep and a refreshing shower, Megan said, "Okay, I'm ready when you are. Where shall we start?"

"Why don't we save the museums for tomorrow?" Carrie asked. "I feel like a change of pace. How about hitting the shopping district today? We can browse through the stores and have lunch at one of those colorful little places with the outside tables."

"Sounds good to me," Megan replied. "I'll get my shopping done early instead of waiting till the last minute the way I usually do. I want to buy some little gifts to take home."

"Me, too. And when we're through, we can pop in at Céleste's. Wasn't that the name of the place where Madame Fouchard said the princess shops? Maybe we'll bump into her."

"You never can tell."

Bienville was experiencing a minor heat wave, so Megan decided to wear a short white sundress instead of her usual pants and T-shirt. She also pulled her hair back and tied it with a colorful scarf, rather than wearing it in a mass of ringlets around her face the way she normally did. The simple hairstyle emphasized her patrician features, and the thin cotton dress moved fluidly over her slender body.

"Maybe I should change." Carrie gazed at her friend consideringly. "You look so elegant."

"In a sundress and sandals?" Megan laughed. "That's scarcely what I'd call haute couture."

"Perhaps I'm just used to seeing you in jeans. Anyway, I think I'll wear a dress, too. Then we can shop at Céleste's and the saleswomen will think we can really afford it." Carrie grinned.

The Rue de Le Havre was a shopper's paradise—guaranteed to max out anyone's credit cards. Exquisite merchandise was temptingly displayed in one shop after another. The two friends kept stopping to exclaim over a glamorous gown in one window, a beautiful silk blouse in another.

They finally managed to find a few stores with prices that didn't require taking out a loan at the bank, and they bought gifts for friends at home. When that was accomplished they decided to have lunch before heading for Céleste's.

The restaurant they chose had a broad outside terrace with red-and-white-striped umbrella tables. A low brick wall decorated with pots of red geraniums separated the diners from the people strolling by.

They were fortunate enough to get a table by the sidewalk where they had a view of both the passersby and the scenic blue sea in the distance. Most of the other tables were filled with men and women dressed in casual chic— definitely not tourists. This was an upscale bistro patronized by the elite of Bienville.

"We have sidewalk cafés at home, but somehow they don't have the same feeling. This place is so Continental," Megan declared happily, gazing around. "Let's order an aperitif before lunch, like the natives do."

"Okay, but I don't think anyone will confuse us with natives."

"Madame Fouchard said they would."

"She isn't exactly a reliable source," Carrie answered dryly. "If we'd taken her advice we'd have skipped the Conservatory of Flowers yesterday."

"Weren't they gorgeous? I especially liked the pink-and-white variegated rose that was named after Gabrielle's mother, Queen Marie."

They were too engrossed in conversation to notice the two men who glanced idly at them as they were walking by.

When the older man stopped abruptly, the younger one

glanced at him and said, "What's wrong, Henri? Did you forget something?"

Henri seized his arm and pulled him over to stand under a nearby tree. "Look at that girl, Robert. What do you see?"

The younger man glanced at a nearby table where a woman and a man were having coffee. "Are they friends of yours?" he asked in a puzzled tone.

"Not that table," Henri said impatiently. "The girl with the scarf around her hair. She's sitting with the redhead."

Robert scanned the tables and found Megan. He sucked in his breath sharply as he gazed at her profile. "Can it possibly be?" He exhaled with a sigh when she turned her head and he got a better look at her face. "No, I should have known it was too good to be true."

"But perhaps it is the next best thing. Beggars can't be choosers."

Robert frowned. "I don't understand."

"Think of the possibilities."

Henri spoke rapidly to his associate, who seemed far from convinced. The two men discussed the matter vigorously for several minutes. Finally Henri prevailed, although Robert still looked apprehensive.

Megan and Carrie were sipping their aperitifs when the two men approached them.

"You were very fortunate to get this choice table," Henri remarked with a smile. He glanced around the crowded terrace. "There doesn't seem to be another one available."

"Why don't you speak to the hostess?" Carrie suggested. She and Megan had heard every pickup line, and they weren't any different in French. "I'm sure a table will be available soon."

"But not one with two such beautiful ladies," Henri said smoothly. "Would you allow us the honor of buying you lunch?"

"That's very kind, but no thank you," Megan said—firmly, she thought.

It didn't deter Henri. "I realize you are approached in this manner all the time, but I assure you this is not what it seems. I am a happily married man."

"How happy is your wife?" Carrie asked dryly.

Ignoring her question, he said to Megan, "I have something I wish to discuss with you. May I sit down?" Without waiting for permission he pulled out a chair, nodding at Robert to do the same.

Megan frowned. "I don't want to be rude, but my friend and I prefer to have lunch alone. Will you please leave."

"Perhaps we should introduce ourselves," Robert murmured.

"Of course! Forgive me for being so intent that I forgot my manners. I am Henri Montelle, and this is my associate, Robert Dubois." He gazed at her expectantly.

The names were clearly supposed to mean something to them, Megan thought, but they didn't. She and Carrie looked back at him blankly.

"You are not from Bienville?" he asked tentatively.

Megan shot Carrie a triumphant look. "No, we're just visiting," she said, thawing slightly at being mistaken for a native.

"You are French?"

"Actually, we're American."

"Amazing!"

"Not really. You must get foreign visitors from all over, especially this week when your princess is getting engaged. That's why we came, to be here for the festivities."

"I see." Henri gazed at her speculatively. "You are interested in Princess Gabrielle?"

"Everybody is. We've heard a lot about her." Carrie grinned.

Henri made a small sound of irritation. "Do not believe everything you read."

"She's very beautiful," Megan said tactfully, to cover Carrie's reference to the tabloids. "We were hoping to catch a glimpse of her around town. Our landlady told us you never know when you might run into the princess."

"How true," Robert said wryly. "Princess Gabrielle is very unpredictable."

"I hope we can count on her to be at her own engagement party," Carrie said. "My friend here would be very disappointed if it was called off and she didn't get to see the prince. Megan thinks he's dreamy."

"Honestly, Carrie!" Megan exclaimed in annoyance. "You make me sound like a teenager. I merely remarked that's he's quite a nice-looking man."

Henri was watching them closely. "Perhaps I can arrange for you to meet Prince Nicholas," he said casually.

"Yeah, sure," Carrie muttered, exchanging a derisive look with Megan.

"I can understand your skepticism, but I really am in a position to introduce you to His Royal Highness. If you were interested enough to visit our country expressly for the engagement festivities, wouldn't you regret passing up such an opportunity?"

"Why would you offer to do a favor like that for two complete strangers?" Megan countered.

"We are a small country, dependent on tourism. I'm sure it would be the highlight of your trip and you would give all your friends a favorable report of us." Before allowing her to examine his explanation for flaws, he asked, "How long do you plan to be in Bienville?"

After hesitating a moment, Megan answered, "For about another ten days."

"Then I'm sure it can be arranged. Prince Nicholas arrives tomorrow. Do you have any commitments for the next week?" When Megan looked at him warily he added, "I mean, are you meeting friends who will be disappointed if you cancel your plans? I can't guarantee when I'll be able to get you in to see the prince, you understand. You might have very little notice.''

It would be very exciting if the man was on the level, Megan decided. She'd heard of things like this happening—a tourist being given the VIP treatment for publicity purposes.

"You could call us at the last minute," she told Henri. "We don't know a soul in Bienville, so we wouldn't have to break any dates."

Henri gave Robert a fleeting look of satisfaction. "Excellent!" he told Megan. "Then why don't we go someplace quieter and discuss the matter?"

Both women were instantly on the alert. "What's the matter with right here?" Carrie asked bluntly.

"Well, actually, there's a little more to it," he admitted. "I'd prefer to conduct our business in private."

"I thought so! What you really mean is, you'll do something for us if we do something for you first."

"You guys are the same all over the world," Megan said disgustedly. "You're never too old."

Robert's face turned bright red. "You do Monsieur Montelle a disservice," he said stiffly.

"I doubt it, but just so there is no misunderstanding, the answer to his proposition is no. Even if he knew Prince Nicholas—which I'm sure he doesn't."

"You really have gotten the wrong impression," Henri protested. "I didn't realize how my request would sound. You must allow me to make amends."

"Certainly. You can start by leaving us to enjoy our lunch in peace," Megan said crisply.

"If you'll just give me a chance to explain."

"What does it take to discourage you guys?" Carrie exclaimed. "If we have to make a scene, we will. How would you explain *that* to your wife?"

"Please don't do anything hasty," Robert pleaded, as a couple stopped at their table.

"Henri, darling, how nice to see you out enjoying yourself." The woman glanced curiously at Megan and Carrie.

Henri stood politely. "Madelaine, Édouard." He nodded at them without introducing his companions.

"I didn't know you took time off for something as frivolous as lunch," Madelaine persisted.

Henri looked at his watch. "You're right, I should be getting back to my office. Thank you for reminding me, and also for stopping by."

After a few more words the couple said goodbye, since Henri didn't leave them any other choice.

When they'd left, Robert said to him, "We should go, too. Perhaps there has been some news."

"I wish I had your optimism. Since I don't, this is our only alternative."

"Surely you aren't still considering this dangerous plan! Not now that we've been seen with her." He nodded at Megan.

"What other choice do I have? If you can think of another way, I'd be happy to listen."

"Excuse me," Megan interrupted pointedly. "Would you mind taking your discussion somewhere else?"

Henri's attitude changed. He was no longer the suave gentleman with the charming manner. His face was hard now, and his voice was authoritative rather than ingratiating.

"I'm sorry I did not handle this affair with greater finesse, but I have no more time to waste. I shall have to strongly request that you come with me immediately."

Megan stared at him incredulously. "You have to be joking! I'm not going anywhere with you. If you don't leave this instant, I'm going to call the police."

He gave her a wintry smile. "That won't be necessary. The police are already here—in a manner of speaking. I am Inspector Montelle, head of National Security, and Robert is my chief deputy."

"If one approach doesn't work, try another, is that it?" she asked derisively. "Aren't you a little old to be playing these games?"

"You wish proof of our identities?"

Both men offered credentials, which Megan brushed aside. "I don't care if you're the king's cousin! Go try your story on some naive soul who will believe it."

Henri stared at her with a frown. "You present me with a problem, *mademoiselle*. The last thing I wish to do is antagonize you. I would hate to resort to stronger methods, but it is imperative that we talk."

"Your threats don't frighten me. I'm an American citizen."

"Even Americans are subject to security checks. We can't be too careful."

"What kind of security risk could she possibly be?" Carrie asked.

"She has shown an inordinate interest in Princess Gabrielle and Prince Nicholas. My job is to prevent any tragic—or even unfortunate—incidents from occurring at their upcoming engagement celebration."

"Are you afraid Megan will try to proposition the prince?" Carrie asked mockingly. "From what I've heard about old Nick, it wouldn't be the first time, and he certainly wouldn't be shocked."

"Enough conversation," Henri stated firmly. "You will come with me," he told Megan.

"And if I refuse?" she asked, tilting her chin.

"Then I will have to insist. I am perfectly within my rights," Henri assured her. "No one will question me."

Megan rapidly assessed the situation and realized he was right. There was nothing she could do at the moment. Turning to Carrie, she said swiftly, "Call Ambassador Hayes in Monte Carlo. Tell him what's happened and ask him to contact the State Department immediately. If he's out of town, his wife, Marla, will know where to reach him."

Henri's eyes narrowed. "You are acquainted with Ambassador Hayes?"

"He's a good friend. Now are you ready to reconsider?" Megan asked triumphantly.

"Yes, I suppose I will have to. I didn't want to complicate matters by involving your friend, but you leave me no choice. It would be awkward if she told her story to the American officials." He nodded toward Carrie. "You will please accompany us."

"No way! You can't get away with this."

"I have already demonstrated that I can," he said impatiently. "If you attempt to make a scene I will inform everyone that you are drunk and disorderly and in need of restraint. Now, please stop wasting time. Robert, summon the car."

The two women looked at each other in consternation. They weren't reassured by the long black limo that pulled up to the curb. Henri and Robert might really be who they said they were—but then again, maybe they weren't.

Megan tried to pull away as Henri led her toward the car. "Can I see your credentials again? You only flashed them by me."

"You can examine them in the car," he said, urging her inside the plush limo.

When they were all seated, the driver locked the doors. It had an ominous sound, especially in conjunction with the tinted windows that prevented anyone from seeing in.

"You *said* this vacation would be exciting," Carrie commented ironically as the car moved smoothly away from the curb.

Megan tried to smile. "That will teach you not to listen to me."

They rode in silence for a while, each occupied with his or her own thoughts.

Finally Megan asked, "Where are you taking us?"

"We will be there shortly," Henri replied.

"That isn't what I asked you!" she exclaimed in exasperation. "You might at least tell me where we're going, even if you won't tell me why."

"If you insist. We are going to the palace."

Her mouth thinned in annoyance. "Okay, be childish about it. Don't tell me."

He looked at her with a mixture of amusement and irritation. "Are all American women this difficult to deal with, or are you an exception?"

"If you think you have troubles now, just wait until you hear from my government," Megan said grimly.

Before he could answer, the limousine turned in between tall wrought-iron gates and traveled down a long, tree-lined drive.

"We really *are* at the palace!" Carrie exclaimed.

"I am sorry to disappoint you by keeping my word," Henri remarked dryly, as the car stopped and they all exited.

They were escorted through a side door into a carpeted corridor with a number of doors leading to various offices. This was evidently the administrative wing of the palace.

Megan and Carrie were led into a spacious office that was rather spartanly furnished, except for the wealth of electronic equipment. The large desk had numerous consoles and phone lines for direct communication with every corner of the principality.

Henri seated himself behind the desk after indicating two comfortable chairs for the women. "I am sorry I had to coerce you into coming here," he began. "I can only hope you will forgive me after I explain the reasons for my behavior. As you will learn, the matter is too delicate to be discussed in a public place."

Both women were too fascinated to be angry. They merely looked at him expectantly and waited.

"You've read about Princess Gabrielle's many escapades. Unfortunately, too many people have." His expression was austere for a moment before he forced himself to relax. "She is young and strong-willed. She doesn't stop to consider the consequences of her acts as a royal princess."

"We already knew all of that from the tabloids," Megan said curtly. "What I'm waiting to hear is, what any of it has to do with me."

"King Claude thought it was time for Gabrielle to marry," Henri answered indirectly. "But she was never one to be dictated to."

"So?" When he paused, Megan looked at Robert. "Maybe you can cut to the chase and tell me what's going on here."

He shrugged. "Why not? Soon everybody will know, I'm afraid. The princess has vanished."

Megan stared at him blankly. "I don't understand. What happened to her? You mean, she was kidnapped?"

"No. She left to avoid becoming engaged."

"She doesn't want to marry Prince Nicholas?" Carrie asked incredulously. "That lady must be seriously disturbed!"

"Unfortunately King Claude gave her a direct order—always a mistake with Gabrielle. They had words and she stormed out of the palace. He thought she would sulk for a day or two and then return, but she has been missing for a week."

"How can that be?" Megan asked. "She's one of the most photographed women in the world."

"That's what puzzles us," Robert said. "I've had legions of people scouring all of Europe for her, without success. It was worrisome enough in the beginning, but now we're running out of time. Prince Nicholas arrives with his entourage tomorrow evening."

"I guess you'd better head him off," Megan said. "He's entitled to know that his bride-to-be is less than eager."

"It's not that simple," Henri said. "The marriage will

form an alliance between the principalities of Beaumarre and Grandalia. Both royal houses are in accord. It would be an affront if Gabrielle were to reject the prince, especially in such an insulting manner.''

''I'll agree that she could have thought of a more tactful way of backing out, but the king can't *make* her get married if she doesn't want to.''

''Gabrielle doesn't know *what* she wants,'' Henri said irritably. ''If her father had forbidden the union, she would have been begging Nicholas to elope. She will come to her senses and agree, but irreparable damage will have been done if the engagement announcement isn't made as scheduled. We can't have rumors starting. It would be a diplomatic nightmare.''

''Yes, I can see your problem,'' Megan said thoughtfully. ''But there's one thing that puzzles me. You certainly don't want the story to get out, so why are you trusting two total strangers with your secret?''

''Because I am hoping you will prove to be the solution. It came to me when I saw you sitting at that sidewalk café. I want you to take the princess's place until we can locate her.''

Megan's mouth literally dropped open. ''You're not serious?''

''Very much so, I assure you.''

''But that's crazy! Who would believe I was Gabrielle?''

Carrie stared at her critically. ''You do resemble her a little bit, now that I think of it.''

''We both have blue eyes,'' Megan said derisively. ''Princess Gabrielle, me, and millions of other women. That's where the resemblance ends.''

''Not really,'' Robert said. ''You're both about the same height and you both have the same...er...excellent figure. I'll admit I had some doubts at first, but if you changed the color of your hair and wore it like the princess does, I think you could pass for her. At least I hope you can," he muttered.

"We'll never know, because I'm not going to do it," Megan stated flatly. "I don't want to become known as one of those weirdos who try to pass themselves off as somebody famous. They always get found out and become objects of ridicule."

"That would be even more of a disaster for us," Henri said. "Therefore, I have a proposition for you. Let our beauticians color your hair and make up your face like Gabrielle's. If you're not satisfied that you look like her when they're finished, I'll be the first to admit it."

"It would be nice to be vindicated, but I can't see spending an entire day of my vacation having my hair bleached."

"I will make it worth your while. You can name your price—anything within reason. As you can see, I am a desperate man."

"I wasn't asking for money," Megan said indignantly. "If I thought your plan had any chance of success I'd be willing to help out for free. I can sympathize with the spot you're in."

"Then, in appreciation, let me offer you the hospitality of the palace. You and your friend will be given our finest suites, a car will be placed at your disposal to take you wherever you wish to go, and tickets will be provided for any events you desire to attend."

"Even if I'm not transformed into Gabrielle?" Megan asked slowly.

Henri nodded. "That is correct."

"And if you're satisfied that I can pass for her? What would I have to do?"

"You will take part in all the planned festivities along with Prince Nicholas. There will be private parties and public balls. A suitable wardrobe will be provided, which will be yours to keep when you leave here, naturally."

"Wow! You can't lose," Carrie told Megan.

"That's a matter of opinion. Even if I turned into a dead ringer for the princess, how do you expect me to fool Prince Nicholas?" she asked Henri.

"He and Gabrielle have never spent much time together. They haven't even seen each other in recent months."

"Not exactly an impetuous courtship," Carrie commented.

"At least he won't be planning a heated reunion," Megan observed wryly.

"Time is getting very short," Henri said. "If you agree to undertake this endeavor, we must start immediately."

"I think there's something you've overlooked," Megan said. "The engagement is already generating a lot of publicity. If I appear at all these functions, Gabrielle will read about it, wherever she is. I don't think she'll be pleased to see somebody else stealing her limelight. What happens if she decides to come back?"

"That would be the best-case scenario—something I'm ardently hoping for."

"I don't think you're quite clear on the concept. What if she just shows up at one of the events and exposes me? It might appeal to her sense of the dramatic. How would you talk your way out of that one?"

"Let us worry about the details." Henri stood, smiling for the first time. "Before I have you shown to your suites, allow me to express my deepest gratitude. You are doing a great service to Beaumarre."

"And not coming out too badly herself," Carrie joked. "She's getting a handsome prince out of the deal."

"Only temporarily." Robert smiled, showing the first sign of humor. "She can't keep him."

"Oh, well. Nothing's perfect." Megan laughed.

She was filled with a bubbling sense of excitement as the full import hit her for the first time. How many women got to live the life of a princess—even for a few days? There would be beautiful clothes, and glamorous parties.

She might even get to borrow some of the fabulous jewelry Gabrielle was always pictured wearing.

And then of course there was Prince Nicholas. He was the icing on the cake. Megan's pulse rate quickened when she pictured herself in his arms. Even if his courtship of Gabrielle had been rather tepid, they would have to appear loving for appearance's sake, if nothing else. She and Nicholas would also have to spend time together and act committed.

Megan supposed she should feel guilty about acting romantic with someone else's fiancé, but she didn't. Gabrielle was a spoiled brat for throwing a tantrum and walking out so irresponsibly. She didn't deserve a fantastic man like Nicholas. Too bad he wasn't on the "available" list, but it would be a lot of fun pretending to be in love with him.

Henri kept his promise handsomely. Megan and Carrie were each given a suite that looked like something out of a period movie and was almost the size of their apartment at home.

Megan's canopied bed had silken draperies flowing from a crown-shaped circlet attached to the ceiling. The linens were decorated with the Montrechet coat of arms, and the royal crest was repeated on a notepad beside the telephone. Against one wall was a huge, cream-colored armoire hand-decorated with a pastoral scene of shepherds and shepherdesses frolicking in a meadow filled with flowers.

Megan opened the tall French windows and stepped out onto a balcony that overlooked the manicured palace grounds. "Did you ever see anything like this?" she asked Carrie, who after a brief glimpse of her own quarters had now come to inspect Megan's.

"I could get used to this kind of living awfully fast."

"How is your suite?"

"Let's just say, they'll need a court order to evict me." Carrie grinned.

"If this is one of the guest suites, I wonder what Gabrielle's quarters look like."

"It sure beats our room at Madame Fouchard's, doesn't it?" Carrie agreed.

"I'm glad you thought of that. We'll have to go back for our things."

"There's no hurry. Henri said he'd provide us with a complete wardrobe."

"I doubt if toothbrushes and underwear were included. We'd better go right away while Madame Fouchard still recognizes me. Do you remember how to get back to Henri's office?"

"No, and I don't think it would be a good idea to wander around alone," Carrie said. "Nobody would ever believe us if we told them why we're here."

"We couldn't tell if we were asked. It's top secret."

Carrie went inside and flopped onto a down-filled couch, smiling beatifically. "Then I guess we'll just have to wallow in luxury until somebody remembers we're here."

A knock came at the bedroom door a few minutes later. Robert had brought a crew to begin Megan's makeover. There was a beauty operator named Alphonse, accompanied by Jeanne, a female makeup artist. The group also included Madame Céleste, who had brought along her assistant and a dressmaker. Each eyed Megan like a lump of clay to be molded to perfection.

"I didn't know you intended to start so soon," she exclaimed. "Carrie and I were planning to go check out of our guesthouse."

"There's no time for that," Robert said. "We have a lot to do in less than twenty-four hours."

"You don't have to go with me, Megan," Carrie told her. "I'll pack up your things."

"That won't be necessary," Robert said. "I'll send somebody to take care of it for you. If there's anyplace you'd like to go, a car and driver are at your disposal."

"Wow!" Carrie exclaimed. "I think I got the best part of this deal."

"Wait until Prince Nicholas arrives." Megan grinned.

"We must get started," Robert said. "Just write a note of authorization to release your possessions."

While Carrie went to look for a sheet of paper in the exquisite eighteenth-century writing desk in the living room, the makeover crew surrounded Megan.

"Don't bother to hurry back," she told Carrie when her friend returned with the note. "This will probably take some time and there's no reason for you to sit around doing nothing."

"Okay, I'll come back for the grand unveiling."

For the rest of the day people fussed over Megan. First her measurements were taken and Céleste conferred with her two helpers without bothering to ask for Megan's input.

When they left, the real work began. A variety of tints were used on Megan's hair before the desired shade was achieved. It was a long, boring process.

"I'll bet I'm going through all of this for nothing," she complained. "When you get finished I'll still look like me, only blond."

The two beauty operators were too intent to answer her. While Alphonse styled her hair, Jeanne worked on Megan's face like an artist painting a canvas. She used a variety of brushes and a seemingly endless amount of cosmetics. Megan wanted to watch what she was doing, but Jeanne was blocking her view in the mirror.

Robert and Henri arrived while Alphonse was combing out Megan's hair. "Are you almost finished?" Henri asked anxiously. "How does she look?"

"You can see for yourself in just a moment," Alphonse said, moving a strand of hair a fraction of an inch before spraying it lightly.

Jeanne applied a last slick of gloss to Megan's mouth,

then stepped back to view her work. The three men stared at Megan in dead silence.

"What?" she asked, slightly alarmed by the incredulous look on all their faces. Her eyes widened as she turned around to look in the mirror. "Good grief! What have you done to me?"

The face that looked back at her wasn't her own. Her long lashes had been lengthened even more with mascara, her lips were full and pouting now, and the long glamorous hair that cascaded around her shoulders was a pale ash blond that shimmered like moonlight.

"Do you still have doubts?" Henri asked Robert with satisfaction.

"I would not have believed it," the other man breathed. "She *is* the Princess Gabrielle!"

"Our problems are solved." Henri beamed.

Megan gazed soberly at the glamorous stranger in the mirror. "I only hope mine aren't just beginning," she muttered.

Michel spent a sleepless night waiting for Nicholas to return—and hoping it wasn't a vain expectation. Had he really driven all the way to Bienville in order to make himself even more miserable? It was just the sort of thing Nick would do, given the black mood he was in. Would he return, though? That was the big question. As the hours passed and dawn approached, Michel started to worry about what to tell the king.

The sun was rising in the sky when the prince finally put in an appearance. Michel hid his concern and pretended it was what he'd expected all along.

"Did you have a good time last night?" he asked casually.

"Surprisingly enough, I did." Nick's eyes softened as he remembered Megan's lovely, natural beauty.

"I knew it would do you good to get out among people.

What did you do all night? Anything you can talk about?''
Michel grinned.

"It was nothing like that. The evening was strictly
G-rated. I met the kind of girl I'd like to marry."

Michel's eyebrows climbed. "After playing the field all
these years, you fell in love in just a few hours?"

"That would be ironic, wouldn't it?"

Michel slanted a glance at him. "It would be unfortunate,
to say the least."

"Don't panic, nothing happened. I merely said she was
the *kind* of girl I'd like to marry." Nick's face hardened.
"Somebody sweet and generous—as different from Gabrielle as possible."

"Anybody would have looked good to you at this point.
She probably wasn't as special as you think."

"You wouldn't say that if you'd spent as much time with
her as I did." Nick's reminiscent smile faded. "But you
needn't worry. I don't have the luxury of getting to know
her better. I have an obligation to produce an heir."

"Most men would consider that a privilege. You'll have
to admit Gabrielle is very beautiful."

"Until you get to know her." Nick scowled. "She has
all the appeal of a rabid polar bear. I realize that I have an
obligation to my country, but our children might have to
be conceived by artificial insemination."

Chapter Three

Megan and Carrie spent all the next day finding out more than they wanted to know about royal protocol and the Montrechet family.

"I can see why Megan has to learn this stuff, but why do I have to?" Carrie complained. "I could be doing a lot more interesting things."

"If you were Princess Gabrielle's close friend, you'd know her family background," Robert explained. "Now, let's continue. What's the name of her mother's sister and how many children does she have?"

The two women were quizzed until it was time to dress for the reception that evening. After being released from "class," they returned to Megan's suite and went out on the balcony for a few moments to get some fresh air. Her balcony had a view of the front entry of the palace.

While they were reviewing all the things they had to remember, three long black limousines appeared on the winding driveway.

"What do you suppose those cars are doing here?" Megan asked. "It's too early for guests to start arriving."

Carrie shrugged. "It's probably just some official palace business."

Her explanation seemed reasonable as several older men with briefcases got out of the lead car. Then the chauffeur of the second car opened the passenger door in the back and a tall dark-haired man in a gray silk suit stepped out.

"It's Prince Nicholas!" Carrie squealed as both women leaned over the balcony for a better look.

Whether he could have heard her from that distance, or whether he was just conscious of their intense scrutiny, Nicholas turned to look in their direction. He stared at Megan for a long moment before turning to the young man beside him and saying a few words.

Then the prince was surrounded by Henri and other dignitaries who bowed and greeted him with short speeches, after which the entire party went into the palace.

Megan turned to Carrie in consternation. "Did you see that? He didn't recognize me. I told Henri we'd never get away with it!"

"Don't get excited. He was too far away to be sure it was you—I mean, Gabrielle."

"We knew who *he* was."

"How could you miss him, with all that pomp and ceremony? Everything here is done according to protocol. He couldn't very well wave and yell hello."

"I hope you're right," Megan answered doubtfully.

"I know I am." Carrie's face lit with excitement. "He's even more gorgeous in person. I can't wait to meet him! Come on, let's get dressed."

Before Megan could change clothes, Robert knocked at the door to tell her the king wanted to see her for a few moments.

As they walked down the corridor Megan said nervously, "What if he doesn't think I look like his daughter?"

"He will. You saw everyone's reaction."

"Her father might feel differently. Why does he want to see me?"

"One doesn't ask the king that question." Robert smiled.

He turned Megan over to a servant who showed her into the king's sitting room. The furnishings were as elegant as she expected, yet the room wasn't used solely for relaxing. Claude was signing papers at an exquisitely carved desk.

His eyes widened as he looked at her. "Remarkable!" he exclaimed. "Henri told me you bore a striking resemblance to my daughter, but I was unprepared for this."

"That makes me feel better. I'm really quite nervous about impersonating the princess," Megan said diffidently.

"You have my deepest gratitude for helping us out of an untenable position. How can I repay you?"

"It isn't necessary. Your hospitality is quite enough."

"Were you given adequate accommodations?"

"Yes, my suite is simply beautiful," Megan assured him.

"Splendid. If there is anything you need, don't hesitate to ask." The king's secretary was hovering in the doorway, waiting to get his attention. "I'll look forward to seeing you this evening, then," Claude said, dismissing her.

Robert had told Megan that the formal events would take place starting the following day. On this first evening of the prince's arrival there would be only a small, informal reception. Megan was afraid of being overdressed when she saw the gown that had been provided for her.

It was simple enough, yet wildly sexy. The long, creamy satin dress was cut on the bias and completely unadorned. It clung to her body like a second skin. Spaghetti straps held up the low-cut bodice, and the back plunged almost to her waist.

The dress was exactly the sort of thing Gabrielle would wear. She'd been pictured in similar outfits. Still, Megan's heart was beating rapidly as she and Carrie paused outside the double doors of the salon where the reception was being held.

"Remember hearing about that old TV show, 'Queen for a Day'?" she joked, to hide her nervousness. "I might be Princess for Five Minutes."

"Try not to blow it until we have a glass of champagne." Carrie grinned.

There were at least fifty people at the "small, informal reception"—all unfamiliar. Except for Prince Nicholas. He was at the far end of the room talking to King Claude and several other people. Megan's pulse raced as she gazed at his lean, handsome face.

Henri led her over to them, giving her last-minute instructions in a low voice. "The man with Nicholas is his equerry, Michel Charbet. You've met him, but you don't know him well, so don't worry about not remembering his background."

"How about the other man with them?" she asked nervously. "The one with the beard?"

"Nobody you need bother with."

Claude was outwardly relaxed, but Megan could tell the king's tension matched hers. His eyes were watchful as he greeted her with a smile. "Ah, here you are, my dear. Beautiful as always. But I'm sure you'd rather hear that from Nicholas."

As the others turned toward him expectantly, the prince's eyes traveled over Megan, lingering on her high, firm breasts. "Gabrielle's beauty has been widely remarked upon," he drawled.

While Claude frowned, Michel said quickly, "It would be hard not to sing Her Highness's praises."

Megan was too relieved to have passed the crucial test to realize that Nicholas might have been alluding to the princess's lurid press notices. Once she was sure he'd accepted her, she was free to look at him more closely.

Nicholas was even better looking in person. Photographs

didn't capture the vitality of the man, or the leashed power in his splendid body. She sensed powerful emotions in his gaze and her pulse quickened. The prince might not have seen much of Gabrielle lately, but he was definitely not indifferent to her. Would it become a problem to hold him off?

Megan couldn't imagine any woman wanting to! He would make love like he did everything else—superbly, satisfying his partner beyond her wildest dreams.

Carrie was hovering in the background, hoping for an opportunity to meet the prince. Henri motioned her over, deciding a diversion would be welcome. The tension in the little group was building.

"May I present Mademoiselle Tolliver, Your Highness," he said to Nicholas. "She is a school friend of the princess's."

After the introductions had been made all around, Michel asked, "Will you be staying for the festivities?"

"I wouldn't miss them for anything. You can just feel the romance in the air, can't you?" Carrie sighed blissfully. "Everybody is in such a happy mood."

"That's one of the duties of royalty—to make one's subjects happy," Nicholas remarked sardonically.

"May I get you a glass of champagne, *mademoiselle?*" Michel asked quickly.

"That's an excellent idea. You young people run along and enjoy yourselves," Claude said.

It was good advice, but difficult to follow. When Carrie and Michel drifted away along with the others, Megan didn't know what to say to Nicholas. And he wasn't giving her much help. He seemed so withdrawn and aloof.

She looked for a way to break the ice. Without knowing any of the friends or experiences he'd shared with Gabrielle, it wasn't easy. Finally, in desperation she remarked, "I guess it's going to be a busy week."

His high cheekbones sharpened. "That isn't the adjective I'd use."

"I know men don't like big fancy parties, but I must admit I'm looking forward to them."

"Why? What outrageous stunt are you planning?"

She looked at him with a slight frown. The prince's tone was definitely hostile. Had he and Gabrielle had an argument? That could be why she took off—not because she didn't want to marry Nicholas, as she'd told her father.

"Whatever happened in the past is over with," Megan said carefully. "I'm sure we can work it out."

He stared at her moodily. "I wish I could believe that."

Before she could reassure him, they were joined by a bejeweled older woman wearing a big smile. "Gabrielle, darling, I'm so happy for you!" She kissed Megan on both cheeks. "And you, too, dear boy. You make a simply gorgeous couple."

"You're very kind, Madame Duchais," Nicholas murmured, providing Megan with a much-needed clue. This must be Gabrielle's Aunt Geneviève, her mother's sister.

"Your marriage will unite our two countries as never before," the older woman continued. "Your parents must be so pleased."

"They're even happier about it than we are," Nicholas replied sardonically. "Isn't that true, Gabrielle?"

"I wouldn't say that." Megan smiled and linked her arm with his. "I'm pretty thrilled about it myself." She could feel his long body stiffen.

His mouth tightened, but he managed a smile. "Would you excuse us, Madame Duchais? I have something I want to say to Gabrielle."

"Of course, run along. I know how it is with lovebirds," she said archly. "You want to be alone."

"You're right." His arm circled Megan's waist like a steel band. "I wouldn't like anyone else to hear what I have to say to Gabrielle."

As he hustled her toward the tall French windows leading to the garden, Megan was very much aware of his angular hip pressing against hers.

Nicholas didn't stop at the terrace. He pulled her down a winding path, past a flower garden to a lacy gazebo set in a grove of trees. She was completely bewildered and slightly uneasy. Was his apparent anger really frustration at their lack of privacy? Did he plan to make up passionately? Megan was torn between anticipation and apprehension. Just how intimate were he and Gabrielle?

The filtered moonlight cast shadows over Nicholas's face, sharpening his high cheekbones and turning his eyes into unfathomable pools. He loomed over her in the semi-darkness, potently male and more than a little dangerous.

Megan tried to tell herself she was being fanciful. He was a civilized, sophisticated man. But she instinctively took a step backward. If Nicholas decided to get physical, she would be no match for him.

"Don't even think about it!" His hands fastened around her arms and he jerked her toward him. "You're not going anywhere until you tell me what kind of game you're playing."

She looked at him blankly. "I don't know what you're talking about."

"That wide-eyed-innocent act is out of character—like the rest of your behavior tonight."

"I thought I was being very pleasant," she said warily.

"That's what I mean."

"You're complaining because I'm acting like an adult? It's more than I can say for you," she couldn't help adding. "Two people can have an argument and still be civil to each other."

"What does that have to do with anything? I want to know why you're giving everyone the impression that you're thrilled about this marriage. What am I supposed to do, play Romeo to your Juliet?"

"You might at least pretend we're in love, even if you've had a change of heart."

"You're not making sense. I feel the same way about you as I always have," he said morosely. "You're a spoiled little brat."

"At least I don't hold a grudge." She slanted a glance at him. "I can't even remember what we argued about."

"I don't recall any particular argument. We disagree on everything, so we've managed to avoid each other most of the time. Maybe we can continue on that way after the public display is over."

"You're not even going to *try* to make this marriage work?" she asked in outrage.

"Spare me your phony indignation. You're as dead set against our getting married as I am."

Megan stared at him in surprise. "You don't want to marry Ga—" She caught herself just in time. "You don't want to marry me?"

"There's no audience, so knock it off," he said disgustedly. "You undoubtedly had as big a fight with your father as I had with mine. I guess we brought this on ourselves by thinking we could simply ignore the paparazzi, but our parents could have picked a less painful way to teach us a lesson."

Megan was shocked by the revelation that both the prince and the princess were opposed to their marriage. They had seemed so perfect for each other—both of them glamorous, rich and royal. But they were also equally spoiled and willful. Megan realized the marriage would be a disaster under those circumstances.

"You'll just have to try harder to convince your parents that you and—I mean, that we're wrong for each other," she said.

He uttered a short bitter laugh. "How far did you get with *your* father?"

While Megan was thinking of a response, Henri appeared. "Ah, there you are. Is everything all right?" His expression was unruffled, but he flicked a glance at Megan. "Your guests are wondering where you disappeared to."

"Surely they can understand our desire to be alone," Nicholas answered derisively.

"Yes, assuredly, and I hesitate to intrude on your privacy. But King Claude wishes to propose a toast to welcome Your Highness to Beaumarre."

"I certainly wouldn't want to miss that," Nicholas drawled.

Megan accompanied the men back to the palace in silence, deeply regretting her part in this sorry affair. If Gabrielle had remained missing, her father would have had to admit it and the engagement would have fallen through.

There might have been diplomatic repercussions, but the monarchies would have survived. Protocol wasn't excuse enough to force two people into a loveless marriage. Unfortunately it was too late now for her to do anything about it.

She was forced to stand next to Nicholas, in front of all the assembled guests while a beaming King Claude held up a glass of champagne.

"First I want to welcome Prince Nicholas to our country and to the Montrechet family. As you all know, tomorrow my daughter and the prince will become formally engaged."

He was interrupted by applause and well-bred cheers.

"I want to thank all of you, family and dear friends alike, for being here tonight to celebrate this very happy occasion with us," the king continued. "I'm sure we all wish this lovely young couple a long and happy marriage."

Megan stole a peek at Nicholas. His face was expressionless, but she could sense the tension in his lean body. *Say something!* she willed him silently. It's now or never. You don't have to go through with it.

But the prince wasn't tuned in to her wavelength. He

stood ramrod straight and tall, gazing out at the crowd with
a regal expression, as Claude concluded his speech.

When it was over, the guests crowded around to offer
congratulations and make enthusiastic comments. They
were mostly polite little platitudes, except for Aunt Geneviève's.

"I know you're dying to kiss her," she told Nicholas.
"Go ahead, dear boy, this is a private party. You can indulge yourself."

Michel was standing next to him. "The prince doesn't
wish to seem disrespectful," he said quickly.

"Nonsense! He's going to marry the girl, isn't he?"

"True, but perhaps he feels a public display is unseemly," Henri said.

"You're getting to be an old fuddy-duddy, Henri," Geneviève said. "A little kiss between an about-to-be engaged
couple is scarcely a public display."

People standing nearby were giving them amused looks.
Nicholas muttered something under his breath and clamped
an arm around Megan's waist, drawing her against his side.
As he lowered his head to kiss her cheek, she turned her
face to look at him. Instead of a chaste kiss on the cheek,
their lips brushed.

It was just a fleeting touch, but she reacted to him instantly. The brief contact made her want the real thing—to
feel his mouth firmly against hers, his lips teasing hers
apart.

Megan turned away abruptly. What was the matter with
her? She was acting like a giddy teenager. A couple of
nights ago she'd felt this way about Philippe. Now, Nicholas.

Suddenly she stiffened and turned to stare at him. Was
it possible that Philippe had really been Nicholas, out for
a last night on the town before his engagement? The resemblance was striking, although Philippe hadn't been this
regal. She remembered him as being slightly shorter, too,

and certainly not this impeccably groomed. And Megan couldn't image Prince Nicholas ever appearing in public needing a shave.

It was undoubtedly only a coincidence that both men were wrestling with a problem that made them unhappy. She didn't even know what Philippe's problem was. Something perfectly mundane like losing his job, no doubt.

Nicholas thought Megan was annoyed at him because of their inadvertent kiss. "I could scarcely help it," he said in an irritated undertone. "I'm damned if I do, and damned if I don't," he muttered.

Geneviève wasn't conscious of any tension. "I'm sure you can kiss her with more feeling than that, but perhaps it's a good thing. You'd only make all the other girls jealous. Isn't that right, Gabrielle?"

Megan gave her a blank look. "Oh...yes, I suppose so."

"Don't tell me you don't know," the older woman said archly.

"May I get you more champagne, *madame?*" Henri took the woman's elbow and expertly led her away.

"Your aunt is quite the romantic," Michel said with a smile after they'd left.

"Dowagers thrive on these big extravaganzas," Megan answered dismissively.

She and Michel made small talk for a few minutes. It wasn't relaxed, however, because Nicholas didn't join in. At least he wasn't making barbed comments anymore, Megan told herself. But she was very conscious of his brooding presence.

Fortunately they were never alone for long. People kept coming over to chat, which made things easier. Nicholas was too well mannered to be surly to the guests. As he accepted their good wishes, Megan got to see the charisma that made him so sought after.

His charm was especially potent with the female sex—

married or single. Megan was amused to see these sophisticated women acting as flirtatiously as young girls.

But Nicholas was almost equally popular with men. He was as knowledgeable about sports and politics as he was about art and the theater—a true Renaissance man.

All of this and the physique of a Greek god. Megan sighed. Why couldn't she have met someone like him who was available?

It was a difficult evening due to all the undercurrents, although the guests weren't aware of them. Everyone was having too good a time to leave.

Megan was relieved when King Claude finally said goodnight, signaling that the party was over. He called her aside as he was leaving.

"Thank you for being here," he said quietly. "You have done a great service to Beaumarre."

"I hope so." She looked at him hesitantly, wanting to say more. But how could she tell a king that he was doing a terrible injustice to two innocent people—one of them his own daughter?

The moment passed as he kissed her forehead, in keeping with the act he was putting on for any onlookers. "Sleep well, my dear."

After Megan and Nicholas had said good-night to the last reluctant guest, he loosened his tie. "I'm going to have a drink. Would you care for one?" he asked her.

She knew he was only asking out of courtesy so she shook her head. "No, thanks. I think I'll go to bed. Tomorrow is going be a long day."

"Yes, well, good night then." He watched moodily as she ascended the broad marble staircase.

Michel followed Nicholas into a paneled den and poured him a drink from the bar instead of ringing for a servant.

"You carried everything off very well tonight," he remarked.

Nicholas raised a dark eyebrow. "Did I have a choice? Gabrielle did suggest that I reason with my father. I couldn't decide whether she was being typically unrealistic, or if she said it to taunt me."

"I thought she was quite charming this evening," Michel protested.

"Yes, and it made me wary. That's not the Gabrielle I remember. I kept bracing myself for some kind of scene."

"You haven't seen her in a long time. People change."

"Maybe." Nicholas's tone revealed his skepticism.

"She's gotten even more beautiful," Michel persisted. "You'll have to admit that."

Nicholas's expression became wholly male. "A man would have to be dead not to appreciate a face and figure like that." He stuck his hands in his pockets and paced the floor restlessly. "My father could be right about me—I have a weakness for beautiful women. How else can I explain the fact that I'm turned on by a woman I don't even like?"

"You never knew Gabrielle more than superficially. She certainly seems to be handling the situation in a mature manner. I was very impressed by her tonight."

"By her, or by her friend, Carrie?" Nicholas joked. "You seemed quite attracted to her."

"She's different from any girl I've ever met," Michel admitted. "More fun and less impressed with herself. Perhaps she's responsible for the change in Gabrielle."

"Whatever the reason, I hope it lasts."

Carrie was waiting in Megan's room to discuss the evening. "Wasn't it a fabulous party? I never saw so many gorgeous men! Of course you got the pick of the pack, but I'd be happy to settle for Nicholas's man Friday. I love that boyish type, even though it's deceiving in his case. Michel must be as sophisticated as the prince."

"He's awfully nice," Megan agreed.

Carrie prattled on about the party without noticing that Megan was saying very little. Finally she became aware of it. "I guess you're tired—and no wonder! It must have been a strain in the beginning, wondering if you could pass for Gabrielle, especially with Nicholas. But he seemed to accept you. He was very austere, though. I guess that was because the king and all the dignitaries were there. According to everything I've read, he's certainly not that way normally."

"Nicholas wasn't just on his good behavior tonight." Megan told her what she'd discovered early in the evening. "I wish I'd never let myself be talked into this charade. If it weren't for me, there wouldn't be any engagement tomorrow. Nicholas would never forgive me if he knew I could have prevented his marriage."

"I'm not so sure you could have. Monarchies are riddled with politics, the same as democracies. They have spin doctors who take over in a crisis and do damage control. King Claude would simply have postponed the engagement."

"For what reason?"

"He'd have found one. It might not have been totally believable, and the king and his crew would have lost a lot of credibility—something they're very touchy about. But you can bet they wouldn't have called off the wedding. It's too important to both countries."

"That's reprehensible, but I'd feel a lot better if I thought you were right," Megan said uncertainly.

"I know I am, so stop blaming yourself. You're only pinch-hitting at the engagement. Something could happen to get them off the hook between now and the wedding date." Carrie grinned suddenly. "Which brings up an interesting question. If Gabrielle continues to be a no-show, do you think they'll ask you to take her place at the altar? And if they did, which one of you would actually be married to the prince?"

"Even if this were my country, which it isn't, that would

be above and beyond the call of duty,'' Megan answered dryly.

"You'd certainly have a memorable wedding night. He's a really virile man. I'll bet he's gorgeous in the nude.''

Having been closer than Carrie to his hard body, Megan didn't doubt it in the least. She remembered his arm around her waist, jerking her against his long length. It had been only an angry gesture, but that didn't lessen his potent attraction.

It boggled her mind to imagine his nude body poised over hers on their wedding night. He would whisper erotic words in her ear while his hands caressed her, bringing her body to pulsating life.

Carrie was unaware of the images she'd triggered. "It wouldn't be ethical to find out, but it's fun to think about.'' She laughed.

"Nothing about this situation is fun. How would you like to be forced on a man who loathed you?'' Megan asked.

"It's nothing personal. He'd probably be crazy about you if you met under different circumstances.''

"Is that supposed to make me feel better?'' Megan sighed. "I'm going to wash off all this makeup and go to bed.''

Carrie tilted her head to stare at her critically. "I'm getting kind of used to you like this. You look like a celebrity. If they teach you how to apply that makeup yourself, you could mingle with the jet set.''

"I'd still be me under all the goop,'' Megan answered, yawning. "I might look like Gabrielle, but I can't keep her hours. I'm going to sleep.''

As the time for the festivities drew near the next day, Megan was surrounded by people. While her elaborate makeup was being duplicated and her hair restyled, Céleste brought out the dress Megan would wear that afternoon.

It was downright chaste compared to last night's gown.

The lavender two-piece dress had short sleeves and a scooped neckline that would skim her collarbones. The skirt was short, with a scalloped hem to match that of the over-blouse.

"Your gown for the ball tonight is in the closet," Céleste told her. "I showed your maid where the circlet is sewn on to the train. Be sure you loop it over your wrist when you dance," she said as she followed the others out the door.

Megan's eyebrows rose. "A train? I only hope I don't trip over it," she remarked to Robert who had remained to give her last-minute instructions regarding the public ceremony.

"You'll do fine," he assured her. "Look how well you managed last night. Nobody suspected a thing."

"Something puzzles me," she said. "Last night was successful, but how do you expect to keep this deception a secret when so many outsiders know about it? Like Jeanne and Alphonse and Céleste. Any one of them could make a fortune selling the story to the tabloids."

"They won't," he answered confidently. "Yes, they'd make a tidy sum, but they would lose more than they gained. Jeanne and Alphonse profit greatly from being official beauticians to the princess. The same is true for Céleste in her line of work. Customers flock to her shop so they can say they buy their clothes where the princess does. Without Gabrielle's patronage all of them would be just ordinary small-business people. It was necessary to enlist their services, but I can assure you we took no risk."

"That's comforting."

"All you have to concern yourself with is the ceremony this afternoon. You won't have to say much. The people just want to see you and the prince together. You'll both stand next to the king on the balcony. After he makes a little speech announcing the engagement, you'll say a few words about how happy you are. Then Nicholas will say something similar.''

"I hope he can make it sound convincing. I don't know if you're aware of it, but Prince Nicholas isn't any keener on this union than Gabrielle is.''

Robert's face became expressionless. "It would be unseemly of me to pry into the personal lives of the prince and princess.''

"You don't have to pry. I'm telling you they don't even like each other.''

"I am sure you got the wrong impression.'' Before giving her a chance to deny it, Robert took two dark blue velvet boxes out of his briefcase. "This is the jewelry you will wear today.'' The square box held a necklace of large pearls with a diamond clasp. Inside the long box was a three-strand pearl bracelet with a matching clasp.

"They're beautiful,'' Megan murmured, touching them gently.

"They are suitable for daytime attire. This evening I will bring you the jewels you will wear to the ball. Do you have any questions?''

"What's the procedure after the engagement is official?''

"King Claude will invite everyone to have refreshments and stroll around the grounds. Then the three of you will proceed down to the south garden for a reception line. People will come up to offer their good wishes, much like last night only on a more extensive scale. I hope your shoes are comfortable.'' Robert smiled.

"I do, too.''

He looked at his watch. "If everything is clear, I have a meeting with Henri.''

After Robert left, Megan untied her robe and started toward the bedroom. When there was a knock on the door she thought it was the maid coming to help her dress.

"Come in,'' she called without retying her belt.

It would be difficult to decide who was the more startled,

Nicholas or Megan. After the initial surprise his eyes started to glow as he gazed at her provocatively clad body.

She was wearing a skimpy lace bra that revealed most of her breasts, and sheer-to-the-waist panty hose that gave a tantalizing glimpse of the rest of her.

Megan was frozen to the spot for a moment by the raw desire in his gaze—and the answering throb in her own midsection. Then her cheeks flamed and she closed her robe and belted it tightly.

"I was expecting the maid. What are you doing here?" she asked brusquely, to cover her momentary lapse. Megan didn't know if she was angrier at him or herself for the unexpected surge of answering desire that had swept through her.

"I came to bring you this." He held out a small square jeweler's box. "I thought it would be better if I gave it to you without an audience. It's your engagement ring."

Her eyes widened after she opened the box. Inside was a very large square-cut diamond set in a frame of sapphires. They sparkled like satellites surrounding a blazing sun. "It's gorgeous!" she gasped.

"I'm glad you like it," he said politely.

"Who wouldn't? I've never seen anything this magnificent!"

Nicholas gave her a puzzled look. "You have a lot of beautiful jewelry."

"Oh... Well, yes, but an engagement ring is different."

He continued to stare at her. "I don't understand this act you're putting on, Gabrielle. Did your father promise you something if you behaved? Is that it?"

"I don't know what you want," she answered impatiently. "I told you to stand up to *your* father and you said it was impossible. That means you're stuck with me. Would it make you feel better if I threw tantrums and made life miserable for everybody?"

"No, of course not. But I can't understand your calm acceptance of a situation that must be as galling to you as it is to me."

She shrugged. "When there's no alternative, you make the best of things."

"Does that mean you want to make ours a real marriage?" he asked slowly.

Any woman in her right mind would want that. But Gabrielle wasn't known for her common sense. If Megan led Nicholas to think his wife would be willing to meet him halfway, what would happen when Gabrielle returned, as difficult and rebellious as ever?

While Megan hesitated, searching for a safe answer to his question, Nicholas's lip curled sardonically. "I thought not. You have some secret agenda you're not telling me about. Daddy must have dug down deep to turn a spoiled hellion into a reasonable human being."

"Are you this suspicious of everyone, or just of me?" she asked in annoyance. "I don't know if this marriage will work out, but if it doesn't, at least half the blame will be yours."

"How can it work when a major ingredient is missing?" he demanded.

"We could learn to trust each other in time."

"I was referring to love," he said curtly. "The main purpose of our marriage is to provide an heir. That's something that happens naturally with other couples. In our case it's a duty."

"Are you telling me you'd find it difficult to make love to me?" Megan asked indignantly.

His gaze transferred to her body, as though he could see under the thin robe. "You're a very beautiful woman. No man would consider it a hardship to have sex with you."

"Thanks for nothing!" she said angrily.

He shrugged. "You asked a question and I answered it.

We might make each other's lives a living hell, but I don't think we'll have a problem in the bedroom.''

"Guess again, pal.'' Her eyes flashed blue fire. "Your ability couldn't begin to match your ego.''

"I wasn't bragging. I was paying tribute to your ability to excite a man—and I'm certainly not immune. When I said I didn't anticipate any trouble, I meant I would try to make the experience as memorable for you as it would be for me.''

"How could it be when we don't even like each other?''

He smiled derisively. "I don't think that's a requirement for sex.'' His smile died. "Unfortunately I always expected to marry for love, as I'm sure you did, too. But I guess I'm willing to make the best of it if you are.''

Megan's anger was replaced by compassion. "You never know what will happen in life,'' she said vaguely, because it was the only comfort she could offer him.

"That's true,'' he answered tonelessly. "Well...I just came to give you the ring.''

"Thank you. I'll wear it at the ceremony.''

He hesitated. "Would you like me to put it on your finger? I guess that's traditional.''

Megan had decidedly mixed feelings as she held out her left hand. She'd always looked forward to falling in love and becoming engaged. But when that happy day finally came, it was apt to be an anticlimax. The ring would pale in comparison to this one, and Nicholas would be a haunting memory. She gazed up at him, unable to keep from envying Gabrielle, as he slipped the ring on her finger.

His hand tightened on hers as he gazed at her parted lips. "This is also traditional,'' he murmured, lowering his head.

His kiss was tentative at first, and Megan's response was the same. She knew she was skating on thin ice. In spite of insurmountable problems on both sides, neither of them was indifferent to the other.

But when his mouth lingered on hers, she swayed toward him. His arms closed around her, molding her to his body. In an instant the chemistry between them ignited, making all their differences seem minor. She felt weightless in his embrace, as if she were actually part of him.

Megan never knew what might have happened if Carrie hadn't knocked at the door. Later she was grateful, but not at the time.

Carrie stuck her head inside, calling out, "I know you're not ready yet but Henri told me to come downstairs early, so I— Oops! Sorry."

Nicholas released Megan and turned to Carrie with a smile. "It's all right. We're almost legal." He gazed into Megan's eyes and said softly, "I'll see you soon."

When he'd left the room, Carrie said, "Not that I blame you, but aren't you throwing yourself into your role a little too enthusiastically?"

Megan was shaken by the intensity of her response, but she pretended to dismiss the incident. "Nicholas and I were merely discussing our—I mean, *his* future relationship with Gabrielle."

"That was no discussion I walked in on. Are you sure you know what you're doing?"

"If I did, would I be here now?" Megan sighed.

"This was supposed to be a lot of fun. But not if you fall in love with the guy. I don't want you to get hurt, Megan."

"I'm not in love with Nicholas. I know that would be disastrous. I'll admit I'm physically attracted to him, but it's nothing I can't handle."

"Just don't try to test your willpower. The guy is awesomely sexy."

"First you tell me to stay away from him and then you

tell me how gorgeous he is,'' Megan exclaimed impatiently.

"There was never any doubt about that. I'm simply advising you to look, but don't touch.'' Carrie started for the door. "I'll see you after the ceremony.''

Chapter Four

It was a perfect day for the festivities. The sun shone brightly, but it wasn't too hot. People had started arriving at the palace grounds early, dressed in their best clothes and in a party mood. As the time for the announcement neared, the grounds beneath the balcony became thickly carpeted with excited people waiting for a glimpse of the royal family.

Megan was a little self-conscious about seeing Nicholas. What had happened between them was incomprehensible and mustn't happen again. But how did she convey that to him without starting up their cold war once more?

Nicholas was unaware of her decision, making it even more difficult. He smiled warmly at her when she joined him and the king a few minutes before the ceremony.

Their appearance on the balcony brought a prolonged cheer from the crowd. They only quieted when King Claude held up his hand. Then they gave him their rapt attention while he announced the engagement of his beloved daughter, Gabrielle Simone, to Prince Nicholas Philippe de Valmontine of Grandalia.

When the roar died down, Megan gave her short prepared speech, which was followed by a few words from Nicholas.

The crowd was so giddy with excitement that a man called out, "Let's see you give her a kiss, Prince!"

They ignored him, but others in the throng took up the chant. Finally Nicholas glanced at Megan ruefully and leaned forward to kiss her cheek.

It didn't satisfy the people. "Is that the best you can do?" another man yelled. "Give her a real kiss!"

Before things could get any more raucous, Nicholas took her hands and kissed her gently on the lips. It was radically different from the passionate kiss in her suite, but it affected her almost as strongly. This kiss expressed tenderness and affection. With the right woman, Nicholas could be a companion as well as a lover. Megan drew back reluctantly, reminding herself that she wasn't that woman.

King Claude made a brief appearance in the south garden and then left Megan and the prince to handle the reception line, which stretched on endlessly.

She became adept at moving people along, but it was more difficult for Nicholas. The men stopped for a moment to express their hearty good wishes, but the women stared at him with dazzled faces, and invented reasons to linger. Older women, young women—it didn't make any difference. His appeal was universal.

Finally Henri took pity on them and ended the reception. He took the sting out of it by inviting everyone to have more champagne and stroll through the gardens.

"I'm glad that's over," Nicholas said as they returned to the palace.

"Don't tell me you weren't enjoying all the attention," she teased as they walked down the hall. "You were mobbed by women gazing at you adoringly."

"You're imagining things. They were just being polite to a stranger."

"They would have been friends with very little coaxing," she remarked dryly.

He looked at her with a tiny smile. "Don't tell me you're jealous."

"Not at all. I thought it was amusing."

"Too bad. I was beginning to think you cared," he said lightly. When they reached the den near the marble staircase he suggested a drink.

"No, thanks, but I'll keep you company while you have one." She sank down on the couch and kicked off her shoes. They'd been comfortable at the start of the day, but not after hours of standing.

"Why don't you lie down and put your feet up?" he suggested, as he poured his drink.

"I might fall asleep."

"What's wrong with that? The ball doesn't start for hours yet. Stretch out," he urged, walking toward her. "Unless you're afraid of getting your dress wrinkled."

She looked at him warily. "You're not going to suggest I take it off?"

"Not here." He smiled sensuously. "My last glimpse of you unclothed almost made me forget I'm a gentleman."

"That was a mistake," she mumbled, remembering his avid gaze traveling over her nearly nude body.

"That isn't what I'd call it." He laughed, plumping a pillow and urging her head onto it. "Relax. I'm scarcely going to attack you with half of Beaumarre within hollering distance."

Megan knew she was being foolish. Nicholas was just clowning around. He could get all the female company he wanted without this much effort. "I'm not being very good company," she murmured as her eyelids drooped.

"You don't have to entertain me. I'm doing what I want to do, too."

Her eyes popped open as he sat at the opposite end of the couch, put his glass on the end table and propped her ankle on his thigh. Before she had a chance to overreact he began to massage her aching foot.

"Does that feel good?"

"Mmm, it feels wonderful," she whispered.

"Then close your eyes. I'll do the other foot next."

Megan was so comfortable she felt like purring. She drifted off to sleep with a smile on her face and his hands gently massaging her.

When she awoke half an hour later, Nicholas was gone and she was covered with a light, fleecy afghan. He was really a very thoughtful man. How could she have misjudged him so badly?

Carrie came bursting into the room as she was putting on her shoes. "I just got the most fantastic news! Ambassador Hayes has the flu!"

Megan raised her eyebrows. "If that makes you happy, you must get euphoric over earthquakes and other disasters."

"I didn't mean it the way it sounded. Naturally I'm sorry that he isn't feeling well. But it isn't anything life threatening, and it means I get to go to the ball."

Henri had told Carrie she couldn't attend because the ambassador would wonder why Megan wasn't there. If he started to ask questions, the whole impersonation could be jeopardized. It was possible he might recognize Megan in spite of her metamorphosis.

"Congratulations, Cinderella." Megan smiled. "Just remember the prince is already spoken for."

"I'll settle for Michel. He might not be as glamorous, but I wouldn't need to keep my eye on him every minute. Gabrielle will have to beat off the competition with a stick."

"Not after the wedding. I think Nicholas will try to make the marriage work."

"A marriage that was forced on him?"

"He's not as adamantly opposed any longer," Megan murmured.

"That's because you look like Gabrielle, but you're not acting like her. Wait until she takes over. He'll wonder what hit him."

"Not necessarily. When she sees how kind and thoughtful he is, she'll change, too."

Carrie looked at her disapprovingly. "You used to be so astute about men. How did you let this one get past your guard? A womanizer like Nicholas never changes."

"It isn't fair to put labels on people. There's a lot more to him than his playboy image. I found that out when I got to know him better."

"If you say so." Carrie shrugged. "It doesn't matter whether you're right or wrong about him, because fortunately he isn't your problem. Let's go upstairs. I have to decide what to wear tonight."

Megan had thought her gown from the night before was elegant, but it paled in comparison to the ball gown provided for this evening. The pale yellow chiffon-and-lace creation had a wide, low-cut neckline that was very revealing. Her shoulders were bare, as well as the upper slopes of her high breasts. The long, fluid column of the skirt flowed from an Empire waistline and culminated in a train in back.

Megan was looking for the circlet sewn onto the skirt when a knock sounded at the door. It was Henri and he was carrying a jeweler's box like the ones Robert had brought in the afternoon, only this one was larger.

"Very nice," he said, circling her while staring at her critically.

Megan tugged at her bodice. "It's a beautiful gown, but I don't think Céleste knew how low-cut this would be on me."

"She knows what she's doing. It's exactly the sort of thing Gabrielle would wear to an affair like this."

"If you say so. What's in the box—more jewelry?"

"These are a selection from the crown jewels."

She gasped when he opened the box. Inside on a bed of white satin was a magnificent diamond necklace that glittered like a burst of fiery stars. The matching bracelet was equally exquisite, but the piece that widened Megan's eyes was a graceful diamond tiara.

"A tiara?" she exclaimed. "Isn't that a bit much?"

"You're a princess and this is the second most important night of your life, outranked only by the wedding celebration."

"That's something we need to talk about. Have you made any progress in finding Gabrielle?"

"She appears to have simply vanished into thin air. I don't understand it." Henri frowned.

"Maybe she had an accident and is lying in a hospital somewhere. Has that occurred to you?"

"We've explored *every* possibility. Fortunately that's unlikely. Gabrielle is instantly recognizable. Someone would have contacted us, even if she was unable or unwilling to."

"Then what are you going to do?"

Henri shrugged. "The only thing we *can* do—keep looking. She can't remain hidden away forever."

"She's done a good job of it so far. Whether you find her or not, I can't stay here indefinitely. I have a job to get back to."

"Perhaps I can discreetly pull a few strings to enable you to stay longer."

"I'm not sure I want to," Megan said slowly. "This whole thing seemed like a lark at first. But I didn't realize I'd be meddling with people's lives. Neither Gabrielle nor Prince Nicholas wants to marry the other. I'm sure you know that. You know everything else that goes on around here."

"The prince is as mulish as the princess," Henri said dismissively, without admitting anything.

"Is it obstinate to want to marry for love?"

"They both fall in love regularly. The newest face attracts them. If you had spent any time with the prince, you would have seen it for yourself."

"You've all misjudged him. Nicholas is actually a warm, kind human being. I realize he's gone from one woman to another, but that will change when he finds the right one."

Henri looked at her without expression. "Prince Nicholas's choices are limited. He must marry someone of royal blood. You would be wise to remember that."

"I don't have any personal stake in this." She could tell what Henri was implying. "I simply object to being the Judas goat that leads them to the altar."

"The marriage will take place—with your help or without it," Henri stated flatly. "You're merely saving everyone a great deal of embarrassment." Without giving her a chance to argue the point, he picked up the necklace and clasped it around her neck. "Robert or I will come to your room after the ball to collect these and return them to the safe."

"I feel very nervous about wearing all this jewelry. These pieces must be worth millions."

"More importantly, they are irreplaceable."

"Thanks, that makes me feel a lot better!"

"You have nothing to worry about. The palace is well guarded. I will leave you to finish getting ready. The prince will meet you downstairs in—" he looked at his watch "—precisely twenty minutes."

When he'd gone, Megan realized how deftly Henri had changed the subject after subtly advising her that the prince was off-limits. Warning her not to fall in love with Nicholas was becoming a cottage industry, she thought resentfully. As though there were any chance of that happening. Yeah, when pigs played piano!

* * *

Megan concentrated on holding up her train as she descended the broad marble staircase. She was so intent on not tripping that she didn't notice Nicholas waiting below.

His eyes held admiration as he gazed at her. "You look exquisite," he said in a deep male voice.

"You're not too shabby yourself." She smiled.

Some of the men she'd gone out with looked uncomfortable when the occasion called for a tuxedo, but Nicholas could have posed as one of those relaxed sophisticates in a men's magazine. His dinner jacket was tailored to perfection, and the formal black-and-white attire accentuated his broad shoulders and narrow hips.

"Are you ready for another mob scene?" he asked.

"Ready if you are." She took the arm he offered.

There were hundreds of people milling around the baroque grand ballroom. They were all dressed splendidly and the women were bedecked with precious jewels.

The noisy chatter died down as everyone faced the doorway expectantly. Megan and Nicholas paused at the top of the stairs while a palace servant in fancy livery stepped forward.

"Princess Gabrielle and Prince Nicholas Philippe de Valmontine," he announced solemnly.

Megan could hardly keep from wriggling with pleasure. It was exactly like a movie and her part was a starring role. She lifted her head regally—hoping her tiara was securely anchored—and accompanied Nicholas down the stairs to the ballroom.

After a few moments the orchestra began to play and people gathered around the dance floor. Robert had told her their appearance would be a signal for the music to begin, but he hadn't told her that she and Nicholas would dance the first number alone.

Megan was self-conscious as she moved into his arms, aware of all the eyes on them. But when he put his arms around her and drew her close, the crowd seemed unimportant.

Nicholas was a marvelous dancer. She followed him effortlessly, almost as if she were part of him. They glided silently around the room, communicating with their bodies. Megan glanced up at his rugged face once and he smiled, sharing her unspoken pleasure.

When the music stopped they were surrounded by people, as always, and she moved reluctantly out of his arms.

That brief interlude was the longest time she spent with Nicholas that evening. Everyone wanted a word with them and they gradually became separated.

Megan glanced around every now and then, looking for Nicholas, but he seemed to be enjoying himself without her. Of course, a lot of these people were his friends, she told herself, and he hadn't seen them recently. She couldn't help noticing, however, that a lot of those friends were female.

Once when she glanced over he was talking to a pretty young blonde, and another time it was a stunning older woman with dark hair dramatically pulled back from her face. He didn't seem to have a preference. He gave all of them the kind of flattering attention any woman responded to. Megan was reminded of Henri's assessment of Nicholas—the newest face attracted him. She dismissed the uncharitable thought. Nicholas was *supposed* to be charming tonight.

One of the most outstanding new faces was that of a redhead with milky skin to complement her flaming hair. She was perhaps in her early thirties and a total knockout.

Megan wanted to know who she was, but she hesitated to ask, in case she was supposed to know. When the redhead managed to get Nicholas alone in a corner, Megan decided to chance it. While she was trying to decide how to frame the question, a woman in the group around her made it unnecessary.

"You'd better watch your fiancé," she said. "Noëlle has a predatory gleam in her eye."

"Nick is the one who'd better watch out," one of the men said with a laugh. "There's no telling what Charles will do if he catches him making nice with Noëlle. The old boy's jealousy is legendary."

"It serves him right for marrying a woman almost twenty years younger," another woman observed tartly. "What did he expect?"

Megan followed the woman's gaze to an older man with a slight paunch and thinning hair.

"Noëlle could be a little more discreet," the first woman said.

"Some women just have a need for attention," Megan remarked.

"You used to speak plainer than that, Gabrielle." The man chuckled.

Some other people joined them and the conversation shifted. Megan forgot about Noëlle until she looked around for Nick a little later and discovered the redhead was still by his side. Not only that, she was clinging to his arm and whispering something in his ear. He nodded and the two of them started for the door.

A white-hot flame of anger engulfed Megan. Henri was right! Anybody would do. How could she have been so taken in by Nicholas? And how could he carry on with another woman right here in the palace at his own engagement party?

Megan was so furious that she didn't stop to realize the prince's behavior shouldn't concern her. He wasn't cheating on her; he was cheating on Gabrielle—and the princess didn't care.

Megan's teeth were tightly clenched as she watched Nicholas and the redhead start up the staircase. Noëlle was leaning against him and he had his arm around her. It would serve them right if her husband did find them together!

She instinctively glanced around to locate the older man, and was appalled to see him starting for the door. The stormy look on his face was evidence that he, too, had seen the couple leave together. Fortunately he was having trouble getting through the crowd.

Megan hesitated only a split second. Nicholas didn't deserve any consideration, but for all she knew, Charles had a gun. He might be just fed up enough with his wife to make an example of her next conquest. At the very least he would cause a nasty scene that would be the talk of the town. She was doing this for King Claude, Megan assured herself.

After excusing herself from the group, she crossed the room more rapidly than Charles. Everybody stood aside to let her pass.

Once outside the ballroom she ran rapidly up the stairs and down the corridor, calling out to Nicholas. Numerous guest rooms opened off the hallway and she didn't have time to look into each one—the outraged husband wasn't far behind.

Nicholas came out of one of the rooms alone. When he saw Megan he managed to look pleased. The man was a quick thinker; she had to give him that.

"Gabrielle! I'm glad you're here," he said.

"That's a little kinky," she answered coldly. "Isn't one woman at a time enough for you?"

He looked at her blankly. "What are you talking about?"

"The redhead in the bedroom. I hope she hasn't had time to take her clothes off. Her husband isn't into sharing. And from what I've been told, he gets pretty ticked off about it."

"You think that Noëlle and I...?" He stared at her incredulously.

"That's good. Hold on to that expression because you're going to need it." Megan glanced over her shoulder at

Charles, who was panting slightly as he made his way up the long flight of stairs.

Nicholas's jaw set. "I can see you've made up your mind without letting yourself be confused by the facts."

"There's no room for confusion." She could see Noëlle standing by the bed in the dimly lit room, hurriedly smoothing her hair. "A man and a woman don't go upstairs to a bedroom in the middle of a party just to talk."

"That's the first thing you've gotten right," he drawled.

Megan's scowl changed to a bright smile as Charles reached the top step. "Have you come to see the engagement present Nick's family sent me? I promised Noëlle I'd show it to her and then I got stuck with old Madame Brouchard. A dear thing, but such a bore!" Megan rolled her eyes. "Finally Nick offered to take Noëlle upstairs for me. It was so sweet of you, darling." She put her hand on his sleeve, digging her nails into his arm.

"Anything for you, my precious," he answered through gritted teeth.

Charles wasn't buying a word of it. He moved closer to Nicholas and thrust out his chin. "Gabrielle might be willing to overlook your disgraceful behavior, but I'm not. If you don't keep your hands off my wife, sir, you're going to regret it!"

If Megan hadn't been so angry it would have struck her as funny. Charles was like a little bantam rooster challenging a hawk. Nicholas towered over him, fit and powerful.

Charles turned away and bellowed, "Noëlle! Come out of there this instant! You've made a fool of me for the last time."

She came out of the bedroom with an edgy smile for Megan. "Charles, darling, I'm sorry if you felt abandoned. I didn't think you'd be interested in seeing Gabrielle's gift or we would have asked you to come along."

"Do you expect me to believe that's why you're up here?" he demanded.

"You're not going to start that again." She sighed dramatically. "When are you going to get over this insane jealousy?"

"When I can trust you out of my sight for more than five minutes," he answered grimly.

"You have to stop imagining these things. You're getting positively paranoid."

"I wish that were true," he answered bitterly. "I don't know how long I can go on like this. It's just one man after another."

"Like the Count de Tremoille? You didn't imagine we were having an affair?"

His anger turned to guilt, leading Megan to surmise that was the one time Noëlle was blameless—or else she and her count didn't get caught.

"I apologized for that," Charles said uncomfortably.

"As well you should! And for all the other things you've accused me of. Let's go back to the party and leave this lovely couple alone."

Megan and Nicholas watched silently as Charles and his wife went down the stairs.

When they were out of sight Megan said, "That was quite a performance she put on. I felt I should applaud."

"You and Charles make a good pair," Nicholas answered morosely. "You're both good at leaping to conclusions."

"*He* might be fooled into believing what he wants to believe, but I'm not blinded by love."

"That's quite obvious. Love means keeping an open mind."

"Or letting yourself be fooled by phony charm," she replied icily. "I realize how much you like variety, but you might at least have had the decency not to carry on right here in the palace."

"I know you won't believe me, but that was never my intention."

"It just happened? You looked into each other's eyes and said, 'Oh, what the hell, let's go make love'?"

A muscle twitched in Nicholas's square jaw, but he didn't lose his temper. "Regardless of your opinion of me, I would never get involved with a married woman. Noëlle and I were simply having a conversation—"

"A *lengthy* one," Megan interrupted.

He frowned. "We were talking, when suddenly she said she didn't feel well. I offered to find Charles and have their car brought around, but Noëlle said she'd be all right if she could just lie down for a few minutes. She said these spells occurred now and then. They were nothing serious, but she didn't want to worry Charles."

"Give me a break! You believed her?"

"I had no reason not to. She seemed so shaky that she had to hold on to my arm."

"You can't be that gullible!" Megan exclaimed.

"Forgive me for being a gentleman," he said irritably. "Perhaps I should have waited until she fainted or something equally dramatic, but it didn't occur to me."

"Okay, so you took her upstairs. Then what? She looked extremely healthy when her husband appeared."

"She made a remarkable recovery," Nicholas admitted wryly.

"Why are you the only one who's surprised?" Megan asked with heavy irony. "You're not exactly inexperienced with women. I could tell from across the room that she was coming on to you."

He stared at her with narrowed eyes. "That bothered you?"

"Not in the slightest! In fact, I was amused. Until you were brazen enough to take her upstairs—in the middle of our engagement party! In the future I'd appreciate it if you'd conduct your affairs more discreetly," she finished coldly.

"It's nice to know you sanction my future dalliances."

"Why not? It's more realistic than expecting you to change your ways."

"If you have such little hope for our marriage, why did you warn me? Your father might have decided he didn't want a notorious womanizer in the family."

"Is that why you made a spectacle of yourself with Noëlle? To get out of the marriage?"

"I already told you that isn't what happened," he rasped. "But since you think it did, I'd like to know why you didn't let Charles catch me with Noëlle. He's too little to rough me up, but he could have made a nasty scene."

"We've both been involved in too many scandalous incidents," Megan answered tartly. "It's time we either resigned ourselves to the marriage, or found some dignified way to avoid it."

Nicholas gazed at her thoughtfully. "I never thought I'd say this, but that's remarkably mature of you."

"I'm sorry I can't return the compliment." She lifted her chin and marched over to the staircase. "I'm going back to the ball. One of us ought to keep up appearances."

"I gather that's your charming way of asking me to join you," he drawled, strolling over to her.

Megan was too angry to answer. She started rapidly down the stairs, forgetting to hold up her train. Fortunately Nicholas was beside her because she caught her foot in the trailing fabric and would have pitched down the entire flight of stairs if he hadn't caught her.

His arms reached out and pulled her against him. She was off balance, so her body leaned heavily against his and her head was cradled in the curve of his neck. A bystander would have concluded that they were embracing, since neither moved for a long moment.

Megan felt the lethargy that always came over her in his arms. It was maddening, considering that she disliked him intensely! But very few women could deny his potent masculinity.

She tried to move away, but he swung her into his arms. "I'd better carry you down. That train of yours is lethal. You could have broken your neck if you'd fallen down these marble stairs."

"That would have solved your problem," she murmured.

"I might not want to marry you, but that's a rather drastic solution."

His reminder was like a dash of cold water. She struggled out of his arms at the foot of the stairs. "Thank you," she said curtly. "I'll be fine now."

The evening seemed endless after that, especially since Nicholas remained by her side. Megan found it difficult to smile when people told her what a handsome couple they were.

Finally she said to him in a low aside, "You don't have to stay with me."

"There's no place I'd rather be, my love. Now that Charles has reclaimed his wife," he added mockingly.

"I'm sure you can find somebody equally cooperative." She turned and walked away.

In contrast to Megan, Carrie was having a wonderful time. She was besieged with attention from a lot of the young single men, which was flattering, but she preferred Michel's company. He danced with her often, so he seemed to share the attraction.

"I hope you'll come to visit Gabrielle after she and the prince are married," he remarked.

"It's possible," she answered noncommittally.

"I find it strange that we never ran across each other before this. At the Grand Prix in Monte Carlo, for instance, or the opening of a new nightclub in Paris or Rome. Gabrielle never misses those things."

"Yes, she's quite the jet-setter," Carrie said brightly.

"Meaning, you're not? What are you interested in?"

"My tastes are simpler. I love elegant parties like this, but I don't think I could take them every night."

Michel arched an eyebrow. "How did you and Gabrielle get to be such good friends?"

"They say opposites attract."

"I've always considered that a cliché. I've found that people prefer to be with other people who share their interests."

"Then Nicholas and Gabrielle should be wildly happy together," Carrie observed dryly. "They both like to party till dawn."

"Nick suffers from a bad press. He takes his responsibilities much more seriously than you're led to believe."

"I'm sure he does," Carrie replied politely.

Michel sighed. "I can tell you don't believe me, but you'll see. He'll be a loyal and faithful husband after he and Gabrielle are married."

Carrie noticed that Michel omitted "loving," but she wasn't supposed to know that Nicholas was a reluctant bridegroom. She changed the subject. "You're his very good friend. You go everywhere with him. Is that why you've never married? At least, I assume you're single."

"That's right, but it isn't because of Nick. Neither of us has ever found the right girl—until he discovered Gabrielle was the one for him," Michel corrected himself quickly.

"That should leave you with a lot of free evenings."

"Maybe you'll help me fill them." He smiled. "Have you ever been to Grandalia?"

"No, this is just my first visit to Beaumarre."

"I thought you and Gabrielle were such good friends. You went to school together?"

"Yes, but we sort of lost track of each other for a while."

"Do you live very far from here?"

"Quite a distance." Carrie glanced away to give herself time to think in case he tried to pin her down, as he probably would. They hadn't thought to invent a background for her. Old school chum had seemed enough. Her glance was caught by activity at the end of the ballroom. "Oh, look, they put out a buffet. Shall we go over and get something to eat? I'm starving."

The buffet was as lavish as the rest of the party. Large bowls with mounds of crushed ice were covered with every kind of seafood, including lobster, giant prawns and oysters on the half shell. Caviar was in a separate crystal bowl, the largest amount Carrie had ever seen.

Farther down the table were salads of every variety, and then giant silver chafing dishes filled with hot food like tortellini stuffed with walnuts and mushrooms, crepes in a Mornay sauce and much more. Servants were spaced along the back of the table to serve the guests, and one man's sole job was to carve thin slices of rare roast beef and arrange them on small rounds of French bread.

"I've never seen so much food!" Carrie exclaimed. "They ought to give out doggy bags."

"I don't think I've ever heard that expression," Michel remarked.

"I doubt if you'd have any occasion to ask for one." She grinned. "People who live in castles don't eat leftovers."

Carrie took the plate he offered her and eyed the buffet happily. The men were heaping their plates, while the women took little dabs of things. Not Carrie. When she reached the end of the table her plate was loaded.

Michel gave it an amused look. "It's refreshing to see a woman enjoy her food. Most of them only nibble at raw carrots or celery to stay thin."

"Life is too short to live on rabbit food," she said dismissively. "Besides, neither Megan nor I have ever had a weight problem."

"Who is Megan?"

"She…uh…she's a friend of Gabrielle's and mine."

Carrie was appalled at herself for becoming so comfortable with Michel that she got careless. "Where shall we sit?" she asked, to distract him.

"Would you like to go outside? It will be less crowded."

As they crossed the room, Michel was still greeting people he hadn't seen in the throng.

A distinguished-looking older man nodded to him. "Good evening, Count. Lovely party, isn't it?"

"It certainly is. Nice to see you again, sir."

As they continued on, Carrie exclaimed, "I didn't know you were a count!"

"Does it make a difference?"

"Sort of. I would have tried to be more dignified."

"Then I'm glad you didn't know. I think you're delightful just the way you are." He led her along a garden path to a white wrought-iron bench beside a tulip garden. "I hope this is the beginning of a beautiful friendship."

"That would be nice. I liked you from the beginning," she said frankly. "But you might as well know up front. I'm not from a titled family."

"Is that supposed to matter to me?"

"Well, those are the people you run around with."

"So does Gabrielle, but you don't hold it against *her*," he teased.

"Okay, I'll overlook your shortcomings if you'll overlook mine." She laughed.

"We'll have to spend an entire day together before I can find out if you have any," he said, gazing at her admiringly.

"Let's see when I can fit you into my busy schedule," she mused. "How does tomorrow sound?"

He frowned slightly. "It sounds great to me, but perhaps I'd better check with Nick first. If he needs me for something, could we make it the next day?"

Carrie hesitated before saying, "Sure, that would be fine."

"Did you have something planned?"

"No, it's just that I don't know how long I'll be here."

Henri had people scouting everywhere for Gabrielle, and it would be just Carrie's luck if the missing woman was found, she thought ruefully. Now that she and Megan had both met fascinating men.

"You can't leave so soon!" Michel exclaimed. "There are all sorts of festivities planned, and then Gabrielle is going to Grandalia for more celebrations."

"I can't very well tag along. I'm just a friend, not a relative."

"I'm sure the king and queen would be delighted to have you."

"Well, we'll see," Carrie said vaguely.

"I'll have Nick extend the invitation personally."

"Let's see how you and I get along after spending the day together," she joked.

He took both of her hands. "I don't think one day with you will be nearly enough," he said in a melting voice.

Later, after saying good-night to Michel, Carrie rushed to Megan's suite, anxious to discuss the party with her friend. She was sure Megan had had an equally smashing time. It was a surprise to find her slamming drawers and closet doors.

"Why are you in such a bad mood?" Carrie asked. "It's been a fantastic evening."

"For you, maybe," Megan answered curtly.

"Forgive me if I don't sympathize with you for wearing a fabulous gown and a million dollars' worth of jewelry. Or for having to dance with a prince who acted like he was in love with you."

"That's exactly what it was—an act! He used that same look on all the other women there."

"Aren't you exaggerating? He was only being charming, the way he was expected to be."

"Does that include making love to one of the guests? A married woman, I might add."

"Is this a joke?"

"Do you see me laughing?" Megan asked grimly.

She told Carrie how she'd seen Nicholas take Noëlle upstairs, and everything that had happened afterward.

"It's possible he was telling the truth," Carrie said hesitantly. "I saw that redhead in action. She's trouble waiting to happen."

"Oh, please! As though *he* isn't. You read the celebrity magazines. You know what he's like. I didn't think he'd be that shameless at our engagement party, though."

"At Gabrielle's engagement party," Carrie corrected her gently.

"Whatever," Megan said irritably. "He's still a womanizing rat!"

"I can't believe Michel could be so loyal if Nicholas is really as unprincipled as you say."

"He's probably just like him."

"They're not a bit alike," Carrie protested. "I spent a good part of the evening with Michel. I know."

"Just this afternoon you were telling me not to be so gullible. It was good advice. You should take it. The two of them have that sincere act down pat. They can make a woman feel she's really special, different from all the others they were only superficially interested in. I believed Nicholas the way you believed Michel."

Carrie's face sobered. "I'd hate to think you were right about Michel. There was an instant rapport between us. I felt comfortable with him, yet there was an undercurrent of excitement, a sexual awareness and anticipation. I kept wondering what it would be like if he kissed me."

"I'm sure he'd be very competent at it. All that practice pays off in any sport."

"I guess you're right." Carrie's soft mouth drooped. "I heard what I wanted to hear."

When she looked at her friend's unhappy face, Megan regretted including Michel in her denunciation of Nicholas.

"Hey, I've been wrong before. Michel is probably every bit as nice as you think he is."

"You don't have to make me feel better. I only spent a few hours with the guy. Nothing could have developed between us anyway. Even if he wasn't a count, which is something I found out tonight. It's unimportant because I doubt if we'll be here much longer. When Gabrielle hears she got engaged in absentia, she's bound to get in touch."

"I certainly hope so. I've had enough of royalty to last me the rest of my life!" Megan turned to look curiously at Carrie. "It's funny that Michel never mentioned being a member of the peerage."

"He's very unassuming. I only found out by accident, and then he played it down." Carrie sighed. "At least he doesn't use rank to impress women."

"I'm sorry I dumped on him. I was really aiming at Nicholas. Enjoy Michel's company for as long as it lasts. You're right, we might not be here much longer."

Carrie stood and started for the door. "Maybe it's just as well," she remarked. "We're both getting a little too involved with men we can never have."

Chapter Five

Megan and Nicholas were scheduled to take a carriage ride through the city the next day to give everyone a chance to see the princess and her fiancé—especially the people who hadn't been able to attend the announcement ceremony at the palace the previous day. Although, judging by the crowds, the entire city of Bienville seemed to have been there.

A small group of people was assembled when Megan went downstairs in the early afternoon, and several open carriages were waiting in the driveway. They were decorated with ribbons and flowers, and drawn by handsome horses that sported their own finery—plumes on their heads and splendid silver harnesses.

Megan would have been enchanted under different circumstances—like not having to share a carriage with Nicholas. She nodded distantly to him and was annoyed when he came over to her, smiling mockingly.

"You shouldn't still be holding a grudge," he murmured

in her ear. "You won last night's round. I had to sleep alone."

"The sheer novelty must have made it interesting," she answered coolly.

"I can't say I'd recommend it. That's one thing you have to say for marriage. You always know you'll have somebody to share your bed. I like to sleep spoon-fashion. How about you?"

Megan knew he was merely baiting her, but she had a flash of their bodies curled up together, his arms enclosing her. Instead of snapping back—which was what he was trying to goad her into doing—she moved away.

Michel came over to join her. Nicholas had evidently told him what had happened the night before, because he gave her a wary smile. "You look lovely today. Did you and Nick coordinate your outfits?"

She had on a sleeveless white eyelet dress embroidered with blue daisies on the skirt and along the neckline. They matched the light blue shirt Nicholas was wearing with pale gray slacks and a white linen sport jacket.

"We didn't get around to discussing clothes last night. We were too busy talking about other things," she replied sweetly.

"I can imagine." Michel hesitated. "It's not a chivalrous thing to say, but Nick really was blameless."

"Carrie told me how loyal you are to him," Megan said noncommittally.

His face lit up. "She's terrific! I hope she'll come to visit you in Grandalia after you and Nick are married. Where does Carrie live? She never got around to telling me."

"I can imagine. It was such a mob scene that it was difficult to carry on a conversation. Did you ever see so many people?" While she was talking, Megan took his arm and steered him over to where Robert was standing. "Isn't it about time we got started?" she asked Henri's deputy.

"We have another ten minutes," Robert said, after consulting his watch.

A servant entered the room and handed Nicholas a small oblong package. "This just came for you, Your Highness. I brought it to you instead of taking it to your quarters because it's marked urgent."

After thanking the man, Nicholas unwrapped the package, then walked over and handed a box to Megan.

She looked at him warily without taking it. "What's this?"

"An engagement gift from my parents. I was supposed to bring it with me, but the jeweler didn't finish it on time. It just arrived by messenger."

Inside the box was a small, exquisite gold medallion set with precious stones—rubies, emeralds and sapphires. It was attached to a thin gold chain.

"It's beautiful," she murmured.

"They'll be happy to hear that you like it," he said politely. "It represents our family's coat of arms. I wear one, too."

Suddenly Megan realized why something had tugged at her memory when she saw the medallion. It was a replica of the one Philippe was wearing the night she met him in the bistro. It *had* been Nicholas that night!

If only he'd told her who he was and what was bothering him. She never would have agreed to this deception if she'd known how he and Gabrielle felt about each other. Poor Nicholas. Their meeting could have changed his life, but all it did was complicate her own. Fate played a cruel joke on both of them.

He was looking at her with a slight frown. "What's wrong? What did I do now?"

"Nothing! I... Should I wear it today?"

"If you like." After watching her fumble with the clasp he said, "Turn around and I'll do that for you."

While Megan held up her long hair, he fastened the intricate catch. It took a few moments and she was very conscious of his fingers on the sensitive nape of her neck. His hands felt sensuous, although she knew it wasn't intentional.

Carrie came over to them, accompanied by Michel. "Thanks for getting me invited to this outing today," she said to Megan.

"I would have, but I didn't know about it myself until this morning," Megan answered. "I forgot to look at my list of events. You'll have to thank Robert or Henri."

"I was the one who asked that you be here—after I found out *I* had to be. No offense meant." Michel cast a laughing glance at Nicholas.

"None taken," he replied. "We all just put up with these things. Noblesse oblige and all that kind of nonsense."

"I think it will be fun," Megan said. "It's a beautiful day for a ride and the carriages look adorable."

Nicholas raised an eyebrow. "I can't keep up with your mood swings. What caused this sudden sweet forbearance?"

She smiled mischievously. "Would you rather we traded insults? I thought of a few I didn't use last night."

He returned her smile. "No, this is definitely preferable."

"It's time to leave," Robert announced. "Gabrielle and Nicholas will be in the lead carriage, with Carrie and Michel in the one behind them. The rest of us will fill up the other carriages." The rest being minor dignitaries brought along to make the procession look impressive.

The streets were lined with people waiting for a glimpse of the happy couple. Their appetite for the young royals seemed boundless.

Megan and Nicholas smiled and waved to the crowd, who cheered and called them by name. One enthusiastic young woman ran alongside the carriage for a few paces and tossed a long-stemmed red rose into Nicholas's lap.

"If the princess doesn't treat you right, just give me a call, Your Highness," she shouted pertly.

He smiled dutifully without responding, casting a side-long glance at Megan. "Even *you* can't blame me for that one," he said out of the corner of his mouth.

"True. You can't help it if you're irresistible to women," she teased.

Megan had decided to give him the benefit of the doubt about last night's incident. She realized belatedly that it could very well have happened the way he claimed. Noëlle was the most predatory female she'd ever encountered.

"You don't seem to have any trouble resisting me," he remarked dryly.

"I could say the same thing about you," Megan replied, continuing to smile and wave.

"You'd be wrong. You couldn't help but notice my reaction to you." He grinned.

Her pulse rate speeded up as she realized what he was alluding to—his obvious desire the previous day when a conventional kiss had turned into something more. For her, too.

"This isn't the time to discuss it," she told him. "What would all these people think if they knew what we're talking about?"

"I don't think they'd be as shocked as you are. We're engaged. They know we're going to make love soon."

"That sounds so unromantic," she protested. "Like it's a duty that comes with the job."

"Any man would consider it a privilege to make love to you."

He could have been reciting the alphabet and any female would have responded to that deep, smoky voice.

Megan was glad they'd finally reached their destination, a tree-lined square in the middle of the city. A lovely marble statue of a woman rose from a splashing fountain set in the center of a circular pool. The statue had been erected in memory of Gabrielle's late mother.

A small stage was set up facing the fountain, and people were gathered expectantly. Nicholas helped Megan down from the carriage and they both ascended the stage where she was to give a short speech.

People pressed forward to hear and see better. When Megan started to speak, all eyes were trained on her. Nobody but Nicholas noticed the toddler teetering on the coping of the pool. His mother's attention was focused on the stage.

Megan had only said a few words when Nicholas jumped off the stage and waded through the crowd. There were murmurs of disapproval, until they discovered the reason. The little boy had fallen into the pool and was lying face-down in the shallow water, momentarily stunned.

Nicholas jumped into the pool and scooped the child into his arms. The toddler was coughing, sputtering and crying, all at the same time, but he wasn't hurt.

"It's all right, little one," Nicholas told him in a soothing voice. "You'll be fine."

The child clutched him around the neck while calling loudly for his mother. "I want my mommy!"

She rushed up and took him from Nicholas, explaining tearfully, "I only took my eyes off him for one minute."

"They're speedy little demons at this age, aren't they?" He chuckled.

"How can I ever thank you, Your Highness? You saved my baby's life!"

Others in the crowd were saying the same thing. They crowded around, offering handkerchiefs and scarves for him to dry himself off. Although the pool was shallow and only Nicholas's shoes and the bottoms of his trousers got wet, holding the little boy in his arms had soaked his shirt and jacket. The fountain had also dampened his hair.

"Don't worry about it," he told everybody. "I'll dry off

in the sun. I know we all want to hear the rest of Princess Gabrielle's speech.''

"That isn't important," she said. Megan jumped down from the podium to join Nicholas. "We should go back to the palace so you can change clothes. You must be terribly uncomfortable."

"I'll survive. You can't disappoint all these nice people." He turned to the crowd. "You'll forgive the way I look, won't you?"

His question was greeted by roars of approval. Nicholas had clearly won their hearts. Even after Megan was through speaking, he insisted on staying to mingle with the people for a short time. Gabrielle's popularity soared along with his.

When they were back in the carriage, Nicholas said, "I think it would be nice to send the toddler a toy of some kind, don't you? It might take the sting out of a bad experience."

"That's a nice idea, but how would we know where to send it?"

"I found out his mother's name."

Megan turned her head to look at him. "You're a very thoughtful man."

"I kept telling you I wasn't as bad as I've been painted." He laughed and squeezed her hand. "You were just a hard sell."

"I'm finally convinced." She smiled.

Henri was very pleased about the way things were going, after Robert told him what had happened that afternoon. Megan was cleaning up Gabrielle's image, and Nicholas was behaving better than anticipated, considering the prince's own reputation as a playboy. Henri only hoped Gabrielle could be persuaded to keep up the momentum—once they finally located her.

He was charged with excitement and relief when the

princess telephoned a few moments later. "Gabrielle! We've been looking everywhere for you. Where have you been hiding?"

"Never mind that. How *dare* you hire somebody to impersonate me?" she asked furiously.

"You didn't leave us much choice."

"That's no excuse. I couldn't believe it when I read about my engagement to Nick. You had no right to do such a thing! I blame you for everything. My father would never have conceived of such an outrageous idea."

"Obviously we couldn't have done it without his acquiescence."

"That's unbelievable! How could he do that to his own daughter? It's like disowning me!"

"He would welcome you back with open arms, I assure you."

"As long as I'm a good little girl and do as I'm told," she said bitterly. "Well, I can be as stubborn as he is. I told him I would never marry Nick and I meant it."

"Why don't you come home and discuss it with your father?" Henri coaxed.

"What good would that do? He wouldn't listen before. I told him how I felt about Nick and it didn't make any difference to him."

"You and the prince haven't given yourselves a chance to really know each other. He's much different than any of us expected. Why don't you come back and see for yourself? You might not be as adamantly opposed after you've spent a little time with him."

"Forget it!" Gabrielle answered curtly. "There's no way any of you can talk me into marrying Nick, so you'd better call off the engagement and fire your actress, or whatever she is. Where did you find her?" In spite of her anger, Gabrielle sounded curious.

"The resemblance is quite remarkable, isn't it?" Henri replied evasively.

"Not to anybody who really knows me, I'm sure. I don't see how you got away with it."

"The young lady is very convincing. Your subjects love her."

"Because they think she's me." Henri's strategy had worked. Gabrielle sounded definitely miffed. "Wait until they find out she tried to take my place."

"You intend to go public with the story?"

"Count on it! Nobody steals my life and gets away with it. I'll see to it that she can't get a job anywhere. She'll end up as a curiosity—the girl who had her fifteen minutes of fame by trying to impersonate a princess."

"That's rather harsh, considering she was only doing your father a favor. Your flight caused him a great deal of worry and embarrassment, and could have had serious diplomatic repercussions."

"That's what this is all about, isn't it? An alliance between Beaumarre and Grandalia. Nick and I are just pawns in the game. Our fathers don't care about us. We're only bargaining chips."

"You can't believe that, Gabrielle. The king worries constantly about you. It isn't only the escapades, with all their attendant publicity. He wants you to know the happiness that comes from a home and a family of your own. The kind of happiness he had with your mother."

"I know I've done some foolish things in the past. Maybe I was testing the boundaries, seeing how much I could get away with. But that's all over with. I've turned over a new leaf."

"I'm delighted to hear it." Henri's polite response didn't hide his skepticism.

"No, really, I mean it. I agree that it's time I settled down. If Father will call off the engagement, I'll come back and he'll see a difference in me."

"If you really are serious, you can prove it by coming home and assuming your responsibilities."

"You haven't been listening to me!" she said in frustration. "I'll get married, if that's what Father wants—but to someone of my own choice, not to Nick."

"I'm sure your father will be willing to talk about it. Why don't you let me send somebody to bring you home? Where have you been all this time?" Henri tried and failed to sound casual.

Gabrielle's conciliatory tone hardened. "Don't insult my intelligence, Henri. Don't you think I know what you're doing? You'd love to find out where I am so you can drag me back like a naughty child. Well, it won't work. I'm not coming back until you announce that the engagement is off. If you don't, the whole world will know about your despicable plot."

"I'd be very careful, Gabrielle. Your impulsiveness could backfire on you badly. If you exposed me, you'd have to explain why the deception was necessary. That you threw one of your tantrums and ran away from home, virtually on the eve of your engagement."

"I had no other choice!" she shouted into the phone.

"People will find that hard to understand. Prince Nicholas is extremely popular in Beaumarre. He and the young lady have been very gracious to the crowds, and just today the prince saved a little boy's life." Henri didn't mind exaggerating slightly.

"Did you stage that, too?" Gabrielle asked witheringly.

He didn't bother to deny it. "The prince is handsome and charming, he cares about others. Your people will begin to wonder just exactly what you want in a man. Or if you know, yourself. They might begin to view your escapades less indulgently."

"Are you threatening me?" she demanded.

"That would be presumptuous of me. I was merely warning you of what might happen if you acted hastily. You've always enjoyed great popularity, but the public is fickle. I don't think you want to lose the esteem of your subjects.''

There was a long silence at the other end of the line. Finally Gabrielle sighed. ''I really don't want to cause any more trouble. I just don't know what to do. Everything is such a mess.''

''Then come home and straighten it out,'' Henri urged.

After another silence she said, ''I'll think about it.''

''Where are you, Gabrielle? I'll arrange for—'' But it was too late. The princess had hung up.

Henri immediately requested an audience with the king. Claude was relieved to hear that his daughter was all right, but depressed that she still refused to return home. Like Nicholas's father, Claude began to have second thoughts.

''We'll have to call off the engagement,'' he said heavily. ''I had no idea Gabrielle was this opposed. I thought she was simply defying me again.''

''Have you thought about the consequences, Your Highness?''

''They'll be horrendous, but what else can I do? My daughter's happiness is more important to me than a diplomatic crisis, no matter how ugly it will be.''

''I succeeded in making her at least consider returning. That would break the stalemate. If she'd just meet with the prince I'm sure she'd change her mind. Everyone is charmed by him.''

''It's a possibility, and that's what I originally thought would happen. But now that she refuses to come home, how long can we continue deceiving Nicholas this way?''

Henri's smile relieved some of the tension on his face. ''The prince seems to be enjoying himself. After a somewhat rough start, he and Megan are hitting it off well.''

''I've noticed that and it's another thing that bothers me. It isn't fair to use the girl like this. I agreed in the beginning because I thought it would only be for a day or two, that

Gabrielle was merely being rebellious. But there's no end in sight.''

"I'm sure Megan won't mind staying longer. We've done everything possible to make her comfortable.''

"That's not what I'm talking about. I'm afraid she's getting too fond of Nicholas, which could only have unhappy consequences for her.''

"He's a very handsome man. It's natural for her to find him attractive, but Megan is a levelheaded young woman. I'm certain that she realizes they could never have a meaningful relationship. Even if he weren't engaged to Gabrielle.''

"It might be the shortest royal engagement on record,'' the king remarked morosely. "We can't wait much longer before telling Nicholas.''

"There isn't any immediate need.''

"When do you propose we tell him? On the eve of his wedding to a woman he thinks is Gabrielle? That's a likely scenario, considering the way things are going.''

Henri knew the king's sarcasm masked his deep concern for all of the parties involved. "The wedding won't take place for months, Your Highness. That's plenty of time for the princess to realize this is in her best interests. Just give her a few days to think it over.''

"I don't seem to have any other choice,'' Claude answered bleakly.

A royal engagement followed strict protocol. During the next three days Megan and Nicholas attended public functions, like making appearances at charity luncheons, or cutting a ribbon to open some civic project.

"This is what I do at home,'' Nicholas complained on the drive back to the palace after a particularly dull ribbon ceremony. "You must get as tired of it as I do.''

"I guess this is what royalty does.'' Megan had never stopped to think that maybe these functions didn't give their lives enough purpose. Perhaps that was why so many of the young royals went on a restless search for a more meaningful existence.

"There has to be something more," he said, confirming her surmise. "These are supposed to be the most productive years of our lives."

"What would you do if you weren't a prince in line for the throne?"

Nicholas told her as he had in the bistro that first night, about his dream of building dams and bridges. It hadn't been just an idle daydream. He'd been serious.

"I know it's unrealistic to think I'd be allowed to climb around a construction site in a hard hat, but there must be some way I can get into the game. I don't know how much longer I can continue to sit on the sidelines."

"What if you started some type of foundation to fund projects in depressed areas of the world? It wouldn't be hands-on, like overseeing the work yourself, but actually you'd accomplish more. You could have several projects going at once—a reclamation project in the desert, a dam in South America, and so on."

"It would take a lot of money," he said slowly.

"You could raise it. You have all sorts of connections with the rich and famous. A lot of people would contribute just to have their names associated with yours. Especially since it would be tax deductible," Megan added with a grin.

Nicholas was staring at her with growing excitement. "It could work! We could start on the Continent and eventually have branches all over the world."

"Nobody will ever accuse you of thinking small." She laughed.

"That's for people without vision," he said dismissively. "Gabrielle, you're a genius! Together we're going to improve the lives of a lot of people."

"This is your project. You're the engineer, not I."

"You don't have to be. You have talent in other fields."

"Like what, other than a fluency in languages?"

"That's important. One of your strengths is communicating with people. You come across just the way you are, warm and sincere. You'll raise a fortune for the foundation, especially when you can give a speech to an audience in their native tongue."

"I'm not sure I'd be as good as you think."

It sounded both fascinating and rewarding, but Megan was wary of agreeing. She had a feeling Gabrielle wouldn't be interested in humanitarian work.

"You're good at everything you do." Nicholas took both her hands in his. "I can't believe what a jerk I was when I first came here. My only excuse is that I didn't really know you."

"We still have a lot to learn about each other," she murmured.

"I'm looking forward to that," he said in a deepened voice.

Megan knew he wasn't talking about an exchange of ideas. Nicholas expected their sex life to be exciting and frequent. It undoubtedly would be, but he would be making love to Gabrielle. Where *was* that wretched woman? It was time to stop this charade. Megan had a terrible feeling that her attraction to Nicholas was becoming more than just physical.

After the public events during the day there were private ones in the evening. All of Bienville society wanted to entertain the engaged couple. Hostesses vied with each other, trying to think of something more novel than just another dinner party or dance. One night the Duke and Duchess of Armante gave a beach party.

"This I can't wait to see," Carrie remarked as she lounged in Megan's bedroom, waiting for her to finish dressing. "Somehow I can't imagine these people getting sand between their toes while they toast marshmallows on pointed sticks.''

''Don't worry, the servants probably laid down red carpets this afternoon. And the marshmallows won't be toasted on sticks—they'll use silver skewers.''

''I could tell this wasn't your average beach party when I heard there would be limos to take us to the shore. I wanted to tell Michel we used to just pile into somebody's van, but I didn't want to blow my cover.''

''Speaking of that, we'd better get together on a background for you—what your father does, where you live, that sort of thing. Michel asked me,'' Megan said.

''He asked me, too, and I managed to avoid answering,'' Carrie said.

''I did the same thing, but we can't keep doing it. Gabrielle went to school in Switzerland, so how about saying you live in Zurich? You've been there, so you can answer general questions.''

''Okay, and let's say my father is a banker. As long as we're inventing him, I might as well pick somebody rich,'' Carrie joked.

They discussed other details, fabricating a whole new identity for her.

''I wish I didn't have to lie to Michel. It would be such fun to exchange stories about our backgrounds—our first date, where I really went to college, that sort of thing.''

''I know. It's difficult to always have to be on your guard.''

''I really like Michel. It's too bad I'll never see him again after we leave here,'' Carrie said wistfully.

''You never know. You could tell him you've been offered a job in New York,'' Megan suggested. ''That way you could keep in touch.''

''There's no future in it.''

''He might invite you to visit him in Grandalia after…after Nicholas and Gabrielle are married." Megan had trouble saying the words.

"I couldn't accept. Gabrielle won't be too pleased with you, or with me, either, when she finds out I was part of the deception. I could scarcely count on her to pretend we were friends."

"I suppose you're right. Well, look on the bright side. There are plenty of other men in the world," Megan said with determined cheerfulness.

"Not like Michel." Carrie sighed.

Or Nicholas, Megan added silently.

The beach party was unlike anything either Carrie or Megan had ever attended. The sand wasn't covered with a red carpet, but every other amenity was provided.

Tables and chairs had been set up around a portable dance floor where a small combo was playing. Waiters in white coats were pouring champagne into crystal flutes, while others passed elaborate hors d'oeuvres.

"Tell me how this is different from a dinner dance," Carrie asked Michel.

"It's held outdoors and the men don't have to wear dinner jackets." He smiled.

Most of the guests were dressed informally in cotton slacks and T-shirts, although the majority of the outfits sported designer logos.

"Where's the bonfire?" Megan asked as she and Nicholas joined the other couple. "How can you have a beach party without a bonfire?"

"I'm sure Claire would provide one if you asked her," Nicholas said.

"I was only joking. Everything is lovely. It's just a little…different."

"A beach party should have hot dogs and potato chips," Carrie explained. "And blankets spread out on the sand, not tables and chairs."

"I don't think I've ever been to a party like that," Michel remarked. "It sounds like fun."

"It is," Megan assured him. "Maybe we can organize one for some other night."

"We're already here, so what's wrong with right now? Claire!" Nicholas called to their hostess. "Princess Gabrielle has a request to make."

"Nick, no!" Megan exclaimed. "She did a lot of planning for this evening. I can't disrupt her entire party."

"It wouldn't be the first time you had a zany idea. Claire won't even be shocked. She doesn't know you've reformed."

Their hostess reached them. "What can I get for you, my dear?"

"Not a thing," Megan answered hastily. "You've provided everything a guest could possibly want."

"Gabrielle is being polite," Nicholas said. "What she really wants is a bonfire and some weiners to roast over it. And buns, I presume?" He looked at Megan questioningly.

"Oh, yes, definitely buns," Carrie answered for her.

Claire looked at them blankly. "You want weiners? Now?"

"If it isn't too much trouble." Nicholas's eyes danced with merriment.

"You do realize that Françoise has prepared a special dinner for the occasion?"

"And I'm sure it will be superb. Nicholas wasn't serious." Megan gave him a reproving look.

"I suppose it *would* be totally inappropriate. Everyone would be talking about how different this party was from all the others that have been given for us," Nicholas remarked blandly.

Claire's eyes began to gleam with satisfaction. "What people think isn't important. If that's what you and Gabrielle want, that's what you shall have." She beckoned to a servant and gave him rapid instructions.

As the man hurried off, Carrie called after him, "And while you're at the market, pick up a load of marshmallows and some long skewers. Oh, and don't forget the mustard."

"How could you do that?" Megan included both Carrie and Nicholas in her reprimand. "The woman had an entire dinner prepared. Did you see her face? She's probably never tasted a hot dog in her entire life!"

"Then we did her a favor." Carrie grinned.

"In more ways than one," Nicholas commented. "She'll be the envy of every hostess in town. It might even start a new trend in entertaining."

"I'll drink to that." Michel chuckled. "I could get used to some informality now and then."

In an amazingly short time, the servants had started a roaring bonfire and spread blankets on the sand.

Initially, the guests were more than a little dubious. But gradually the novelty of it started to appeal to them and they became enthusiastic. It was probably the first time they'd ever eaten finger food, except for hors d'oeuvres.

"Leave it to Gabrielle to introduce us to something new," one man remarked, slathering mustard on his hot dog.

"Wait until you get to the entertainment," Carrie said. "She's going to teach you to sing along."

"This one was your idea," Megan said. "You can lead them."

"Carrie must be a very good friend of yours," Nicholas observed. "The Gabrielle I used to know didn't play second banana to anyone."

"You never met Carrie before. She taught me all I know about outrageous behavior," Megan said lightly.

Carrie got everybody to sing and then she showed them how to toast marshmallows. Claire was almost wriggling with glee at the success of her party.

After a while the crowd around the fire dispersed. Some

of the couples strolled along the beach, others drifted over to the dance floor, and many just stood around chatting.

"Would you like to dance?" Nicholas asked Megan.

"In a minute." She stood and held out her hands. "First I want to wash off my sticky fingers. Those marshmallows are good, but they're messy."

"I'll be right with you," he called, pausing to roll up the cuffs of his jeans.

The water had been calm earlier, but it was getting rough. Waves were building farther out, and even the shallow water was choppy. A light wind had sprung up, too.

Foaming water hissed around Megan's ankles as she bent down to rinse off her fingers.

"Gabrielle! Watch out!"

She heard Nicholas's warning, but almost simultaneously a wave broke over her. Not only her clothes were drenched, but her hair as well.

He raced over and led her out of the surf to dry sand. Brushing the wet hair away from her face, he said, "I tried to warn you when I saw it coming."

"I should have been paying attention. I must look a mess," she said ruefully.

Nicholas's gaze shifted from her face to her body—and froze there. Suddenly Megan was conscious of how her wet T-shirt was clinging to her breasts. She couldn't have looked more provocative if she were completely nude. Her hardened nipples were clearly visible, pressed against the wet shirt.

His desire was all too obvious, but she couldn't move. Nicholas's avid gaze lit a small flame deep in her midsection, immobilizing her. As he took a step toward her, she shivered out of mounting excitement.

He stopped and dragged his eyes back to her face. "You're cold. Come back to the fire and I'll wrap you in a blanket."

She didn't want a blanket. She wanted him to strip off

her shirt and take her in his arms. Her breasts ached with desire for him, for the touch of his hands, the hot, moist suckling of his mouth.

The extent of her passion brought Megan to her senses. She folded her arms across her breasts and mumbled, "I'd better do something about my hair."

"First we have to get you dried off." He put his arm lightly around her shoulders, as though the last few moments hadn't been charged with tension.

A servant brought towels, and Megan turned her back to Nicholas while she toweled her hair dry. Then she allowed him to wrap a blanket around her.

"Sit down here by the fire," he said. "I don't want you to catch cold." He wrapped her up, mummy-fashion.

"I have to get my arms out so I can do something about my hair," she complained.

"I like it this way." He combed his fingers through the damp strands. "You look more approachable, not so picture-perfect."

"I'm far from perfect," she said sadly. "I do really dumb things." Like falling in love with a man she could never have. Megan couldn't pretend any longer. At least, not to herself.

"Anybody could get hit by a wave—or were you talking about some of your more memorable escapades?" he teased.

"You're not in any position to be judgmental. You've been involved in a few incidents yourself."

"Overblown or taken out of context," he said dismissively. "I'm an innocent victim of the paparazzi."

"Those pictures of you in Rome with that actress didn't look so innocent."

He eased her down on a blanket and stretched out beside her. "Why are we talking about the past when it's the future that matters? Our future together."

Megan wanted Nicholas to be happy, even if it had to

be with someone else. When you truly loved someone, you wanted the best for them. But had she set him up for disappointment? Gabrielle would come back full of anger and bitterness. She wouldn't give herself a chance to get to know him. And he wouldn't know why she'd seemed to change so radically. Megan decided she'd better try to prepare him.

"Nicholas," she began hesitantly.

"Nick," he corrected her. "We don't have to be formal with each other in private." He traced the shape of her mouth with his forefinger before leaning forward to kiss her sweetly.

"I wish you wouldn't do that," she said faintly.

"How about this?" His lips slid down her neck to the hollow of her throat.

"I'm trying to talk to you," she pleaded.

"I can't say much for your priorities. But okay, go ahead. What's more important?"

"I wanted to talk about us."

"That's a subject I'm vitally interested in. What about us?"

"We've been getting along really well, but it won't necessarily last," she said carefully.

"I suppose we'll argue eventually. We're both very volatile people. But think of the fun we'll have making up." He unwrapped the blanket and drew her into his arms.

Megan tried to keep her mind on what she needed to say to him, but it was difficult. His hard body was seducing her with its blatant masculinity. She wanted to feel its full power, filling her with joy. It took a great effort to draw away.

"You have to listen to me, Nick. Most of what you've heard about me is true. I'm stubborn and headstrong and spoiled. You haven't seen that side of me much because I've been trying very hard to change. But don't be surprised if I have a relapse."

"I don't expect you to be sweet and docile. I want a partner, not a cocker spaniel. Of course we'll argue, but only because we care about each other. And for the same reason, we'll work things out."

"Oh, Nick, you're too good to be true." She buried her face in his shoulder to hide the tears that blurred her eyes.

Carrie had been having a wonderful time. She enjoyed the fancy dress balls and all the beautiful clothes that were provided for her, but tonight was fun, too. She was especially pleased that Michel felt equally at ease in a tux or a T-shirt. He was one man in a million.

They were strolling hand in hand on the beach when Carrie noticed Megan and Nicholas lying on the sand together.

"Come over to the fire," she told Michel. "I have something to tell Gabrielle."

"I don't think they'd appreciate being disturbed at the moment." He smiled.

"I can't think of a better time." When Michel looked at her in surprise she modified her grim tone. "I mean, this won't wait. I just thought of something important that I forgot to tell her. Gabrielle!" Carrie said urgently when they reached the other couple.

Megan looked up vaguely, as though she didn't recognize her.

"I have to talk to you," Carrie insisted. "Walk down the beach with me."

"Now?" Nicholas frowned. "Can't it wait?"

"No, it can't. Are you coming, Gabrielle?"

Carrie's timely appearance helped Megan shake off the spell she'd been under. She rose to her feet, avoiding Nick's eyes.

"What happened to your hair?" Carrie was curious in spite of her concern.

"I got hit by a wave," Megan explained as they walked away.

When they were out of earshot, Carrie said, "I don't know if you're annoyed with me for breaking up your clinch, but I thought I should remind you that you're gathering bouquets in somebody else's garden."

"I know that. We weren't doing anything wrong," Megan said defensively. "Nick just kissed me a couple of times. It's perfectly natural for a man to kiss his fiancée. It would have seemed odd if I'd made a big deal out of it."

"From what I could see, you weren't just passively enduring," Carrie observed dryly.

"Not many women would be indifferent to him."

"That's a good point, but you aren't doing either of you a favor. If he falls in love with *you*, he isn't going to be happy with Gabrielle."

"I was trying to prepare him for her when things sort of got out of hand."

"Well, I had to say what was on my mind, but it's your life. I won't nag you about it anymore."

"Feel free." Megan managed a smile. "My judgment is slightly impaired these days."

"It's only temporary insanity." Carrie returned her smile. "You'll recover."

Megan could only hope her friend was right.

Chapter Six

As the week wound to a close, the social events were scheduled to culminate in a house party at the country estate of one of the king's ministers. After that, the engaged couple and their entourages would travel to Grandalia for another round of public and private festivities to give Nicholas's subjects a chance to see his fiancée.

"Do you think you can stand another week of my constant company?" he asked her with a grin.

Megan doubted it. Not without her willpower failing her. That Friday, she went to Henri's office to have a word with him.

"After the house party this weekend, I have to go home. I'm not going to Grandalia," she told him firmly.

"I hope it won't be necessary," he said. "We have every indication that Princess Gabrielle will be back by then."

"You've located her?"

"Well, not exactly, but it isn't important. She's coming back of her own accord."

"That's what you've been hoping for all along, but it didn't happen. What makes you think she's changed her mind?"

"The princess telephoned and we had a lengthy conversation."

"She agreed to marry Nick?" Megan asked intently.

Henri hesitated imperceptibly before saying, "She realizes it's the right thing to do."

Megan stared at him suspiciously. "When is she returning? What specific day?"

"I didn't attempt to pin her down," he said smoothly. "Gabrielle doesn't like to be questioned. But I explained things to her, and I'm sure she's going to be a lot more cooperative."

"I don't know what kind of blackmail you used, but from all I've heard about her, it won't work."

"Let me worry about that." He gave Megan a small, confident smile. "It's my problem."

"And mine," she answered evenly. "You led me to believe this impersonation would only last a few days. It's been going on for almost a week now and there's no end in sight. I don't have your faith in the princess's reliability."

"The king deeply appreciates your cooperation. If there is anything I can do to make you more comfortable, please don't hesitate to ask."

"You've both been more than generous, but that's not the point. I have a life of my own that I'd like to get back to."

"I understand completely. Nobody wants that more than we do," Henri said fervently. "If you'll just be patient a little longer, I'm sure this entire affair will work itself out."

"I'll give you until Sunday night," Megan said adamantly. "After that, Cinderella turns in her time card."

"I'm sure the princess will have returned by then."

"If that's the case we have no problem. Please make

reservations for Carrie and me on a flight to New York on Sunday.''

"That can be done at the last minute. Why don't we hold off—just in case there are any little last-minute glitches," Henri said with elaborate casualness.

"I have no doubt there will be. You don't really know when Gabrielle is coming back, but I know when I'm leaving. You'd better start inventing some lingering illness for the princess. If she does show up, you can suddenly discover a miracle cure."

"I can certainly understand your impatience. You've done a marvelous job of impersonating the princess. If your departure precipitates a diplomatic crisis…well, so be it. We have no right to impose on you any longer."

"Don't try to make me feel sorry for you, Henri. I've been around enough foreign ministers to recognize a snow job when I see one." Megan went to the door. With her hand on the knob she turned and said, "Sunday night, no later."

Gabrielle hadn't put in an appearance by Saturday morning, so the two young couples drove to the country in a convertible provided by the palace. They were all in high spirits. Nicholas and Michel because they didn't have a care in the world, and Megan and Carrie because they'd decided to make the most of their last two days in Beaumarre.

Carrie had reluctantly agreed with Megan's decision to set a deadline. They couldn't let Henri keep her dangling indefinitely. Besides, it wouldn't get any easier to leave, no matter how long they stayed. This luxurious weekend in the country would be a wonderful way to end their stay.

"Is it too windy for you?" Michel asked Carrie. "I can put the top up."

"Not for me. I love the wind in my face."

"You're very unusual," he said admiringly. "Most women don't like getting their hair mussed."

"No problem. After a session with the princess's hairdresser we'll both be new women."

He reached over and took her hand. "I hope not. I like you just the way you are."

Nicholas put his arm around Megan. "That's my feeling exactly. I can't wait to show you off to my parents and the people of Grandalia."

She smiled vaguely and said, "How much farther is it to where we're going?"

He looked at her with a puzzled frown. "You must have been there before. Simon Dumont is your father's minister."

"Oh...yes, of course, but I haven't been to their country place in a long time."

"According to my directions it's right around this bend," Michel said.

Megan stifled a gasp as the house came into view. She'd been expecting something luxurious, but nothing like this. It was a stone castle with a vast courtyard partially enclosed by two wings that, together with the house, formed a U shape. Ivy covered the high walls, and the roof was decorated with turrets and cupolas.

"This place must be hundreds of years old," Carrie exclaimed. "Just look at those front doors. Aren't they magnificent?"

Michel had driven up to the entry. As soon as he turned off the motor, the massive double doors opened and servants came out to take their luggage inside.

A majordomo greeted them formally and led them to a paneled library where their hosts were waiting.

Claudette Dumont was an accomplished hostess, used to anticipating anything a guest might desire. A long table against one wall held a coffee urn and a silver tea service, along with tiered serving dishes filled with pastries and snacks. These were in case a guest got hungry between breakfast and lunch. There was also a well-stocked bar cart, with something for every appetite.

Several of the guests who had arrived earlier were drinking Bloody Marys, but Megan and the others chose coffee.

"I don't know what's gotten into you, Gabrielle," a woman named Brigitte drawled. "You're no fun at all anymore."

Nicholas was about to disagree, but Carrie came to her defense first. "Maybe Gabrielle has just outgrown your kind of fun," she said sweetly.

"Yes, well, let me tell you what we have planned for this evening," their hostess said hastily.

Every kind of party had already been given for the royal couple, which had really taxed Claudette's ingenuity. As the final event in a week of festivities, she wanted hers to be especially unique. The entertainment she'd planned was certainly memorable.

"We're going to have a costume ball tonight," she announced. "Everyone will come as someone from the court of Louis XVI of France. Gabrielle, you'll be Marie Antoinette, and Nicholas will be Louis."

"I'm not sure I like the casting." Megan laughed. "Both of them were beheaded."

"Marie lost her head over a man she wasn't even in love with," Brigitte observed. "Her marriage to Louis was arranged to form a closer alliance between France and Austria."

"She wasn't the mate *he* would have chosen, either," a man in the group commented. "That's one drawback to being a king. You can't marry for love."

"Sometimes you can," Nicholas said softly.

Megan stood abruptly. "I think I'd like to go to my room and freshen up."

"Of course, my dear." Claudette rang for a servant. "I've given you your usual suite. Carrie's is the one next to it and Nicholas and Michel are across the hall."

"I'll go with you," Carrie told Megan. "I need to comb my hair."

Their suites were comparable to the ones at the palace in Bienville and the service was equally good. Their suitcases had been unpacked, their clothes put away in huge armoires and their toiletries arranged in the bathroom.

Carrie reappeared with a disbelieving look on her face after going to check out her own suite. "Have you looked in your closet yet?"

"No. What's the matter? Aren't your clothes there?"

"Yes, but you should see what else. There's a costume for this evening's masquerade ball."

"I wasn't told I'd need a costume. I wonder if my maid packed one for me, too."

"You don't have anything like this. Claudette evidently provided them for all the houseguests. See for yourself. She must have spent a fortune on these outfits."

Megan walked over and opened her armoire. Inside was a pale blue satin gown embroidered all over with gold thread and studded with faux jewels. The bodice was minuscule, but the long sweeping skirt had enough fabric to drape a living room. The accessories meant to be worn with the gown were even more extravagant.

A tall, elaborately coiffed white wig was perched on a hat stand, with a small blue satin mask and a lace fan propped up on the base. Everything was authentic for the period. The blue satin shoes had square buckles and Louis heels, even though they would never be seen under the voluminous skirt.

"All the hostesses have been trying to outdo each other, but I think Claudette deserves the grand prize," Carrie said.

"She certainly put a lot of thought into the entertainment." Megan was eyeing the low neckline of her gown. "She didn't have to be this authentic, though. The French court of that period was known for being licentious, and this dress would have been right at home there."

"Some of the crown jewels of Beaumarre would come in handy right now. You wouldn't look so bare if you wore one of those eye-popping necklaces they own."

"I think Robert brought one. That could be why he and those bodyguard types came along."

"Ordinary people don't realize the freedom they have," Carrie mused. "It must be difficult to be surrounded by a retinue wherever you go."

"I'll remind you of that tonight when you're having your hair styled by the hairdresser we brought with us," Megan teased.

"My hair won't show under the wig, so why bother? I can't wait to see Michel and Nick in satin breeches. I'll bet they're less delighted than we are."

"At least they don't have to wear corsets." Megan looked dubiously at the boning in her gown.

"It will be worth it," Carrie assured her. "This will be a night we're not likely to forget."

Megan needed help getting into her gown that evening. It had tiny hooks halfway down the back where she couldn't reach. "Claudette didn't have to be *this* authentic," she grumbled to Carrie, who had finished dressing earlier and was waiting for her. "A zipper would never show."

Carrie was watching in amusement. "I can't understand how those people back then had so many affairs. You'd think by the time a guy got one of these gowns unhooked he'd be out of the mood."

"I guess they didn't have other distractions then, like television. I guarantee you a man's passion would dim if it was a toss-up between a hundred hooks and Monday-night football," Megan said dryly.

"You have to admit the style is becoming, though. That panniered skirt takes inches off your waist."

Megan was tugging at her neckline. The low bodice was barely an inch above her nipples. "Robert left some jewelry for me to wear. I just hope it covers up some of this bare skin."

Carrie's eyes widened as Megan opened the velvet jeweler's box. Inside was a magnificent necklace that glittered like cold fire. A series of huge sapphires surrounded by large diamonds were suspended from a loop of smaller diamonds. A matching bracelet and drop earrings completed the set.

"Wow!" Carrie exclaimed. "You don't have to worry about your cleavage. Who's going to look at that when you have a million dollars around your neck?"

"I've never worn the same jewels twice. The past queens of Beaumarre must have shopped till they dropped," Megan remarked as she tucked her hair under the wig. The transformation was astounding. "I look like a different person!" she exclaimed. "I wonder if Nick will recognize me?"

"I *know* Michel won't recognize *me*," Carrie said.

The change from her formerly flaming red hair was the most pronounced, but both women looked totally unlike themselves. Especially when they put on their masks.

"Let's go flirt with them and see if they flirt back," Carrie said mischievously.

"I think we can safely assume they will," Megan answered evenly.

"You still don't trust Nick? He seems quite devoted."

"I'm sure he is." Megan sighed. "But all this intrigue has made me suspicious of everyone."

"I know. The lies and half-truths are wearing me down, too. The one good thing about leaving here is that I won't have to watch every word I say." The two women were silent for a moment. Then Carrie squared her shoulders.

"Well, we might as well adopt Marie Antoinette's philosophy. Live for the moment, because tomorrow might be a bummer."

Megan couldn't help laughing. "No matter what happens, I don't think they'll send us to the guillotine."

There were only about twenty houseguests, but Claudette had invited more than a hundred outside guests. The ballroom was crowded when Megan and Carrie went downstairs.

It was like stepping into another world. The huge room was decorated to look like a forest, with live trees in camouflaged pots and green carpeting covering the floor like moss. Only the dance floor in the middle of the room was a concession to the modern age.

The musicians were dressed like minstrels, and the guests looked like a page out of the past. Both men and women had on towering white wigs, and the men wore knee breeches and froths of lace at their wrists and throats.

"I'll never complain about a necktie again," a man muttered, brushing his white lace jabot out of his face.

"Be careful of that," his wife warned. "It has to go back to the costumer on Monday."

Megan looked over the crowd for Nicholas, but she couldn't find him. She wasn't alone for long, though. Men came over to ask her to dance and to try to find out who she was.

That meant they were attracted to *her,* not her title. Megan began to get a glimmering of the doubts that might have plagued Gabrielle and accounted for her outrageous behavior.

A few moments later she spotted Nicholas on the dance floor. His height and superb physique made him instantly recognizable, in spite of the mask and foppish clothes. But unlike some of the other men, he didn't look at all silly. He wore his satin waistcoat and lace cuffs with the same elegance as his custom-tailored suits. Nicholas would have looked like a prince in any era.

Megan couldn't help feeling a slight twinge of jealousy at the attention he was giving his partner, but she was determined not to overreact this time. Although it would have been nice if he'd been looking for her, she thought a little forlornly. She watched him go from partner to partner until finally she concentrated on her own partners.

A small shock of awareness went through her when she heard Nicholas's voice as she chatted with some people on the sidelines.

"Has anyone told you that you're the most beautiful woman here tonight?" he asked, drawing her aside.

"I wonder how many women you've told that to," she answered lightly.

His eyes gleamed with mischief behind his mask. "You mean in total, or just tonight?"

"Don't bother counting. It isn't important," she said dismissively and changed the subject. "You would have fit right into the French court."

"Because you think I'm insincere?" he teased, leading her onto the dance floor and taking her in his arms.

"I wouldn't know about that. I was referring to the way you look in that outfit. You seem quite comfortable."

"I am, although I wouldn't want to wear it on a daily basis. The lack of a zipper could get to be a problem." He chuckled.

"Women weren't much better off in those days. I could never get in or out of this gown without help."

"I'm sure you'd never lack for volunteers," he murmured, gazing at the creamy skin revealed by her deep décolletage.

The pressure of his close embrace was making her breasts swell even more over the low-cut gown. Megan was afraid they would break free at any moment. She drew away slightly, but that only gave him a better view.

"I've never known anyone like you," he said in a husky voice. "You're utterly bewitching,"

"You must be very susceptible. We just met."

"I've been searching for you all my life."

"You don't know anything about me. You can't even tell if I'm a blonde or a brunette under this wig."

He brushed his knuckles gently against her cheek. "This creamy skin could only belong to someone with pale silken hair the color of moonlight."

"Do you prefer blondes?"

"I wouldn't care what color your hair was." He inclined his head to kiss the corner of her mouth where she'd penciled a small black beauty mark.

Megan wanted to turn her face so their lips met, but she laughed breathlessly instead. "You'd better not get too amorous. What if I have a jealous husband or boyfriend watching?"

"I'm the one who's jealous—of every other man you've ever known. But you're mine now, and nobody else matters."

She looked at him uncertainly. "Do you know who I am?"

Instead of answering, he took her hand and led her off the dance floor and through the make-believe forest to the French windows beyond.

The terrace was brightly lit, so he continued on into a small grove of trees bordering the lawn. Moonlight filtered through the leaves, making Nicholas's tanned face appear pale. But even in the semidarkness his eyes were brilliant as he gazed at her.

"Darling Gabrielle, I'd know you in a pitch-black room. By the perfume of your skin, the graceful way you move, so many different things. I enjoy just watching you."

"Not tonight, you didn't," she pouted. "You were too busy to care where I was."

"Not true. I saw you dancing with the young dandy in

purple satin, and the handsome fellow in damask. The men were lined up waiting to dance with you.''

''Didn't that bother you?''

He shrugged. ''You seemed to be enjoying yourself. I didn't want to be too possessive and spoil your fun.''

Megan felt guilty over her own possessiveness. ''That was very thoughtful of you, but I'm glad you finally got around to me.''

''I wasn't trying to qualify for sainthood.'' He grinned. ''Besides, I couldn't stay away from you any longer.''

His expression changed as he drew her into his arms and kissed her—gently at first, then with growing passion. Megan flamed to instant life. This was where she longed to be. How could she deny what she wanted so desperately?

Nicholas's embrace tightened at her response and he parted her lips for a deep exploration that left her clinging to him. She made a soft sound of satisfaction as his tongue tantalized her with its symbolic possession.

Dragging his mouth away, Nicholas said in a thickened voice, ''I've never wanted anyone as much as I want you.'' His lips trailed a path of fire down her neck to her deep cleavage.

Megan's muscles were taut as she tried to resist the hot tide of passion that was urging her to listen to her heart, not the voice of reason.

''I want to kiss every inch of your beautiful body,'' he murmured, sliding his lips along her bodice.

''Not here,'' she whispered.

''No, someplace completely private where I can undress you slowly and gaze at the perfection of your body. You're like a work of art that deserves appreciation.''

She shivered at the thought of being naked in his arms and having his eyes wander over her, discovering her intimate secrets. It would be unbearably arousing even before he touched her. Like he was doing now.

His teeth gently tugged at her bodice, pulling it down so

one nipple was exposed. Megan drew in her breath sharply as his lips closed around the hardened little bud.

"Nick, you mustn't," she protested, although she didn't have the will to pull away.

"Why not, little angel?" His warm tongue circled her nipple, sending a thrill through her. "Don't you like it?"

"Yes, I... But this isn't the..." Megan couldn't think straight with his mouth driving her to distraction.

"This isn't the place?" He finished her sentence. "We could go upstairs."

His hand had slipped inside her bodice, cupping her breast while his mouth suckled on the nipple that was exposed. Megan's legs were trembling. They felt as liquid as the rest of her.

"You want me, too, don't you, darling?" he murmured.

She couldn't have denied it convincingly. All of her cried out for him. As she was about to admit it, there were voices along the path. Nicholas put his arm around her and drew her deeper into the shadows so she could straighten her gown.

When the voices had receded down the path, he stroked her cheek and said in a smoky voice, "Shall we go in now?"

She nodded silently, letting him take her hand as they started back to the house. But the interruption had given Megan a chance to think clearly. Making love with Nick under false pretenses was dishonest. A man who did that would be taking unfair advantage of a woman, and it wasn't any more acceptable when the sexes were reversed. Her problem was how to tell him she'd changed her mind, after evidencing a desire as strong as his own.

As they approached the house he said, "Perhaps you'd prefer to go up first. I'll join you in a few minutes."

"I don't think we should," she said, avoiding his eyes.

"I don't understand." He gave her a puzzled look.

She explained with difficulty. "This ball is being given in our honor. It wouldn't be right for us to leave early."

"Do you honestly think anyone would miss us in that crowd of people? They don't even know who we are in these getups."

"Claudette would know. She supplied our costumes. Besides, everyone's going to unmask at midnight."

The fond impatience in Nicholas's eyes turned to coolness. "I could say we'd make sure to be back by midnight, but I imagine you'd find another excuse," he said evenly.

"This is your obligation as much as mine. You don't have to sulk like a little boy." Megan's tone was sharper than she intended, because she shared his disappointment.

"My emotions at this moment are far from juvenile," he answered with a wintry smile.

When they had returned to the crowded ballroom Nicholas asked with cool courtesy, "Can I get you some punch, or a glass of champagne?"

"No, thank you. I'm going to fix my makeup." She walked away, conscious of his eyes on her back.

Several bathrooms had been provided for the guests and the one Megan chose was blessedly empty. She didn't want to talk to anyone. When the door opened a few minutes later she was relieved to see that it was Carrie, not someone she would have to trade small talk with.

"I saw you come in," Carrie said. "Are you having a good time?"

"Oh, yes, it's a marvelous party," Megan replied brightly. "Are you enjoying yourself?"

"Don't I always?" Carrie stared in the mirror for a moment before turning to her friend. "Who are we kidding? We're both miserable about having to leave tomorrow night."

"You agreed with me that it was the right thing to do."

"Knowing something is right and actually doing it are two different things. If I stayed, I think a relationship might develop between Michel and me. He wants me to meet his parents.''

"How would that make you feel? You'd have to lie to all three of them.''

"I know.'' Carrie sighed deeply. "But I wish I could at least tell Michel I'm leaving. It seems so cowardly to just disappear without any explanation.''

"You're doing him a favor. He'll realize it was only a summer romance. That's actually what it was. You wouldn't be this reluctant to leave if it weren't for all the glamour.''

"That's where you're wrong,'' Carrie said soberly. "Michel is the man I'd like to spend the rest of my life with. It wouldn't matter if he didn't have a penny or any prospects.''

"I'm sorry,'' Megan murmured. She certainly understood.

They were both caught between a rock and a hard place. Carrie couldn't marry Michel because if she did, sooner or later the lies they'd told would start to unravel. Her American passport was enough to betray her.

Megan was even worse off. Nick could never marry anyone but a royal princess, even if he wanted to—which wasn't a certainty.

"It wouldn't change anything if I agreed to stay,'' Megan said hesitantly.

"I know. It would only prolong the misery.'' Carrie tried to smile. "We'll have plenty of time for that when we get home.''

"That's negative thinking. We're going to look back on this trip with nothing but fond memories.'' Who knew? Maybe in time that would be true, Megan tried to tell herself.

The rest of the evening dragged on endlessly. Nicholas stayed away from her, but he didn't seem to be sulking. She saw him dancing and circulating around the ballroom, trying to have a few words with as many of the guests as possible.

Megan followed his example, being as charming and gracious as Nicholas. To all outward appearances, they were supremely happy. More than a few guests commented on the fact.

"Love certainly has done wonders for Gabrielle," one woman observed. "She hasn't thrown a tantrum or made any cutting remarks all evening."

"It's a little hard on the nerves," a second woman said with a laugh. "I keep waiting for the inevitable explosion."

"I guess love has had a softening effect on her."

"It had just the opposite effect when she was going with that tennis player, Jacques Duvalle. I don't know which was more passionate, their arguments or their reconciliations."

"That was just sexual attraction. This is real love. You can tell when they're together."

"Nicholas will be good for her. Gabrielle needs a strong man who won't put up with her antics. That must be why she's been on her good behavior all night."

"I just hope it lasts." The subject was dropped as they were joined by their escorts.

As midnight approached, Claudette brought Megan and Nicholas together. "You two have hardly had a moment alone tonight," she said. "It was good of you to go along with my little masquerade, but it's almost time to take off our masks. Then everybody will know who you are and you can spend the rest of the night together."

"I suggested that to Gabrielle, but she turned me down," Nicholas drawled.

"Naughty boy." Claudette tapped him with her fan. "You're trying to embarrass me."

"I thought you wanted me to stay in character," he said. "Louis and Marie would have been in bed long ago. Perhaps we're miscast."

"It's possible," Megan said evenly. "Louis was a mature man. He didn't sulk when something was denied him."

"He didn't have to. He simply called in an understudy."

"Is that what you've been doing? Auditioning?"

Claudette was alarmed by the note of anger underlying their brittle repartee. Was Gabrielle's notoriously short temper going to erupt now, when everything was going so well?

She signaled hastily to the orchestra leader, who gave her a drumroll. "Attention, everyone! It's time to remove your masks and find your partners. Now you'll know if you guessed everybody's identity correctly."

"I was beginning to have doubts about yours," Nicholas murmured to Megan. "But you're the same old Gabrielle."

A couple approached them, saving her the necessity of a reply. "I knew it was you, Gabrielle," the woman said.

"What gave me away?" Megan managed a smile.

"Yes, how did you guess?" Nicholas asked mockingly. "I thought I knew her, but I didn't."

"It was that magnificent necklace," the woman said. "I do hope you plan to wear it on your wedding day—or is that a big secret?"

"I haven't really thought about it yet," Megan answered vaguely.

As the woman pressed her for details of the wedding, Nicholas drifted away.

The party lasted quite late. When it was over, Megan went upstairs alone. Nicholas had disappeared right after the midnight supper, and she hadn't seen Carrie in some time.

It was just as well, Megan thought wearily as she closed the door of her suite. She wasn't in the mood to talk to anyone, even her best friend.

She kicked off her shoes and walked out onto the balcony, enjoying the silence after all the hubbub of the party. The formal gardens looked almost eerie in the moonlight, like a surrealist painting in shades of gray and black. Gravel paths fanned out in several directions, giving no clue as to where they led. Like life, Megan thought poignantly. You could take the wrong path quite innocently. With a sigh she went back into the bedroom.

She'd discarded the heavy wig along with her shoes. That was the easy part. Getting out of her gown was the challenge. Although the hooks at her waist were tiny and hard to unfasten, at least they were within reach. The ones higher up were not. After struggling mightily, she had to concede defeat.

What to do now? Gabrielle would have called a maid to undress her, but Megan hated to disturb anyone at that late hour. In any case, she didn't know how to summon the maid. There were several buttons by her bed, but she hadn't listened when the butler had told her what each one was for. Her only option was to hope Carrie wasn't asleep yet.

Holding her gown together at the waist in back, Megan went into the hallway. Her stocking-clad feet didn't make any sound on the carpeted floor and she knocked softly. Too softly, because there was no answer.

Knowing Carrie was a sound sleeper, Megan was forced to knock a little louder. When that brought no result, she called to her and still didn't get any response. The situation would have seemed funny at any other time, but Megan was tired and she wanted to go to bed.

Out of sheer frustration she called out louder than she intended, "Carrie, will you please wake up!"

Carrie's door remained shut, but the one across the hall opened. Nicholas stood in the doorway, wearing only black satin pajama bottoms that rode low on his lean hips. His hair was tousled, as though he'd been asleep.

"What the devil's going on out here?" he demanded.

"I'm sorry I woke you," she murmured.

Nicholas looked tremendously sexy with his sleepy eyes and half-naked body. Megan tried not to stare at the triangle

of dark hair that curled on his broad chest, tapering to a V
before disappearing into the drawstring of his pajamas.

"What are you doing out in the hall at this time of
night?" he asked.

"I was just going to bed, but I have to see Carrie first."

"Can't it wait until morning? She's obviously asleep."

"I know, but I need her help. I can't get out of this
wretched dress."

He looked at her with a slight frown. "Why didn't you
call a maid?"

"Because I forgot which button to push and I didn't want
a whole gaggle of servants showing up at this hour. I feel
foolish enough."

"Since I'm already up, there's no point in waking Carrie.
Turn around and I'll unhook you."

She did as he said, because it was only sensible, but
when he fumbled with the tiny hooks, Megan wasn't so
sure. She was very conscious of him, so close behind her
that she could feel the warmth of his body on her bare back.

"This thing must have been designed by the Marquis de
Sade," he muttered. "What you need is someone with little
fingers and a lot of patience."

"It's all right, I'll wake Carrie," Megan said with relief,
starting to move away.

Nicholas stopped her by putting an arm around her waist.
"I didn't say I couldn't do it. Just give me a minute."

"We're going to wake up the whole house," she protested.

"Not if you stop fidgeting." He grinned suddenly. "Although I suggest we go into your room. The lighting is
better, and if anyone came walking down the hall, this
would look quite suggestive."

Megan didn't want to be alone with Nick, and certainly
not in her bedroom. But making a big thing of it would
only provoke sarcastic remarks. She didn't feel up to re-

suming hostilities at this time of night, so she silently led the way.

"Did the party just break up?" he asked after closing the door and resuming the intricate task of unhooking her dress.

"Weren't you there?"

"By one o'clock I felt I'd done my duty, so I went to bed. You didn't even miss me," he teased.

"I didn't see that much of you during the second half of the evening," she answered evenly. "But I'm sure all the single women missed you."

He didn't respond for a moment. Then Megan breathed a sigh of relief, realizing her gown was finally unfastened. She held the top so it wouldn't slide off her shoulders.

Nicholas turned her around to face him. "I want to apologize for my conduct tonight. I acted like a petulant schoolboy. You have every right to be angry."

"*I* wasn't the one who got angry. *You* did."

"*Disappointed* is a better word for it. I thought you wanted me as much as I wanted you."

"I did! It just wasn't—"

"You don't have to explain. No means no. A real man accepts that."

Megan felt he deserved more of an explanation, but what could she say?

"It's all right, darling." He stroked her hair tenderly. "I overreacted because I want you so much, but I think I understand what you were trying to tell me."

She gave him a cautious look. "You do?"

"You want our relationship to be different from the ones we've both had in the past. There's more to marriage than just the physical side—although I must admit that part is irresistible." He smiled sensuously. "I want to take you to bed and make love to you night and day for a week."

It was torture to be offered something she wanted so

much, yet couldn't have. Megan made a tiny sound of protest.

Nicholas misunderstood. "Don't worry, angel. I'm not going to try to change your mind. I don't know if I can wait until our wedding night, but if that's what you want, I'll try."

"You would do that for me?"

He framed her face in his palms and gazed at her tenderly. "I love you, sweetheart. It's taken me years to discover it, but I never really knew you before. Whatever you want is all right with me. I want to make you as happy as you've made me."

"Oh, Nick, I can't do this to you," she whispered.

"I'll survive." He smiled. "It will take a lot of cold showers, but you're worth it, my love."

Unshed tears made her eyes as bright as stars. "You're too good to be true," she said in a choked voice. As she reached out for him, the front of her loosened dress slipped to her waist.

He drew in his breath sharply at the sight of her exposed breasts. The raw hunger in his eyes couldn't be refused. When Megan made no attempt to cover herself, Nicholas reached out and cupped her breasts in his hands.

"You're irresistible," he muttered, caressing her compulsively.

He pulled her into his arms and parted her lips for a deep, inflaming kiss that made her long for his full possession. When his hands moved across her bare back, then lower to cup her buttocks and lift her into the juncture of his thighs, Megan moved urgently against him.

"You don't know what you're doing to me," he groaned. "I've never wanted anyone this much. I can't leave you alone."

"I don't want you to," she whispered. "Love me, darling."

"Yes, sweetheart, I'm going to fill you with joy. I'll hold you in my arms and we'll be joined in every way."

They clung together for long moments, their passion rising as they caressed each other with increasing intimacy.

"Ah, Gabrielle, Gabrielle..." He murmured her name over and over. "My beautiful bride."

The reminder registered, even in Megan's heated state. Her body told her to ignore it, but the damage had been done. Passion didn't justify what she was doing—even though her feelings for him were more than merely physical. But it would still be a betrayal of the man she loved. He would never forgive her.

Nicholas could feel her tense in his arms. He raised his head to look at her searchingly. "What's wrong, Gabrielle?"

Her lashes swept down to fan her flushed cheeks. How could she do this to him again? There was no easy way except the truth, which couldn't be told. "You can tell how much I want you, Nick," she began haltingly.

"But you still want to do it the right way," he finished for her.

She glanced up swiftly, dreading the anger she expected to find on his face, but she found only tenderness tinged with regret.

"It would make our marriage...significant, somehow," she explained hesitantly, hoping he would accept that.

He nodded. "More than just a night of passionate lovemaking—although I can't think of anything better at the moment." He smiled wryly. "But our marriage is going to be so much more than that. We'll be partners as well as lovers, sharing everything."

"It sounds wonderful," Megan answered wistfully.

"It will be," he said in a vibrant voice. Putting his hands on her shoulders, he kissed her without taking her in his arms. When her disappointment showed, Nicholas laughed. "I've used up most of my self-control for tonight. I have just enough left to take me out the door.'' He kissed the tip of her nose. ''Sleep well, angel. I'll see you in the morning.''

After he left, Megan undressed slowly and climbed into bed. If she hadn't listened to her conscience, Nick would be lying here with her, their naked bodies joined together. She turned over on her stomach and buried her head under the pillow to blot out the erotic image.

Doing the right thing might be good for her character, but it didn't do a lot for the rest of her.

Chapter Seven

A light tap on Megan's door woke her the next morning, which was surprising. Gabrielle's maid usually waited until she rang for breakfast.

"Please come back later," Megan called.

The door opened and Nicholas came in carrying a tray loaded with covered dishes and a pot of coffee.

"It's time to get up, sleepyhead," he said. "You're wasting the best part of the day."

Megan sat up in bed, pulling the covers up to her neck. "What are you doing here?"

"I came to have breakfast with you."

He put the tray over her knees and started to remove the silver covers from plates of crisp bacon and eggs. There were also croissants, butter rosettes and a crystal dish filled with strawberry jam.

She sniffed the aroma of coffee appreciatively. "Why are you bringing it? Did the servants all go out on strike?"

"Not that I know of. This is a labor of love."

"You just wanted to see what I looked like first thing in the morning," she joked.

"I didn't have to. I knew you'd be gorgeous."

He walked around to the other side of the bed and stretched out next to her, but on top of the covers. After propping some pillows behind his back, he took one of the plates from the tray and picked up a piece of bacon.

She gave him a startled look. "What are you doing?"

"You didn't intend to eat both breakfasts, did you?"

"I meant, what are you doing in bed with me?"

"Technically I'm *on* the bed, not in it. Not as satisfactory an arrangement as I'd like, but I'll settle for what I can get."

He didn't seem to be affected by the suggestiveness of the situation, but that could be because he was fully dressed, while she was wearing only a skimpy chiffon nightie. Nick looked very virile in a navy turtleneck pullover and fawn-colored slacks. Megan was intensely conscious of his long, lean body stretched out next to her, tantalizingly close.

"We must be the only two people who are up this early," she said hastily. "Outside of the servants, that is."

"The others don't know what they're missing. It's too nice a day to stay inside. What would you like to do today?"

"I guess we'll have to wait and see what our host and hostess have planned."

"Probably something dull like bridge and rehashing last night's ball." He reached for another croissant. "We can think of something better to do than that."

"Like what?"

"How about getting a couple of horses from the stables and going for a ride in the countryside?"

"I didn't bring any riding clothes." She was glad of the excuse.

Nicholas and Gabrielle were both known to be superb

horsemen. He played polo and she'd won ribbons at riding exhibitions. But Megan couldn't hope to pass herself off as an expert rider. She hadn't been on a horse since summer camp many years ago. And she hadn't been any good at it even then.

"You don't need riding clothes," he said. "You can wear jeans."

"I didn't bring those, either."

"Claudette can probably scare you up a pair, or send somebody out to buy them."

"That's so much trouble. Why don't we just go for a walk instead?"

"All right, if you'd rather," he said reluctantly.

"We can have the cook pack a basket for us and we'll have a picnic under a tree. Won't that be fun?" she coaxed.

"Just being with you is a slice of heaven."

He leaned over to kiss her tenderly, then with increasing desire. When Megan parted her lips receptively, Nicholas's hand slipped under the covers to caress her warm body. Her awakened senses responded instantly and she uttered a tiny sound of pleasure.

After a tantalizing moment he groaned and drew away. "I promised myself I wasn't going to torment us like this, but I lose all control when I'm around you." He got off the bed and started for the door. "You're the one who's to blame, though."

"How is it *my* fault?" she asked indignantly.

"No woman should be that beautiful."

"Okay, I'll try to be ugly today." She smiled.

"You couldn't if you tried," he said fondly. "Get dressed and meet me in the library in half an hour."

Megan rushed to shower and dress, grabbing a pair of cream-colored pants and a matching shirt with long full sleeves. She was glad Nick had wakened her so they could have a long day together. She didn't allow herself to dwell on the fact that it was the last one she would have with him.

On the way downstairs she knocked softly at Carrie's door, but there was no answer. That was slightly strange. She would have thought Carrie would want to make the most of her last day with Michel, also. But then, Megan told herself, everybody except Nick had gone to bed awfully late last night.

Nick was waiting with a picnic basket at the foot of the stairs. "The cook assures me it's a lunch fit for a princess," he said.

"How did you get her to make it so fast?"

"No problem. I simply went into the kitchen and asked."

"Guests aren't supposed to go into the kitchen. Proper protocol would have been to ask your valet, who would have asked the butler, who would have asked the cook," Megan joked, although it was true.

"That's nonsense. We had a nice talk. Her name is Roselle, and her husband is the head gardener here. They have two children, a boy and a girl."

That was one of the many things Megan loved about Nick. He was genuinely interested in people, no matter what their status, and he refused to allow the rigid rules of society to keep him from getting to know them. He would make a wonderful king when the time came, Megan thought wistfully.

As they went out the front door, Nick suggested they stop by the stables before starting on their walk. "Just to see the horses," he said hastily when Megan gave him a wary look. "The duke recently acquired a new Arabian stallion with superb bloodlines. I'd like to take a look at him."

She couldn't think of any reason for refusing, so she went along without protest. While Nick talked with the stable boss, Megan walked down the line of stalls, looking at the horses.

They were superb animals, sleek and high-spirited. Some tossed their heads and snorted loudly, but one bay-colored mare was more placid. She stuck her head over the gate and nuzzled Megan's hand.

"That's Lady Jane," a groom told her. He handed Megan a couple of lumps of sugar. "This is what she's looking for."

Megan stroked the horse's soft nose as it ate the sugar. "She's a beautiful horse."

"That she is, but Lady Jane is too tame for Your Highness. You'll be wanting something more high-spirited, like Rex here." He gestured at a huge black stallion who tossed his head and stamped the ground.

"He's a splendid animal, but actually I prefer Lady Jane."

Before she could stop him, the man opened the gate and led the mare outside to where Nicholas was chatting with the stable boss.

"I'll have her saddled up for you in a jiffy, Your Highness," the groom said.

Nick turned with a pleased expression on his face. "You changed your mind."

"No, I didn't!" Megan insisted as the groom put a saddle on the mare. "I merely said she was a beautiful horse. I didn't mean I wanted to ride her."

"I can see why." He gazed at the horse disparagingly. "She doesn't look very spirited."

"Just because she isn't pawing the ground?" Megan asked indignantly. "Who needs a macho horse? I think she's lovely."

"Okay, but you don't mind if I choose a mount with more 'enthusiasm,' shall we call it?" he teased.

"Choose anything you like, but you'll be riding alone."

Nick looked at her with a puzzled frown. "You love to ride, Gabrielle. Why this sudden aversion? It's almost as if you're afraid."

"You know better than that," she said swiftly. "I'd love to go galloping across the countryside with you, but not in these clothes. I dressed for a walk."

He continued to look at her strangely. "You never let something like that stop you before," he said slowly. "You attended the opera in jeans and a tank top once."

Megan knew she wasn't behaving like Gabrielle, but she thought Nick had accepted the change in her. It would be ironic if the whole deception started to unravel on her last day in Beaumarre.

That couldn't be allowed to happen. Megan eyed Lady Jane grimly, hoping she wouldn't break anything major if she fell off.

Keeping her voice light she said, "I was trying to live down my lurid past, but you've tempted me once too often. Come on, pal, let's ride."

"Wouldn't you know *this* was the temptation you couldn't resist," he said wryly, cupping his hands to help her into the saddle.

As the groom led out a handsome brown stallion for Nick, Megan tried to remember the little she'd learned about riding a horse. Grip with the knees was one thing, and there was something about positioning your feet in the stirrups.

She clutched the reins tightly as they rode away and Lady Jane started to trot to keep up with the other horse. Staying astride was only half of Megan's problem. She was being jarred unmercifully. With every step, her bottom rose in the air and then slammed back onto the saddle.

Besides the discomfort, she was afraid Nick would discover what an inept rider she was, but he was enjoying himself too much to notice. He kept up a running commentary on what a beautiful day it was and how much he liked being out in the country.

Megan didn't have time to appreciate it, although as they got farther from the castle the scenery was spectacular. The meadows were filled with wildflowers and many of the trees were covered with blossoms.

She was just getting used to the mare's gait when Nick said, "This is too tame. I'll race you to that clump of trees out there."

"I don't want to beat you," she answered lightly. "It would ruin your disposition for the rest of the day."

"You have to be joking! I could give you a ten-minute start and still be there ahead of you."

"What's the big rush to get to a clump of trees? I'll get there almost as fast and I won't be all hot and sweaty when I do."

"You'll look even sexier—if possible. Come on. No more excuses."

Nicholas reached over and flicked her horse's flank with his reins. It startled the mare. She reared, then took off at a gallop. Megan was caught by surprise, too. She managed to stay in the saddle by grabbing the horse's mane, but the reins slipped out of her hands. Lady Jane was in full gallop when she raced under a tree. A low, leafy branch obscured Megan's vision for an instant. She reached up instinctively to brush it out of her face and lost her precarious balance.

One minute she was holding on for dear life, the next minute she was lying on lush grass in a field of daisies, with flower petals from the tree drifting down on her head. It happened so fast that she was surprised rather than hurt.

Nick galloped up only seconds behind her. He slid off his horse and knelt beside her in one fluid motion. Trying to hide his panic he smoothed the long pale hair out of her eyes and said, "Lie still, darling. I'll get a doctor. You'll be fine."

"I don't need a doctor. There's nothing wrong with me." She struggled to a sitting position, in spite of his restraining hands on her shoulders.

"You can't be sure. I want an expert opinion."

"I just gave you one. I'm the one who knows how I feel."

"Nothing hurts?" he asked anxiously.

"Only my dignity." She smiled. "Can you imagine *me*, an expert rider, falling off a horse?"

"It was all my fault. I didn't realize she spooked so easily. If anything had happened to you I'd never have forgiven myself!" Nick took Megan in his arms and held her so tightly she could hardly breathe.

It was always heavenly to be in his arms, but her nose was wedged into the curve of his neck. "Could you loosen up just a little?" she asked in a muffled voice. "You're squashing me."

His punishing embrace loosened immediately and he drew back to look at her ruefully. "I seem determined to injure you in one way or another. But I just want to hold you and know you're all right. When I saw you go sailing through the air, my heart stopped!"

"I can imagine how klutzy I looked," she remarked wryly.

"You do everything with style," he said fondly. "Who else would have landed in a field of flowers? You look like a beautiful wood nymph with all these petals in your hair."

As he leaned forward to remove one, Megan's mouth brushed his cheek. He turned his head so their lips touched.

"Don't ever leave me, my love," he murmured.

She linked her arms around his neck and kissed him yearningly. "I don't know how I can. You're everything I ever hoped for."

"Darling Gabrielle, you're everything I've ever wanted in a woman. I don't know what I'd do if I lost you." He kissed her tenderly.

It was a bittersweet moment for Megan. This would be the last time she had alone with Nick. Once they returned to the house party they would be surrounded by people for the rest of the day. And then she would leave for home.

The thought of never seeing Nick again was unbearable—never knowing what it would be like to have him fill the aching void inside her. Would it be so terrible to find out, just this once? Nick was the only man she'd ever loved and it was all she would have of him for the rest of her life.

Megan's arms tightened around his neck and she lifted her hips in a need for closer contact with his. Nick's response was immediate. His legs scissored around hers and he slipped one hand under her to mold their bodies tightly together.

"This is the way I want to make love to you," he said huskily. "In the sunshine so I can see your face and know when I'm pleasing you."

"Everything you do pleases me," she whispered. Megan turned liquid inside as Nick's warm mouth trailed kisses down her neckline.

"You're so exquisite," he muttered, fondling her breast. "I want to kiss every secret part of you."

She quivered with anticipation when he gently nudged her legs apart and unfastened her zipper. His hand scorched her as it glided over the soft skin of her stomach, then moved lower. Megan cried out with pleasure when he caressed her intimately, then probed the hidden core of her desire.

"You're so receptive, darling," he said with delight. "You can't know how it makes me feel to see you come alive like this in my arms."

Megan was reaching out to unbutton Nick's shirt when the silence around them shattered. The stallion that had been grazing nearby lifted his head and neighed loudly in answer to the sound of horses' hooves and voices calling in the distance.

Nicholas lifted his head and swore softly. With a few swift movements he straightened Megan's clothing, smoothed her hair and helped her to sit up.

"We'll have to find a deserted island," he said wryly "That's the only place people will leave us alone."

She looked at him in a daze. It was difficult to be abruptly thrown out of paradise. "Why are they calling us?"

"Lady Jane must have returned to the stable and they're worried about you." Nick got to his feet as several rider galloped up.

The stable boss reined to a stop and jumped off his horse "Is the princess all right, Your Highness? The mare came back alone." He looked down at Megan with deep concern

"I'm fine." She stood and brushed herself off. "We stopped for a picnic and I forgot to tie Lady Jane to a tree."

"She doesn't usually bolt for home," the man said doubtfully.

Nick shrugged. "You never know what a horse will do Thanks for your concern. We'll be all right now," he said in a dismissive tone.

"Yes, Your Highness. I'll leave a spare mount for Princess Gabrielle."

There was no way Megan was getting on another horse Before she could think of an excuse, Nick made one for her. "It's such a nice day, I think we'll walk back. You can take my horse with you," he told one of the grooms.

After the men had ridden away he said to Megan, "I hope that was all right with you. I don't want to take chance on any more accidents today."

"It's fine with me," she said. "I preferred walking in the first place, but it's a long way back."

"I'm in no hurry. Are you?" He gave her a sultry look

The respite had given Megan's passion time to cool With deep regret she realized that what almost happened would have been a mistake. One idyllic act of love wouldn't be enough, and it would have made it even harder to leave Nick.

"I'm not in a hurry, but I was looking forward to

picnic," she said, ignoring his tone. "What happened to the picnic basket?"

"I had it fastened to my saddle. It must have fallen off when I raced after you. Maybe we can find it."

Nick didn't try to rekindle the mood, once Megan indicated she was unwilling. He took her hand instead as they started back through the meadow.

The picnic basket was lying not far from the tree that had unseated Megan. Containers had tumbled out onto the grass, but the lids hadn't come off.

"The pâté got a little mashed, but it will taste just as good," she said after removing the top of a small carton.

"The wine survived. That's more important." Nick laughed.

"There's enough food here for ten people!" she exclaimed. "What was the cook thinking of? We could never eat all of this."

"Speak for yourself. I'm famished. Frustration always makes me hungry."

He grinned to show it was a joke, but Megan knew he was serious about the frustration part.

When she gave him a troubled look, he raised her hand to his lips and kissed it. "Don't worry, darling," he soothed. "I'm not going to sulk or throw a tantrum. Every inch of me aches for you, but we have a lifetime of happiness ahead of us. I can afford to wait."

Too bad she didn't have that option, Megan thought poignantly, but she refused to dwell on it now. "I don't want you to be frustrated *and* hungry," she said lightly. "I'll put out the food while you open the wine."

It was a sumptuous picnic. The cook had provided both cold salmon with dill sauce, and herbed chicken breasts. Little watercress sandwiches and two kinds of salad rounded out the menu, and there were petits fours and fresh fruit for dessert.

After they'd eaten, Megan dabbed at her mouth with a

linen napkin, sighing happily. "That was fantastic. I don't think I could eat again for a week."

"You'll be hungry again by dinnertime," Nick predicted.

"I doubt it. I hope Claudette doesn't have something lavish planned."

"Usually after a house party there's just a buffet laid out for anyone who is still around. People leave at different times during the afternoon and evening." He reached over and took her hand. "I wish you were coming home with me tonight. I hate the thought of being separated from you for even a day. Why do you have to go home first?"

"Women have things to do before a trip," she answered vaguely.

"Like what?"

"Well... Deciding what clothes to bring, for one thing."

"You can always have your clothes sent to you. Just call and tell your maid what to pack. Grandalia is only a couple of hours away. Come with me, angel," he urged. "We can have a day to ourselves before all the mandated state functions begin."

The strain was beginning to fray Megan's nerves. Not only because of her sadness at having to leave Nick; she felt guilty over the suffering she was about to cause him. He would be devastated and bewildered over her desertion. If he never trusted another woman, it would be her fault.

She tried to keep the tension out of her voice. "We've spent most of today by ourselves. We should be getting back to the house party."

"Do you really want to?"

"Not especially, but it isn't polite to just disappear for the entire day."

"That's one of the perks of royalty. When you're rude, nobody dares to criticize." He grinned.

"We've turned over a new leaf, remember? I'm going

to stop throwing tantrums, and you're going to do something meaningful with your life.''

He reached over and gripped her hand. "With your help, sweetheart. That's another reason for you to come with me tonight. We have so much to talk about. The foundation will take up a lot of our time, so I suppose we'd better get settled in our own home first. I have an estate just outside the city that I want you to see. I spent most of my summers there as a boy. It's a wonderful place to bring up children, and we can also keep an apartment at the palace. But if that arrangement doesn't suit you, there are a lot of other choices.''

"I'll have to think about it," she murmured.

"Of course. I don't expect you to make up your mind right now. We'll find someplace where you'll be happy, my love.''

He was twisting the dagger in her heart and Megan didn't know how much longer she could stand the pain. She busied herself putting the remains of the picnic back in the basket to avoid looking at him.

"Just leave that here," he said when he finally noticed what she was doing. "I'll tell one of the grooms where to find it.''

Nick was so caught up in his plans for the future that he didn't realize Megan was saying very little. She suffered greatly on the long walk back as he told her about the huge fireplace in his castle, and described how they would make love in front of the fire on cold winter nights. There was also a lake on the estate where they would teach their children to swim. Megan breathed a sigh of relief when the manor house came into sight.

The houseguests were assembled in a large den on the main floor, judging from the buzz of conversation coming from there. But Carrie and Michel were in the front hall, talking very seriously.

Nick raised an eyebrow. "Is there a problem?"

"I've been waiting for you to get back," Michel said with relief. "I have to speak to you alone for a minute."

After the men had excused themselves, Megan turned to Carrie. "What's going on?" Before her friend could answer, she continued, "Are you feeling okay? I knocked on your door last night and again this morning, but you didn't answer either time."

Carrie's cheeks flushed and she avoided Megan's eyes. "I guess I was asleep and didn't hear you."

It was a reasonable explanation, except for her strange behavior. Megan's gaze sharpened. "You weren't in your room, were you?"

Carrie took a deep breath. "All right, no, I wasn't. There's no reason to lie about it. I'm not ashamed of the fact."

"You were with Michel, weren't you?"

"Yes, and it was wonderful." Carrie's face was soft with remembrance. "He's everything I've ever wanted in a man. I'm in love—*really* in love—for the first time in my life."

Megan hesitated. "Ordinarily I'd be thrilled for you, but I don't want to see you get hurt. We talked this over. You and Michel have no future together."

"That's where you're wrong! *You* have no future with Nick. Unfortunately he can never marry you, no matter how you feel about each other. But it's different with me. Michel doesn't have to marry royalty. There's nothing standing in our way."

"Except a phony identity. Can you marry him without telling him who you are? Or did you already tell him last night?" Megan asked tensely.

"No! I wanted to, but I thought I should talk to you first. Michel wouldn't tell anyone if I asked him not to," Carrie said earnestly.

"You don't really believe that. He's utterly devoted to Nick. Do you honestly think he'd let this deception go on?"

"Maybe Nick *should* know," Carrie said uncertainly.

"Of course he should! But it's too late now. The engagement has been announced and the two of us have been on display all week. Nick would look like a fool for being taken in by a phony Gabrielle, and King Claude would look even worse for perpetrating such a fraud. Relations between the two countries would be irreparably damaged, all because of me."

"You're not solely to blame," Carrie protested. "It wasn't your idea."

"But I went along with it. I'm the one who ruined Nick's life," Megan said somberly. "How do you think Michel would feel if he found out? Do you really think he'd keep it to himself?"

"No, and he'd blame me, too, for keeping quiet," Carrie said sadly. "Now I'm glad that I didn't tell him. At least we had one perfect night together."

Which was more than *she* had had, Megan thought wistfully.

"It won't be much consolation to you, but the marriage between Nick and Gabrielle might not go through," Carrie said.

"What could prevent it?"

"That's what Michel was waiting to talk to Nick about. I wanted to warn you, too. It might be very—" Carrie paused as a group of people came out of the den.

One of them was holding a newspaper and they were all talking animatedly.

"I don't care how rich or handsome he is," a woman said. "I certainly wouldn't put up with a thing like this."

"You women are too hard on the poor chap," a man protested. "After all, he was a footloose bachelor at the time."

"This is more than just a case of boys will be boys," his wife answered sharply. "If I were Gabrielle, I'd—" She stopped abruptly and rolled up the newspaper when she saw

Megan and Carrie in the hall. "Oh...you're back, Gabrielle. We all wondered where you'd gotten to."

"Nick and I went on a picnic," Megan said. "Is there something going on that I should know about?"

The men looked uncomfortable and the women exchanged meaningful glances. "It isn't our place to say anything," the first woman answered. "But on the other hand, you'll find out anyway."

"Find out *what?*" Megan was losing patience.

"Perhaps it would be better if you read it for yourself." She held out the newspaper.

It was one of the more lurid tabloids, one that regularly dished out details on the less savory escapades of the rich and famous. Dominating the front page was a large picture of Nick beside an exotic brunette. The headline above it read: The Prince and His Paramour. Does Princess Gabrielle Know About Nick's Secret Love Child?"

Megan's first reaction was shock. It couldn't be true! She glanced up in bewilderment to find the others staring at her avidly, waiting for her reaction.

Lifting her chin regally she said, "I thought these yellow rags couldn't sink any lower, but it appears they have. I'll put this thing in the garbage where it belongs." She walked gracefully up the staircase, followed by Carrie.

When they were in Megan's suite with the door closed, Carrie said, "You carried that off royally. I'm proud of you. Gabrielle couldn't have done any better."

"They were just waiting for me to make a scene. I wasn't going to give them the satisfaction," Megan said disdainfully. "Did you know about this?"

"I found out about it just a short time ago. Somebody went into town and came back with that tabloid. They've all been discussing it. It's the high point of the weekend," Carrie commented sardonically.

"You don't believe it, do you?"

Carrie hesitated. "Maybe you should read the article."

"I don't have to read it. I know what sort of trash those yellow rags print."

"I know they exaggerate, but there are a couple of things that almost have to be the truth. Nick could sue the pants off them otherwise."

"Even if you win, you lose. A lawsuit only gives the story wider coverage. That's what they count on."

"Maybe you're right, but you still should read the article."

"All right, if you insist."

Megan handled the paper as though it were contaminated. Her face was filled with disgust, but as she read further, her expression changed.

The article described Tanya Tremaine as a sometime "model and actress." She'd told the reporter that she and Prince Nicholas had been intimate for over a year. Three months ago she'd borne a child by him—a little girl she'd named Nicole for her father, Nicholas. Tanya had said she and the prince were very much in love, but they both realized he could never marry her.

Nicholas was very generous, however. He was paying the rent on her luxury apartment and also supporting his daughter. To back up her story, Tanya had given the reporter a photocopy of a generous check made out to her and signed by Nicholas. The check was pictured in the article.

That was numbing enough, but Megan was really wounded by the woman's final claim. Tanya said Nicholas had assured her that he would visit her and their daughter regularly, and of course continue to support them. She said she and the prince had a special relationship that his marriage would not change—the implication being that the affair would go on.

Megan's face was pale as she put down the paper. It didn't matter that Nick hadn't betrayed *her*. He thought she was Gabrielle, so it was the same thing. How could she have been so badly taken in by him?

After a look at Megan's expression, Carrie said, "I'm sorry you had to find out like this."

"I was so trusting I didn't even want to read the article," Megan said bitterly.

"I'm sure some of it is overblown."

"Which part? They have a picture of the woman, the baby and the check. You're right, he doesn't have grounds for a lawsuit."

"I meant the part where she intimates the affair will continue after Nick is married. I don't think he'd do a thing like that."

"Oh, really? If he'd keep a separate family tucked away secretly, he's capable of anything. He *should* see his daughter. A man should have more responsibility than to just scatter his seed."

"He is supporting them," Carrie reminded her.

"How generous of him! Maybe they'll pin another medal on his chest."

Carrie gave her a curious look. "Nick never even hinted that he'd fathered a child?"

"Believe me, it never came up. He was too busy telling me I was the only woman he'd ever loved, and how he'd been looking for me all his life. He didn't mention that he'd made a detour here and there."

"Well, luckily it isn't your problem. Everything will really hit the fan when his parents and King Claude get wind of this. That's why I said the wedding might not take place."

"And all of this was for nothing," Megan said dully.

"I guess so." After a few moments of silence Carrie said, "For what it's worth, Michel said the story isn't true."

"Why doesn't that surprise me? Nick has the ability to inspire loyalty—among men, anyway."

There was a light tap at the door and Nick called, "Are you in there, Gabrielle?"

Megan crossed the room with a set face. She opened the door, but didn't invite him in. "What is it?" she asked coolly.

He sighed when he saw her expression. "You've seen the newspaper article." It wasn't a question.

"Yes, some of the guests couldn't wait to show it to me."

Nick swore under his breath. "You'd think they'd have more to occupy their time. I wanted to tell you about it myself."

"But you never found an opportunity all week?" she asked derisively.

He frowned. "Don't tell me you believe what that yellow rag printed? You, of all people, know they don't let the truth get in the way of a juicy story."

"Maybe. But it's a little more difficult to make up photographs."

Michel had accompanied Nick, but he wasn't immediately visible in the shadowy hall. As an argument seemed imminent, Michel stepped forward and said, "Why don't we all go inside where we can discuss this without an audience."

"There's nothing to discuss," Megan replied. "I read enough about it in the paper. I don't care to hear any more details."

"You're sure everything you read is true?" Nick demanded.

"Please," Michel coaxed. "We really need to talk about this in private. Carrie?" He tacitly asked for her assistance.

"Michel is right," she said. "Why give those gossipmongers more to talk about?"

Megan stood aside reluctantly, and Nick entered with the same lack of enthusiasm. "This is fairly pointless," he said. "You've already made up your mind about me."

"How can I ignore the fact that you're having an ongoing affair with another woman?"

A muscle twitched in his square jaw. "You're not asking me if I am, you're telling me."

"Do you deny it?"

"Would you believe me if I did?"

"That's no answer," Megan said angrily.

Before they reached a complete stalemate, Michel said pacifically, "You've had experience with the tabloids, Gabrielle. You know they mix lies with half-truths."

"What part is a lie—the affair, the baby? He isn't writing out checks to her for no good reason."

"It doesn't have to be for the one you're thinking," Michel replied.

"Give it up," Nick said distantly. "Let her think what she wants."

"You're both being pigheaded," Michel said impatiently. "If you won't tell her, I will. Nick dated Tanya once or twice, but they were never involved," he said to Megan. "They knew a lot of the same people and ran across each other frequently in different clubs. She was having an unhappy love affair and she cried on Nick's shoulder. He felt sorry for her, so he was sympathetic."

"That's a polite way of putting it," Megan commented cynically.

Nick scowled. "You see? Why are you even bothering?" he asked Michel.

The other man ignored him and continued doggedly. "Tanya became pregnant and the father of the baby ran out on her. She was broke and desperate. She didn't even have money to pay her rent, so Nick helped her out. That's what the check was for."

"And she was so grateful she named her baby after him?" Megan asked derisively.

Nick threw up his hands in frustration. "The child wasn't

named after *me!* She just happened to like the name. It's very popular at the moment.''

''Even if I accepted that explanation, there's one thing that doesn't add up. If you simply befriended her, why would she give such a damaging interview to a tabloid reporter?''

''For money,'' Nick answered succinctly. ''Maybe she thinks it will be publicity for a book she plans to try and peddle. Everybody who's ever had the most casual encounter with a celebrity writes a book about it. Why would Tanya photocopy the check I gave her? Who does that unless they plan to use it in some way at a later date?''

Carrie hadn't taken part in the conversation, but she now remarked, ''That's a good point. The normal thing would have been just to deposit it.''

''Don't confuse Gabrielle with logic,'' Nick said sardonically.

''If you want unquestioning acceptance, get a dog,'' Megan snapped back.

''I'd settle for an open mind,'' he replied.

''Why don't we all calm down,'' Michel pleaded. ''Something like this is very stressful, but we can work it out if we don't lose our perspective.''

''It's already worked out. Nick didn't want to marry Ga—'' Megan caught herself just in time. If she revealed her own deception, Nick would think his was justified—which it certainly wasn't! ''You didn't want to marry me in the first place,'' she told him. ''Now you don't have to. Your girlfriend has provided a reason to call off the wedding.''

His jaw set grimly. ''If that's what you want, it's fine with me.''

''Don't pretend I'm being unreasonable,'' she flared. ''How did you expect me to react?''

''I expected you to realize I was being set up,'' he said austerely. ''In a way, I'm glad this happened. Our marriage

wouldn't stand a chance if we couldn't trust each other."
He turned and strode out of the room.

Michel gave Megan a troubled look. "You're making a big mistake," he told her. "Nick really loves you."

"How gullible do you two think I am? You heard him. When I told him we had grounds for breaking the engagement, he couldn't agree fast enough."

"That was simply anger and hurt pride. He's innocent, Gabrielle. Stand by him." Michel left to find Nick.

After a moment of silence, Carrie said, "Nick could have been telling the truth. It could very well be a frame-up."

Megan wavered for the first time, remembering the tender as well as the passionate moments she'd shared with Nick. Wouldn't he have prepared her for something that damaging to a relationship, rather than have it come out after the marriage? She honestly didn't know what to think.

"It doesn't really matter whether I believe him or not." Megan sighed. "It's what Gabrielle thinks that counts. She'll break the engagement so fast he'll get whiplash."

"That's undoubtedly true," Carrie said. "Well, maybe it's for the best."

"There isn't anything good about this whole situation," Megan said somberly.

Chapter Eight

Megan and Nick weren't the only ones affected by the tabloid article. The royal houses of Beaumarre and Grandalia reacted with shock and anger.

King Claude was fuming when Henri arrived at his chambers in response to an urgent summons. "What do you know about this wretched matter?" the king asked. "Is there any truth to it?"

"I just found out about it myself, Your Highness," Henri replied cautiously. "I haven't had time to investigate."

"Well, get on it, man!" Claude snapped. "I want to know if there's any truth to the woman's allegations."

"I have people working on it at this moment," Henri assured him.

"Do you realize what an embarrassment this is?" Claude paced the floor restlessly. "I sanctioned the engagement of my daughter to a worthless young pup who publicly humiliated her."

"The story might not be true," Henri said cautiously.

"Prince Nicholas doesn't seem like the sort of man who would continue to carry on an affair after he was married. Which, according to the young woman, is his intention."

"If it's true, we have a real mess on our hands. Can you imagine Gabrielle tolerating a mistress? What Nicholas did when he was a bachelor was his own business. I'm a man of the world, I understand these things. But once he's engaged, that should have been the end of it."

"Perhaps he tried to end the affair and the woman was reluctant to accept the fact."

"She has a compelling reason! If Nicholas is the father of her child, he's no longer an acceptable choice for Gabrielle."

"I do think the prince deserves a chance to explain," Henri said tentatively. "Would you like me to talk to him?"

"No. I want to hear for myself what he has to say. Phone him in the country and ask him to kindly return immediately!"

King Damien also wanted an explanation, but unfortunately he demanded one, instead of asking for it. By the time he reached his son by phone, he'd worked himself into a state. Without any preamble, the king lit into his son.

"That article about you was an absolute disgrace! I've overlooked your past escapades because they were relatively minor, but this latest episode is inexcusable! What do you have to say for yourself?"

Nick immediately lost his own temper. "What do you want me to say? You've already held a trial and found me guilty."

"Are you denying you had an affair with the woman, or that she bore your child?"

"That's what you're telling me, isn't it?" Nick drawled. Damien made an effort to rein in his temper. "I'm asking you if the story is true," he said in a more reasonable tone of voice.

"You don't want the truth," Nick said bitterly. "You've made up your mind that I'm irresponsible. Isn't that why you arranged to marry me off? So I'd settle down and stop being an embarrassment to you? Unfortunately you'll have to search for another bride. Gabrielle shares your opinion of me."

"The girl is understandably hurt. It must be humiliating to read that your fiancé is deeply involved with another woman. But I'm sure that isn't the whole story."

"You're certainly changing your tune," Nick remarked derisively. "A minute ago I was a disgrace to the royal house of Valmontine."

"You know that's not so. I'll admit I should have calmed down before I called you. You're aware of what a rotten temper I have. It's one of the traits I passed on to you." The king smiled for the first time. "I'm sorry for forgetting for just a moment how proud you've always made me. I'd like to hear the truth, if you'd still care to tell it to me."

"I suppose I can understand how upsetting it was to have something like this hit you out of the blue," Nick said grudgingly. "I didn't have any warning, either. I was as shocked as you were."

"You don't know the woman?"

"Not as well as she claims." Nick told his father the same story Michel had told Megan.

"That's incredible! Is there really a baby?"

"So I've heard, but I don't know whose it is. I only know it isn't mine."

"This is an outrage! You can't let her get away with it."

"I don't intend to," Nick said grimly. "Tanya made a mistake when she picked me for her fall guy. There are any number of men she could have chosen. She wasn't very discriminating when it came to lovers. That was one of the many reasons I never slept with her."

"Do you think the publicity about your engagement gave her the idea? She wanted to bask in the limelight?"

"It's possible. She'll get even wider exposure when the news breaks that the engagement is off," Nick said sardonically.

"You can't do that, son! It will give credence to her story. Everybody will think you're still lovers."

"I couldn't care less. The people who count will know it's a lie."

"I realize you're angry and upset, but don't make any hasty decisions," Damien pleaded.

"You don't understand, Father. It isn't my decision. Gabrielle doesn't want to marry me. She never did. It was an arranged marriage that was a bad idea to begin with."

"I thought you were starting to care about her," Damien said slowly. "Your mother said you sounded very happy when she spoke to you on the phone."

Nick's eyes were bleak, but he kept his voice unemotional. "Gabrielle wasn't as bad as I'd expected, but we're not right for each other. I can't see spending my life with a woman who doesn't trust me."

"Surely if you told her what you just told me, she'd realize you're blameless."

"I did tell her—or at least, Michel did. It didn't shake her conviction for an instant. I'm sorry for the embarrassment this has caused everybody, but that's *all* I'm sorry about."

Damien sighed heavily. "All right. If you're sure you don't want to try reasoning with Gabrielle, I'll speak to Claude."

Nick's square jaw set. "No, I'm a mature man. I'll clean up my own mess. But Father, in the future, please trust me to make my own choice."

"I'm not likely to do something like this again," Damien muttered as he cradled the receiver.

* * *

The return trip to the palace was a lot less joyful than it had started out on Saturday. Megan and Carrie rode in the limousine with Robert, and Nick drove Michel in the convertible.

Nobody talked much in either car. Robert tried to make casual conversation at first, but only out of a sense of duty. His heart wasn't in it, either.

When they reached the palace he said to Megan, "King Claude is waiting to see you and the prince."

"I can understand his wanting to talk to Nick," she said. "But I think they'd be more comfortable talking alone. I only came back here to pack my clothes."

"My instructions were to escort you to the king's chambers," Robert said stubbornly.

"This farce is played out," she exclaimed impatiently. "I told King Claude I was going home today and I meant it. We have nothing further to talk about."

They argued back and forth, but Robert was even more adamant than Megan. He'd been given an order and he intended to obey it.

Finally she said, "Oh, all right! It will be faster than standing here arguing with you. Tell the maid to start packing my things, Carrie. Only what I brought with me. I'm not taking any of the others."

"Isn't that a little foolish?" Carrie asked. "What are they going to do with them?"

"That's not my problem," Megan answered curtly.

She didn't want to take home outfits that would remind her of the days and nights she'd spent with Nick. As though anything could keep her from remembering, she thought despairingly. But at least she didn't need to have constant reminders every time she looked in the closet.

As she walked down the hall with Robert, Megan said, "I don't know if you're planning to tell Nick the truth about me, but—"

"Oh, no!" he interrupted hastily. "Things are bad enough now, without complicating the situation."

"You mean, King Claude wants to be the only wronged party here?" she asked mockingly.

"If the engagement is broken, nothing would be gained by telling the prince. I implore you not to say anything."

"Don't worry, he won't hear it from me." Her eyes were bleak. "I'm not proud of my part in this thing."

Nick was already in the king's chambers. He looked at Megan without expression. "We can get started now. Court has convened."

"I think you'll agree that I'm due an explanation, but I'm sorry you feel this is a tribunal," Claude said.

"Your daughter has decided I'm guilty as charged, and I assume you have, too."

"I like to think I keep an open mind."

"It doesn't run in the family," Nick said, with the first sign of emotion.

As Megan was about to answer angrily, Claude said, "It will be a lot easier for all of us if we try not to lose our tempers. Sit down, both of you." When Megan and Nick had reluctantly complied, in two chairs far removed from each other, the king continued. "First of all I must ask you, Nicholas, is the story true?"

"No, it is not," Nick said curtly.

"The woman must have had some basis for naming you the father of her child."

Nick told the same story he'd told several times before.

"If what you say is true—and I'm not doubting you," Claude added hastily, "then the woman must be made to recant her story. It's very damaging to your reputation."

"I intend to get a retraction." Nick's eyes sparkled dangerously. "I'm going to demand a blood test. There's no way that child could be mine, and Tanya knows it. I want her to admit it publicly—like she made the accusation."

"What if she refuses?" Megan asked slowly. Nick's

complete confidence was convincing. He wouldn't chance a blood test if the results might be inconclusive, at best.

"If she tries to stonewall or shake me down, I'll get a court order forcing her to have the baby tested. I'm also going to make the tabloid publish a retraction or face a lawsuit that will enrich some charity beyond its wildest dreams," Nick said with satisfaction. "I'll make it the beneficiary of the money I win."

"I hope it doesn't come to that," Claude said. "I'd like to put this thing behind us as soon as possible so we can get back to normal."

"Meaning no disrespect, sir, but my problems aren't your concern any longer, now that the engagement is off."

"That's ridiculous!" the king said impatiently. "You've explained everything fully. There's no reason to call off the engagement."

"Gabrielle already did," Nick replied laconically.

Claude looked at Megan in outrage. "You took it on yourself to do this?"

"She *is* one of the people most directly affected," Nick reminded him.

"I didn't exactly break the engagement, but I think it's the thing to do," Megan told the king. "Nick and I never wanted to marry each other. It was your idea and his father's."

"You don't know anything about—" Claude began furiously. Realizing belatedly that he'd almost said too much, he stopped short and began again. "Every couple has problems in the beginning, but you'll work yours out. You and Nicholas will be good for each other."

Megan stared at him incredulously. "How can you make your daughter marry a man she doesn't love?"

Nick flinched for an instant, then his face set in austere lines. "The question is academic because we've both decided we can't go through with it. Isn't that right, Gabrielle?"

She nodded mutely.

Claude looked at them speculatively. They both looked more miserable than they should have, considering they were getting what they wanted. The king was convinced that he'd made the right decision in the first place. He felt guilty about the obvious feeling Megan had developed for Nicholas, but he also felt she would get over what was surely only an infatuation. Once he coaxed Gabrielle back, she would see the qualities in Nicholas that Megan had. The engagement mustn't be allowed to fall apart.

"I certainly wouldn't want to force you into anything you were really opposed to," Claude said in a reasonable tone of voice. "I realize you didn't fall in love the way I'd hoped, but I honestly thought you both liked and respected each other."

"That's a valid assumption on my part," Nick said. "I'm glad I got to spend this time with Gabrielle. It wasn't all bad." His eyes met hers. "I'm just sorry things didn't work out."

"I am, too," Megan said. "I really hope you find the right person for you."

"As long as there is no animosity between you, it's a shame you're not willing to help Nicholas clear his name, Gabrielle," Claude said smoothly.

"Tanya is the only one who can do that," Megan protested.

"Not really. If you stood by Nicholas, people would begin to wonder if the story was true. But if you break the engagement, they'll be sure it is."

"Not after he proves he isn't the baby's father. When that turns out to be a lie, nobody will believe the rest of her story, either."

"There will always be a lingering doubt. Everyone who has seen you in public considers you a happy couple. What other reason would you have for breaking up?"

"People decide they're not right for each other," she said uncertainly.

"Just coincidentally, after the fiancé has been accused of being involved with another woman?"

"Don't pressure her," Nick said after gazing at Megan's troubled face. "It doesn't matter what people say."

"Yes, it does!" she replied earnestly. "What he said is true. Everybody will automatically assume you were mixed up with that sleazy woman."

Nick shrugged. "There's not much I can do about it." He slanted a glance at her. "I can't ask you to take part in a charade."

The intrigue was getting even more complicated, Megan thought despairingly. The sensible thing would be to get on the first plane for home, but how could she do that to Nick? It was her fault he was in this position. The least she could do was not leave him here alone.

"No matter what happens from now on, I'd like to think we became friends," she said. "And a friend is supposed to be there when you need one. I would never forgive myself if I deserted you now," Megan said truthfully.

"That's very sweet of you, but this thing could drag on endlessly." Nick looked at her intently. "How long are you willing to stick by me?"

"That's not something that has to be decided right this minute," Claude said quickly. "The two of you should go to Grandalia as planned and just concentrate on enjoying yourselves." When Megan gave him a mutinous look, he said, "You have to go with him."

"Only if you want to," Nick said firmly.

"Of course I want to," she answered, knowing it was unwise, yet true. But she couldn't help wondering if somehow the King had manipulated her.

"Good. Then that's settled." Claude stood and walked them to the door. "We'll all meet in the library for a farewell toast before you leave."

* * *

After the entourage had left for Grandalia, Claude relaxed over a drink with Henri. It had been a stressful time and both men were relieved that the situation had resolved itself without rupturing relations between Beaumarre and Grandalia. Claude had received a phone call from Damien, during which the two men expressed their continuing faith in Nicholas.

Claude realized, however, that only this latest crisis had been averted. A much more serious one was still unresolved. "I can't understand why you still haven't been able to find my daughter," he said to Henri. "Gabrielle is one of the most instantly recognizable young women in the world. Your people must be either stupid or incompetent." The king scowled as his frustration mounted.

"Everybody is making an all-out effort, Your Highness, but we're hampered by having to be extremely circumspect. Still, I'm as puzzled as you. We've sent people to all the luxury resorts the princess frequents. We've questioned her friends discreetly. We've even enlisted the help of bartenders and headwaiters, but nobody has seen her."

"Or else they're not telling you."

"I don't believe that's the case. My people have been very careful not to arouse suspicion. They're trained to get information without giving any away."

"She can't have just vanished off the face of the earth! Gabrielle telephoned from *somewhere!* What about a private yacht? She could be cruising to God-knows-where!"

"It's a possibility, but there are a limited number of larger private yachts that can offer the luxury that the princess prefers. I managed to obtain the guest lists for every one that's on a cruise at this time. A lot of the princess's friends are aboard various ships, but Gabrielle's name isn't on any list."

"I'd like to know what she's living on. You told me she

hasn't used any of her credit cards—which is astounding in itself,'' Claude said ironically.

"The princess undoubtedly knows we could locate her through her purchases."

"She must be found," Claude stated imperiously. "This stalemate can't go on any longer. I want results, not excuses."

"I understand, Your Highness." Henri hesitated. "When we do find your daughter, I'm afraid she will be very angry at being forced to return. Has it occurred to you that she might tell Prince Nicholas he's been duped?"

"Gabrielle is willful and headstrong, but she loves her country. She knows any such revelation would destroy the peaceful relations that have existed between us and Grandalia for generations." Claude's smile was wintry. "She'll make my life miserable, but she won't betray me."

"Will she marry the prince, though?" Henri persisted. "Her return won't automatically solve everything. Megan could be the princess's twin, but they're nothing alike." He chose his words carefully. "Gabrielle has a…a more volatile personality than Megan."

"*Explosive* is the word for her," Claude agreed dryly.

"Prince Nicholas will be bound to notice the difference. If he was attracted to Megan—who is perhaps a little more understanding, shall we say—then he might not be compatible with Princess Gabrielle."

"I'm hoping that despite her anger with me, Gabrielle will discover for herself what a charming young man Nicholas is. Everyone else is captivated by him."

"He *has* been quite a hit with the court as well as the people of Beaumarre," Henri conceded.

"Gabrielle can't help but be impressed," Claude said eagerly. "We've had a few setbacks, but the original idea of a marriage was sound. My daughter and Nicholas might not know it now, but they'll thank us someday."

It was Henri's private opinion that the king was whistling

in the dark. The two young royals would be like gasoline and matches together.

The only bright spot was that Megan had helped them avert a major scandal.

The castle at Grandalia was larger and more imposing than the palace in Beaumarre. Flags flew from turreted towers, and ivy clung to the ancient bricks. Beyond the massive front portals was a lofty entry hall hung with priceless tapestries.

Megan and Carrie weren't given a chance to look around. Servants were waiting in the great hall to show the entourage to their quarters.

"Wow, this place makes Gabrielle's palace look like a tract house," Carrie muttered to Megan as they followed one of the staff up broad marble stairs carpeted in midnight blue.

"It's not your average two-bedrooms-and-a-den," Megan conceded.

"The housemaids probably have apartments larger than that," Carrie remarked as they reached Megan's suite where a maid was already unpacking for her.

"If there is anything you require, Your Highness, please ring." The manservant gestured to a long tapestry pull next to rose-colored damask drapes. The drapes were looped back from tall windows, which overlooked lush green lawns that were bordered in the distance by an old-growth pine forest.

"The king and queen request the honor of your company in the library in one hour," the man said. "My name is Édouard, and I will return to escort you there if that is agreeable to Your Highness."

"That will be fine, Édouard," Megan said.

"Do you feel as if you're five years old again and your mother is going to hold your hand and walk you across the street?" Carrie asked, after the man left.

"It's better than getting lost and having them send out a search party for us," Megan remarked.

"I wasn't included in the invitation. Nick's parents only want to see you."

"I'm sure that was just an oversight on Édouard's part. He meant he'd come back for both of us."

Carrie shook her head. "I'm getting the hang of this protocol thing. The king and queen will meet all their guests at dinner tonight, but you're not an ordinary guest. It's natural that they'd want to talk to you privately."

"This is the part I hate." Megan sighed. "I don't know what to say to them."

"Just be your own sweet self," Carrie teased. "They'll love you."

"That's the whole point. I don't want them to love me!"

"Then be rude. Tell them your accommodations are terrible and demand new ones. It's probably what Gabrielle would do."

"You're a big help," Megan grumbled.

Nick had waited until his guests were taken care of before going to look for his parents. He found them in the library where they all embraced warmly.

"It's good to have you back, my boy," King Damien said fondly. "We missed you."

"I can't imagine why, considering the way I sulked like a teenager for days before I left." Nick smiled. "I wouldn't have blamed you if you'd changed the locks on the front doors."

Rosamund returned his smile. "Parents learn to grin and bear it. Payback time will come when you have children of your own."

"I'm happy to tell you that's not the case yet," Nick said, a trifle grimly.

"I've already spoken to my attorneys," Damien said. "They'll proceed on the matter first thing in the morning."

"There's to be no compromise," Nick warned. "I'm

sorry for the additional publicity this will cause if I insist on complete vindication, but I won't settle for anything less."

"I wouldn't consider it, either," Damien said. "As for publicity—I welcome it. I intend to issue a press release telling the world we won't stop until we get a retraction on the front page of that yellow journal."

"They can't buy us off the way they do a lot of their other victims. Our pockets are as deep as theirs." Rosamund smiled mischievously.

Nick's face was charged with deep emotion. "I can't tell you what it means to have you stand behind me like this."

"We know what a principled young man you are," his father answered fondly. "I'm just glad that Gabrielle recognizes it, too." When Nick's expression changed, Damien looked at him sharply. "This hasn't caused trouble between you two, has it?"

"Don't be naive, darling," Rosamund chided. "The girl would have to be a saint not to have been furious with him. It wouldn't be surprising for relations between them to be a little strained at first. The important thing is that she stuck by Nick."

"Did she?" Damien continued to stare at his son.

"Gabrielle returned with him, didn't she?" Rosamund asked impatiently. "That should answer your question."

"Actually, her father talked her into coming," Nick said with reluctance. "When Gabrielle heard what I was accused of she went ballistic. I suppose I can't blame her. It really blindsided us. We'd gone out alone for a picnic and when we returned, everybody was talking about that damn article. She was hurt and embarrassed."

"But you explained that it was a pack of lies," Nick's father said.

"Not exactly. She was too angry to let me explain. Then I lost my temper and let her think the story was true."

"How could you do that?" Damien exclaimed.

Nick shrugged. "I figured if she didn't trust me, nothing I said would make any difference. When she said we had grounds for breaking the engagement, I said that was fine with me."

"The engagement is off? Why wasn't I informed of this?" the king demanded.

"I'm not sure whether it's on or off." Nick stood to pace the floor restlessly, jingling some coins in his pocket. "Or which one I want it to be."

Damien's rising indignation died as he gazed at his son. "Now would be the worst possible time to announce that the engagement is over, but your future happiness is a more compelling reason for doing so. I take full responsibility for this fiasco, if that's any consolation to you."

"I'm not blaming you, Father."

"You're more forgiving than I would be in your place," Damien said wryly. "I played God because I thought I knew what was best for you. I won't compound the error by forcing you to see it through. I'll call Claude right now and discuss the most diplomatic way to end the engagement."

Rosamund was watching her son intently. "Is that what you want, Nick? You don't feel you can be happy with Gabrielle?"

"I'm afraid it's the other way around," he answered somberly. "She's the woman I always dreamed of meeting. I fell deeply in love with her, and I thought she cared for me, too. It hurt more than you'll ever know when she seized the first chance to get away from me."

"She must care for you if she's willing to continue on as if nothing had happened," Rosamund protested.

"Gabrielle is a kind, decent human being. She wouldn't desert me when I needed her. But pity is no basis for a marriage. I suppose we'd better bite the bullet and get it over with. Make the call and do whatever damage control

you feel is necessary, Father. For your sake, not mine,"
Nick added. "I really don't care anymore."

"There's no need to act immediately," his mother said
hastily. "Gabrielle has shown great generosity by coming
here and facing down the gossip. You can't trivialize her
gift. Festivities have been planned for the whole week. Why
don't you wait until they're over to make the announcement?"

"How can I ask Gabrielle to go on pretending for another week?" Nick asked hesitantly.

"She's expressed her willingness." Damien had picked
up on his son's reluctance to sever the relationship. "By
the end of the week the celebrations will be over and the
spotlight will be off both of you. After a suitable period,
Claude or I can announce that by mutual consent, you've
changed your minds."

"I suppose that would be all right," Nick agreed, looking a great deal more cheerful.

"It's the only sensible way to handle the matter," Damien assured him. "By then we should have our retraction
from the tabloid, and the whole thing will simply fade
away."

Rosamund looked at her watch. "Now that that's decided, you'd better go freshen up, Nick. We've asked Gabrielle to join us for a private chat before dinner."

When their son had left the room, Damien shook his
head. "Does Nick really believe all those fairy tales I just
told him?"

"At this moment all he cares about is spending another
week with Gabrielle. I think he really loves her," Rosamund answered her husband.

"That would be cause for celebration if she felt the same
way," Damien said soberly.

"Don't be too sure she doesn't." Rosamund smiled.
"The Valmontine men are irresistible. I can vouch for
that."

* * *

Megan was interested in meeting Nick's parents, in spite of her nervousness. He hadn't told her much about them, but she gathered they had a close relationship.

The king and queen were very gracious to her, giving no indication that they knew about her problems with Nick. They referred to the story in the tabloid only indirectly, and they didn't dwell on it.

"It was good of you to come, Gabrielle," Rosamund said.

"I've been looking forward to meeting you—I mean, seeing you again." Megan corrected herself hastily.

"It has been quite a while, hasn't it?" the queen remarked.

"You've grown even more beautiful, my dear," Damien said to Megan. "I hope my son realizes how lucky he is."

"You're very kind," she murmured.

"We're grateful to you for being so understanding," Rosamund said quietly. "I hope this week will make up for any unpleasantness you've suffered because of Nick."

"It was a lot worse for him," Megan said. "He deserves a public apology from everybody involved."

"He'll get it," Damien stated grimly.

Rosamund changed the subject. "I know you've been in a social whirl all week, so I thought you might enjoy an informal evening, for a change. We've planned a simple family dinner for tonight."

Megan wondered if it would be like the "small informal reception" in Beaumarre when she made her first appearance as Gabrielle. That had turned out to be a party on a grand scale.

But Rosamund hadn't misled her. There were only eight people for dinner. The outsiders, besides Megan and Carrie, were Michel and his parents—they were evidently considered family.

Michel's father was a pleasant, easygoing man. He had

none of the imperiousness that sometimes went with a title. André Charbet was a person everyone liked immediately, like his son.

Michel's mother looked young to have a son in his late twenties. She was a vivacious, attractive woman with naturally red hair that was just beginning to show a few threads of gray.

"You didn't tell me your mother was a redhead," Carrie exclaimed when they were introduced.

"It never occurred to me. I guess you didn't remind me of my mother." Michel smiled.

Helena Charbet gave her an interested look. "How long have you two known each other?"

"Not long," Carrie answered. "We only met last week when I came for Gabrielle's engagement. I'll be going home soon."

"Surely you'll stay for the week," Rosamund protested.

"I'm hoping to," Carrie replied, exchanging a glance with Megan. "But I'm really not sure yet."

"You can't leave," Michel told her. "We have too many things to do."

"Yes, we'd love to get better acquainted," Helena said. "Is there any way we could all get together for dinner at our house, Rosamund?"

"I'm afraid every night is already scheduled," the queen replied. "This promises to be a very hectic week."

"I realize that. Well, perhaps we could have a ladies' lunch, or even tea one day."

"Please don't go to any trouble for me," Carrie said swiftly.

"You're no trouble. You're pure pleasure," Michel said affectionately.

Megan could sympathize with Carrie. It made matters even worse that both sets of parents approved of them.

It was an enjoyable evening. The conversation was witty and the atmosphere relaxed, but scarcely casual. Dinner was served in a small dining room—small by royal standards, at least—but it was as elegant as the rest of the castle.

A long polished table was set beautifully with the finest china, crystal and silverware. In the middle of the table was a centerpiece of deep red roses that echoed the maroon-and-gold band around the Coalport china plates.

A corps of unobtrusive servants filled wineglasses and glided in and out of the room, silently serving or removing plates.

The group was small enough for everyone to join in the conversation. Megan enjoyed listening to stories about Nick when he was a boy, but they created some difficult moments. Occasionally she was supposed to know certain people, or things that had happened in the past.

"You remember my thirteenth birthday party," Nick reminded her. "You were the one who insisted we play kissing games."

"*Insist* is a strong word," Megan protested. "I'm sure I just suggested it."

"You said you'd tell everybody I was afraid to kiss you." Nick grinned. "I call that insistence. What thirteen-year-old boy could live with an image like that?"

"You were macho even then," she said lightly.

"Maybe you blackmailed me into letting you have your own way, but then I discovered I liked kissing." He laughed.

"To think I started you on your downward spiral." She gave a mock sigh.

It felt wonderful to joke around with Nick again. Since the article appeared they'd been so stiff with each other. Maybe they could get back on their old footing for this last week. But it would mean being more than friends, and Megan didn't know if she could manage that.

While they were having coffee, Helena returned to the subject of the party she wanted to have. "Surely you can find me a couple of hours on one of the afternoons," she told Rosamund.

"The only possible time would be on Thursday from about three to five or six," the queen said. "I thought Nick and Gabrielle deserved a little time to themselves, so I set aside that short period for them."

Helena appealed to the young couple. "I know it's selfish of me, but could I prevail on you to come to a garden party instead? You won't be alone, but you will be together," she coaxed.

Megan knew she was better off not being alone with Nick. "It sounds lovely," she said. "I'd like very much to come."

"That's extremely generous of you," Helena said happily. "I'm sure Carrie will be visiting you often after you're married, so I thought it would be nice if she met some of the other young people here."

"You're very thoughtful, but I doubt if I'll be back anytime soon. Newlyweds don't really welcome houseguests." Carrie smiled brightly.

"Then you can stay with us," Michel said. "That's a better idea anyway. I'll get to see more of you."

"We'd be delighted to have you," Helena said.

"You almost have to say that," Carrie remarked wryly. "Michel didn't leave you much choice."

"You don't know my wife very well." André laughed. "She's quite adept at avoiding anything she doesn't want to do."

"So now you have an official invitation," Michel told Carrie.

"It would be great fun," Helena said. "The house is always so much livelier with young people around. When Michel is busy, you and I can go shopping together."

"Be careful she doesn't try to talk you into mother-daughter outfits," her husband teased.

"Mother always wanted a girl," Michel explained. "But all she got were three boisterous sons."

"I wouldn't call that a hardship." Helena smiled.

"She'll get her daughters when you boys marry," Rosamund said.

"I didn't know you had brothers." Carrie turned quickly to Michel. "Do they live here in Grandalia?"

"Off and on," he replied. "Roger is in the navy. He's away at sea, and René is traveling in Europe."

"Young people are never home anymore," Helena complained. "Your brother didn't even return for your engagement," she said disapprovingly to Megan.

"He felt badly about it, but his trade mission is very important," Megan explained.

"I'm sure he'll be back for the wedding," André said. "That's the important event, right, Gabrielle?"

"Yes, it is," she murmured, without looking at Nick.

After they'd had second cups of coffee Rosamund said, "You young people don't have to sit around here any longer. Why don't you go to one of the clubs and dance?"

"Carrie and Michel can go, but I'm perfectly happy right here," Megan said. "It's been a long week. I think I'll make this an early night."

"That sounds good to me, too," Nick said. "Would you like to take a stroll in the garden before you turn in?"

Megan agreed reluctantly, because she couldn't think of any polite way to refuse. As they left the room together she was aware of the king and queen watching them. They were hoping, no doubt, that everything had been smoothed over between herself and Nick. Too bad this was one fairy tale that would not have a happy ending.

Chapter Nine

It was a beautiful, star-spangled night. The moon was almost full, and a gentle breeze perfumed the air with a dozen different floral scents. Megan and Nick walked silently down a mossy path, suddenly constrained now that they were alone together.

When they reached a secluded spot ringed by some fragrant jasmine bushes he asked, "Would you like to sit here for a few minutes?"

As they sat on a garden bench, she said, "It was such a nice evening. Almost like the ones ordinary people spend."

"What do you know about ordinary people?" he teased.

"I know we aren't like them," Megan answered soberly.

"People are pretty much alike. We all want the same things out of life."

"But ordinary people are free to do as they like. They don't have any restrictions on them."

Nick's face was suddenly austere in the moonlight. "I'm

sorry you were coerced into coming here. I never should have permitted it.''

"That wasn't what I was talking about. You yourself said you couldn't take a job like a normal person. That's the kind of limitation I was referring to,'' she lied.

"There's no real reason why I can't do the work I was trained for. Father is a very open-minded man in most cases, but he has a blind spot when it comes to the monarchy and my place in it as heir to the throne. Perhaps it's because I'm an only child.''

"I assume your mother couldn't have any more children.''

"That's correct. They wanted a big family. Not merely because there would be no one to succeed if anything should happen to me, although I'm sure that's a constant worry. It's one of the reasons they want me to marry and have children. I can understand that.''

Megan stared down at her clasped hands. "I guess royalty has its obligations as well as its privileges.''

"True, but I thought I was one of the lucky ones. I thought I was marrying for love,'' he said in a husky voice. "Unfortunately, you weren't struck by the same magic.''

Couldn't he see how wrong he was? Megan thought in despair. It was lucky that he wasn't more perceptive, but she didn't think she could possibly feel any worse.

Nick's expression was gentle as he glanced at her bowed head. "Don't worry about it. In another hundred years it won't make any difference.'' He rose and held out his hand to her. "Come on, I'll take you back to the house.''

The next day Megan was too rushed to worry about her tangled relationship with Nick. She was kept busy from morning to night, making appearances with him at state functions and private parties.

Everyone expected them to be ecstatically happy, so they were forced to hold hands, at the very least. Then Nick began to put his arm around her, sometimes almost without thinking. Gradually it began to seem natural and the reserve between them disappeared.

The king and queen watched silently, not wanting to meddle in their lives any further. But finally Rosamund said one morning, "You don't have to stay at the fair this afternoon, Nick. After you both say a few words, you and Gabrielle can leave."

"I thought we had to stay until the bitter end to award the prizes."

"I'll explain that you had another commitment and you had to leave. Unless you're pining to judge the best sow and heifer."

"No way! I don't know one from the other, except that they're both female."

"Why is it you're never confused about sex?" Megan teased.

"I don't think there's any safe answer to that question." He laughed.

Rosamund nudged them back to the subject. "You'll do your duty just by showing up. All people really want is to see the two of you together. After that you can do as you please. Maybe you'd like to take Gabrielle to see your house in the country," she added casually.

Nick's eyes brightened. "That's a great idea! Would you like to do that?" he asked Megan.

After a moment's hesitation she said, "I'd love to see your house, and I know Carrie would, too. Why don't we invite her and Michel to join us?"

"I was going to ask them to award the prizes in your place," Rosamund said swiftly.

"Better them than us." Nick grinned.

"You're a fine friend," Megan scolded, with mock disapproval.

"Shall I call the staff and have them prepare a late lunch for you?" Rosamund persisted.

"Not for me, thanks," Megan said. "It seems all I've been doing lately is eating."

"Me, too." Nick patted his flat stomach. "It won't hurt me to miss a meal."

Megan's eyes were drawn to his lean length. Nick looked especially virile that morning in tight jeans and a black turtleneck that molded to his broad chest. He was lounging in a chair like a sleek black panther, in complete control of his splendid body.

Megan looked away quickly as memories made her heart beat faster. The feeling of his arms holding her a willing captive, his pulsing loins echoing her own passion.

"Is there any chance we can skip the fair entirely?" Nick asked his mother, unaware of Megan's fantasies.

"Don't be greedy," Rosamund chided. "I made you a gift of an afternoon."

"It never hurts to ask," he joked. "Okay, we'll settle for whatever time we can get. Right, Gabrielle?"

"Right," she echoed, since she'd decided that for herself.

It was a perfect day for a drive in the country, especially in an open convertible. Although they hadn't started out that way. Originally Nick had left the top up on his sleek red sports car.

When Megan suggested he put it down, he said, "Your hair will get all windblown."

"I don't care," she assured him. "Put the top down. I don't want to miss anything."

She was enchanted by the little villages they passed through. The diamond-paned windows of the shops sparkled in the sunshine and the streets were lined with shade trees.

"Everything is so old-world," she remarked. "Like something out of the past."

"If you think this is old, wait until we get to Chandoreaux." Nick laughed.

"Is that your country estate?"

He nodded. "It's the ultimate fixer-upper. Once I have one thing repaired, something else needs doing. Of course it's hundreds of years old, so I guess I shouldn't complain. If I was that old I'd need a lot of work done on me, too," he joked.

"Do you go there often?"

"Not as often as I'd like."

"But you keep the place fully staffed?" Megan still couldn't get used to the idea of having unlimited money.

Nick shrugged. "The house and grounds need to be kept up year-round." He glanced over at her. "Are you sure you don't mind the wind? Your hair is getting blown pretty badly."

"Is that your way of saying I look a mess?" she teased.

"Not at all." He reached over and brushed a silky strand of hair off her cheek. "I like you this way. You look just as beautiful, yet more approachable." He frowned slightly. "You remind me of someone, but I can't quite decide who."

Could Nick possibly be thinking of their meeting in the bistro on the night before his engagement? It seemed unlikely, even though there had been a certain chemistry between them even then. To be on the safe side, Megan changed the subject.

"How long does it take to drive to Chandoreaux?"

"Half an hour if I have my mother in the car. Less if I'm by myself." He grinned.

"I wonder why driving fast is such a macho thing?" Megan mused.

"Perhaps because we have control over a thousand pounds of automobile, but a hundred-and-ten-pound woman can leave us clueless. It's compensation."

"You're rich, handsome and royal. I can't feel sorry for you," she said lightly.

"Thanks for the 'handsome' part, but pity wasn't the emotion I was hoping to inspire."

Megan couldn't imagine anyone pitying him. Nick was everything a woman dreamed of and a man wished he could be. Unconsciously, her yearning showed on her face.

He drew in his breath sharply. "Do you think we could start over, Gabrielle?"

There was that name again, jerking her back to reality. "I honestly don't know, Nick. But we have today and the rest of this week together. Let's enjoy it and not worry about what will happen next week."

"Fair enough." He gripped her hand. "If all the days are like today, I can't complain. I'm really eager to know what you think of Chandoreaux."

"I'm sure I'll be impressed."

"I don't want you to be impressed, I want you to like it. I've modernized the house to a certain extent—put in central heating and updated the bathrooms, that sort of thing. But it's still a fourteenth-century manor house."

"Does it have ornamental turrets and those huge fireplaces?"

"Tremendous. The one in the dining room was used for cooking. It's big enough to roast a whole ox."

"I want the entire grand tour."

Nick gazed dubiously at her high-heeled pumps. They matched the white linen suit she wore with a silk blouse printed in jewel tones.

"I'm afraid we'll have to save the more rugged parts for another time," he said. "Those shoes weren't made for climbing down stone steps to the dungeon, or up them to the sentry towers."

"You have a dungeon?" she asked delightedly.

"Actually I've converted it to a wine cellar, but there are still some iron cuffs bolted to the walls and a couple of pairs of leg-irons."

"I definitely have to see it," Megan declared.

"The stairs will be tricky in those heels, but I suppose it will be all right. I wish now that we'd changed into something more casual, but I didn't want to waste time going back home after the fair."

"We'll improvise. For starters, take off your tie," she said as she removed her jacket.

"Maybe I will when we get to the house."

"Why be uncomfortable until then? Here, I'll do it for you." She leaned over closer to him.

After unknotting his tie and putting it in the pocket of his jacket, she unfastened the top buttons of his shirt.

He glanced down at her and smiled. "I always hoped you'd undress me one day, but I had someplace more private in mind."

"I'm beginning to think there's no place private in all of Grandalia," she observed lightly.

"With enough incentive I'll find one," he murmured.

Megan inhaled the heady scent of his sun-warmed skin and tangy after-shave lotion. It was like an aphrodisiac. She wanted to kiss the hollow in his throat and open his shirt deeper so her lips could trail down his tanned chest to his flat nipples.

"Gabrielle?" he asked softly when she remained silent.

Megan sat back in her seat, fighting his powerful appeal. "How can you get amorous in an open convertible?" she asked in as light a tone as she could manage.

Nick chuckled, unaware of the effect he was having on her. "I don't have any inhibitions when I'm around you. Too bad I can't convince you to lose a few of yours."

"One of us has to act royal."

"You never used to worry about your image." He turned his head to look at her speculatively. "You've changed so much you almost seem like a different person."

Megan gave a nervous little laugh. "Father was furious over my last escapade. He threatened to cut off my charge accounts if I didn't clean up my act."

"It wouldn't be an escapade if we made love. We're legal."

"Not yet."

"Does that mean you've decided not to marry me?" he asked soberly.

"We agreed to enjoy the here and now. Don't spoil things, Nick."

"You're right. If it isn't the answer I'm hoping for, I don't want to hear it just yet. Maybe that's living in a fool's paradise, but I have a feeling you'll realize we were meant to be together."

"Anything is possible," she murmured, wishing it was true.

Nick's country home was a vast estate. The house itself was smaller than the family castle, but almost as impressive. It was set in the center of acres of land, surrounded by high stone walls. The grounds around the house were colorfully landscaped with carefully tended flowers and clipped grass that softened the imposing stone structures.

Nick gave Megan the requested tour, pointing out the fireplace he'd described and some improvements he'd made. The renovations were more obvious upstairs, where the bathrooms had been modernized and some of the stone floors carpeted.

"This wing will be the nursery someday," he said, leading her into a large room that connected with several others.

"You must be expecting to have a lot of children," Megan remarked in an attempt at humor.

"I hope to," he answered without any suggestiveness. "This will be the common playroom, with the children's bedrooms and the nanny's interconnecting. In the opposite wing is the master suite. I'll show you that and then we'll go down to the cellar."

The master suite was very masculine. The furniture was massive, with few softening touches. The bedside table held a lamp, a telephone and two books, but no ornaments or plants. The dresser and a tall chest were similarly uncluttered. Only the large desk had the normal amount of disorder.

Nick watched Megan's face as she glanced around. "You don't like it," he commented with disappointment.

"I do," she protested. "It's a very handsome room—for a man. Anyone can tell a woman doesn't live here."

"If you shared this room, what would you change?" he asked in a casual tone.

She glanced around thoughtfully. "For starters, I'd bring in some color in the bedspread and drapes. And then I'd reupholster that couch and those chairs in a print with a white background. Those are the major changes, but I'd also fill the room with flowering plants and some personal touches. That ormolu clock on the mantel downstairs, and the lovely Wedgwood bowl, perhaps."

"I didn't realize I was living in such austerity." He laughed.

"It's your room. You're entitled to furnish it any way you like. You asked me what *I'd* do and I told you."

"If you decide to marry me—and I'm by no means pressuring you—but *if* you decide, you can redecorate any way you like."

"Sure, and then you'd move to one of the spare bedrooms." She smiled.

"I can guarantee that would never happen," he said in a velvet voice.

"Didn't you promise to show me the dungeon?" she asked, moving toward the door.

"If these were the old days, I'd keep you there until I wore down your resistance," he joked.

"You're too civilized for that."

"Keep reminding me of the fact." He put his arm around her as they walked down the hall. "I have stirrings of my caveman origins when I'm around you."

The dungeon wasn't easy to get to. Beyond the cavernous kitchen was a room with a trapdoor in the floor. Nick grasped a metal ring in the door and pulled it open, revealing a flight of hand-hewn stone steps leading to the basement below. It was dark, and a dank smell rose from the depths.

"You want to change your mind?" he asked Megan.

"No, I really want to see it." She couldn't tell him, but this might be her only chance to see an authentic dungeon.

"All right, if you're sure." Nick flipped a switch and nothing happened. "Damn! The light must have burned out. Stay here and I'll turn on the lights in the cellar."

She stared down into the black hole. It was a little eerie. Were people actually imprisoned in the dark in those long-ago, brutal days? She hoped not. Nick's footsteps sounded faintly from below, like those of an animal prowling. And then the lights came on, dissipating the feeling of danger.

"Stay there and I'll come up and get you," Nick called.

But Megan had already started down the stairs. "It's all right. I can make it on my own," she called back.

There was no railing, so she clung to the wall with one hand as she picked her way gingerly down the uneven stone steps.

"Wait for me," he ordered. "You might fall."

Before Megan could answer, her heel caught in a crevice between two rocks and she pitched forward into space.

Nick raced up the stairs and caught her, breaking her fall, but her knee scraped painfully across one of the rough stone steps.

He held her tightly, his heart racing against hers. "You never listen to me," he scolded. "This is exactly what I was afraid of. You could have broken your neck!"

"You were right about the high heels," she said meekly. "Next time I'll take your advice."

"It's a nice fantasy, anyway." He smiled wryly. "I'm just thankful you didn't get hurt."

Megan didn't want to tell him her knee was throbbing. But as they started back up the stairs, Nick noticed that she was trying not to limp.

"What's the matter with your leg?" he asked sharply.

"Nothing. I'm fine."

"No, you aren't." He knelt down to see for himself. "You're bleeding! Why didn't you tell me you were hurt?"

"I just scraped my knee, that's all. No big deal."

"What am I going to do with you?" He swung her into his arms and started for the central staircase. "You need somebody to take care of you."

"You mean, like a keeper?" she teased.

"It's not a bad idea." He smiled wryly. "Your father would agree with me."

"He did. He chose you."

"I'm not doing a very good job of it." Nick carried her to the bed in his suite and set her down gently. "Let me take a look at that leg."

He uttered a sharp exclamation when he examined her more closely. Her panty hose were shredded and blood was oozing out of the scrape on her knee.

"Take off your panty hose," he ordered.

"Certainly not!"

"This is no time for false modesty," he said impatiently. "All I'm going to do is clean off that bruise and bandage it so it doesn't get infected." He disappeared into the adjoining bathroom before she could object.

Megan knew he was right. The tiny particles of stone in her knee had to be cleaned out or it might very well become infected. Scowling in annoyance, she hastily wriggled out of her panty hose while he was still out of the room.

Nick returned, carrying a variety of first-aid supplies. He raised an eyebrow when he saw she'd done as he instructed. "This must be a first."

"Just do it and get it over with," she muttered.

"That's scarcely the kind of thing a man likes to hear," he remarked mischievously.

"I'm not noted for my patience," she said pointedly.

"Tell me something I *don't* know." He put a towel under her leg and picked up a bottle of alcohol. "This might hurt a little." When he swabbed her knee with a wad of cotton she flinched. "I'm sorry," he murmured.

"It isn't your fault."

"I know, but I never want to hurt you," he said softly.

Megan's heart filled with so much love that she lowered her lashes, unable to answer.

"The worst is over," he said. "I'll put on a bandage and you'll be as good as new."

She looked at the large square of gauze he was taping to her knee. "Does it have to be that large? I don't want to make a big deal out of this."

"I didn't want you to get blood on your white skirt, but the cut should stop bleeding soon. You can take off the bandage when we get home."

"All of this and I didn't even get to see the dungeon," she commented ruefully.

"When you've seen one, you've seen them all. If it's a high priority you'll just have to come back again."

"But next time I'll wear flat shoes," she agreed, knowing there wouldn't be a next time.

Nick's smile faded and he gripped her hands. "When I saw you come plunging down those stone steps I felt real terror for the first time in my life. I don't know how I could have gone on if anything terrible had happened to you."

"Nick," she began hesitantly.

"I'm not asking you to love me." He framed her face in his palms and gazed at her with deep emotion. "It would be like a dream come true if you did, but if that isn't to be, I'll settle for knowing you're alive and happy."

Megan threw her arms around his neck. "Oh, Nick, darling, I don't deserve you!"

He held her close and stroked her hair. "Don't feel badly, sweetheart. I'm a grown man, I can cope with it. You can't help the way you feel."

"You don't understand about me. I never meant to hurt you. No matter what happens, please believe that."

"You don't have to apologize. Love is a rare and wonderful thing. It hit me hard, but you can't make somebody love you in return," he said sadly.

"Nick, my dearest, don't you know what I'm saying? I love you so much it hurts!" Megan decided nothing was worth the pain she was inflicting on him. If he hated her for the cruel trick she'd played on him, it couldn't be helped. He deserved to know the truth.

Nick was staring at her with a mixture of incredulity, joy and belated caution. "You know that's what I want to hear, but you don't have to say it, angel."

"Yes, I do! I can't pretend any longer!"

"Why would you want to? You have to know I'm mad about you!" He drew back to look at her searchingly. "Is it because of Tanya? You still think I'm involved with her?"

"No, I trust you completely, Nick. I know you're not capable of anything callous or underhanded."

He gathered her into his arms and held her tightly. "My dearest love. I never knew I could be this happy!"

His fervent kiss expressed all the pent-up longing he'd been keeping in check. Megan responded with an equal lack of restraint. It had been so difficult to deny him, when he was everything she'd ever wanted.

They clung to each other, murmuring passionate declarations of love between frantic kisses. Gradually Nick's caresses became more sensual and his mouth trailed down her neck to the valley between her breasts.

Megan arched her body as he unbuttoned her blouse and strung a line of kisses over the soft slopes above her bra. Then his teeth nipped gently at the hardened nipple strainng against its lace covering. She moaned softly as his warm tongue circled the little bud, creating a burning desire.

"My beautiful princess," he said huskily. "You're all mine, aren't you?"

Megan struggled to resist his powerful allure until she established complete honesty between them. Nick had to know the truth before they made love; otherwise she would be taking advantage of him. Maybe he wouldn't want her once he found out what she was capable of. That was a chance she had to take.

She captured his tormenting hand, but it remained curved around her breast. "We have to talk, Nick," she said faintly.

"I can't say much for your timing." His chuckle had a deep masculine sound.

"There's something I have to tell you," she persisted.

"I don't want to hear anything except I love you, Nick."

"You know I do, but I can't—"

"I can see there's only one way to get your full attention."

His mouth took possession of hers, effectively ending all conversation. While his tongue probed deeply, his hands caressed her body sensually.

All of her senses were under siege. Megan tried to remember why this was wrong, but when his hand slipped under her skirt to stroke her bare thighs, nothing else seemed important.

"Your skin is so warm and smooth," he murmured. "I want to touch every inch of you."

She flung her arms around his neck as his fingertips made erotic circles over her stomach. When they moved to the damp curls at the apex of her thighs, she held her breath in anticipation.

She was tantalized by his deliberate exploration of her body as he fulfilled his desire to know every inch of her.

When his hand finally slipped between her legs and h
probed intimately, she cried out in delight.

"Do you like that, my little darling?" he asked in
husky voice. "I want to bring you more pleasure tha
you've ever known."

"You do, my love," she whispered. "It's never bee
like this."

"Do you know how that makes me feel?" He stare
down at her with blazing eyes. "You're all the woman I"
ever want."

He positioned her body under his and scissored his leg
around hers. Sliding his hands under her hips, he joine
their bodies even closer. Megan was molded to his lon
length, the hard proof of his desire raising the pitch of h
own excitement almost unbearably.

He raised his head to say exultantly, "You're finally g
ing to be mine. There's no turning back now."

She couldn't have if she'd tried. As Nick tugged h
blouse out of her waistband, she reached eagerly to do th
same with his shirt.

The harsh ringing of the telephone was an unspeakabl
intrusion into their private paradise. They stared at eac
other for a moment in disbelief.

"Do you have to answer it?" she asked in a muted voic

Nick hesitated. "Mother is the only one who know
we're here. She wouldn't disturb us unless it was reall
important."

Megan nodded wordlessly. As her passion slowly ebbe
she realized it was for the best, even though her achin
body disagreed. She would have had to tell him the trut
afterward, and it would have tarnished the beautiful expe
rience.

It was Nick's father on the phone, not his mother. "
have wonderful news, son." Damien sounded euphoric.

"Couldn't it have waited till we got back, Father?" Nic

gritted his teeth, trying to control his frustration. "This is the first free time Gabrielle and I have had in weeks."

"I realize that, but this is urgent. As you know, our attorneys have been negotiating with that tabloid newspaper. The publisher tried to stonewall us, but we've had detectives looking into the matter. They've uncovered enough unsavory evidence against that Tanya woman to discredit her even without a blood test. She has agreed to hold a press conference recanting her entire story."

"Fantastic!" Nick's frown was replaced by a broad smile.

"But that isn't all. When we presented our evidence to the newspaper and told them the amount we were prepared to sue for, they agreed to publish a retraction—on the front page!" Damien finished jubilantly. "That was one of our conditions."

"You were always a tough negotiator." Nick chuckled.

"It helps to be in the right, but this was one fight I didn't intend to lose. If money was all those people understand, then we'd have hit them where it hurts."

"I appreciate your support, Dad. Thanks for telling me the good news."

"Don't hang up, I'm not finished yet. The newspapers got wind of the story. You know how dogged they are about something this sensational. Reporters have been calling from all over, asking for a statement, so we set up a news conference. It's scheduled for two hours from now. That will give you time to get home and also confer with our attorneys before you face the press."

"You want me to come home *now?*" Nick turned to look at Megan.

"It's imperative! You want to clear your name and put this all behind you, don't you?"

"Of course," Nick answered, but with reluctance.

"Then you have to meet with the press, tell them how

confident you were that you'd be vindicated, and answer the questions they're bound to have.''

"I suppose it has to be done." Nick sighed. "I just wish it didn't have to be right now.''

"I know, but it can't be helped. You'd better start for home immediately so our attorneys can brief you before you face the reporters.''

Nick put down the phone slowly. "As you heard, that was Father.'' He told Megan what had happened.

She had already tucked her blouse back into her waistband. "That's good news." She slid off the bed without looking at him.

"It would have been even better news an hour from now,'' he said wryly.

"You can't have everything." She tried to keep her voice light.

"I almost did.'' He took her into his arms and cradled her chin in his hand, gazing down at her tenderly. "I wish I could tell them to have the news conference without me.''

"You can't do that.''

"No—for your sake as well as mine. I need to erase any doubt in people's minds. Although I don't know how anyone could think I would even look at another woman when I have you, my beautiful princess.''

"We'd better go,'' Megan murmured.

"In a minute.'' He sighed and nestled her head on his shoulder. "I want to hold you just a little longer.''

"We don't have time,'' she said as he kissed the corner of her mouth.

"Not for what I'd like to do. I don't want our first time to be a hurried affair. When I make love to you it will be slowly, the way you deserve. I'll hold you in my arms and bring you joy, over and over again, all night long.''

"Oh, Nick,'' Megan groaned.

"You're right, I'm just tormenting both of us. But our time will come, sweetheart. I promise you.''

"I'd like to think so," she said wistfully.

"Count on it! After the final ball, you and I are going away together for the weekend. Lord knows, we deserve it! We'll go someplace where we can be completely alone without these constant interruptions."

"I don't think there is any place like that," she said wryly.

"As a matter of fact, I happen to know of one."

"Where is it?"

"You'll find out when we get there. I want to surprise you."

Megan didn't allow herself to think about how wonderful it would be. When this week ended, so would her relationship with Nick. King Claude would have to figure out some other solution to his problem. She couldn't go on living a lie any longer.

Nick's parents were sure the promise of the printed retractions had patched up any rift between Megan and their son. Nick was obviously mad about her, and she couldn't hide her feelings for him. The chemistry between them was evident.

Michel and Carrie were equally in love and had much the same problem as the other couple, although Michel wasn't aware of it.

"Michel asked me to marry him," Carrie told Megan that evening.

"What did you say?"

"What *could* I say? You were the one who pointed out all the reasons why I couldn't accept."

"I'm sorry," Megan said quietly.

"It isn't your fault." Carrie sighed. "You have your own troubles. It's so frustrating, though, when Michel and I both love each other. Sometimes I'm tempted to tell him the truth—but it's a no-win situation. He'd undoubtedly hate me for what we've done to Nick."

"You aren't to blame. I'm the guilty one."

"Not entirely. I was the one who urged you on. But it doesn't matter who was more at fault. We've backed ourselves into a corner and there's no way out."

"This thing has gotten out of hand and too many people are getting hurt. I won't let Nick be victimized any longer." Megan's chin set firmly. "If Gabrielle hasn't surfaced by the time this week is over, I'm going to tell him the truth. And this time I won't let myself be talked out of it."

"What about the repercussions between Beaumarre and Grandalia?"

"King Claude will just have to deal with it," Megan answered grimly. "I'm prepared to do everything in my power to convince Gabrielle of how wonderful Nick is. But I won't let her and her father keep him dangling. The longer he lives with great expectations, the more it will hurt when everything comes crashing down around him."

"You'd be taking an awful chance by telling him," Carrie warned. "He might never forgive you."

"I'll just have to risk it," Megan replied bleakly. "Nick asked me to go away with him for the weekend after the grand ball. If there's no word from Gabrielle by then, I'm going," she said, making up her mind.

"Think about it before you do something you might regret," Carrie pleaded.

"It's something I should have done days ago, but that's hindsight."

"Well, maybe Nick will understand how it happened."

Megan tried to smile. "Do you believe in the tooth fairy and the Easter bunny, too?"

"No, really. He might take it a lot better than you think. You could at least part friends." Since she realized Megan couldn't be dissuaded, Carrie tried to sound convincing.

"Sure, it might be the best weekend of my life," Megan said mockingly. "Or the worst."

Chapter Ten

The week in Grandalia was winding to a close and most of the major events, including the public ones, were over. Helena's garden party was Thursday afternoon, the time Rosamund had allotted her. Someone else was hosting a private dinner in the evening and the grand ball on Friday night would climax the festivities.

Helena's party was as organized as if she'd planned it for weeks instead of just a few days. A corps of waiters circulated among the guests on the lawn, serving an endless supply of tiny sandwiches and pastries. Tea was dispensed from huge silver urns under a red-and-white-striped tent, which also sheltered a long, fully stocked bar.

Carrie gazed at the lovely château that overlooked the meticulously groomed lawns. "Your parents' home is beautiful," she remarked to Michel.

"You've only had a glimpse of the inside," he said. "After the party I'll show you around. I especially want you to see my apartment."

"You also have a suite of rooms at the royal castle, don't you?"

He nodded. "As equerry to the prince, I have to spend a lot of time there. But now that Nick is getting married I'll have more time for my own life." He smiled and squeezed her hand.

Carrie quickly turned to look around at the groups of guests dotting the lawn. "There must be almost a hundred people here, but it isn't a bit crowded."

"My parents have had three times as many people at parties. This is just a last-minute thing."

"That's even more amazing. I don't know how your mother does it."

"Mother will be delighted to share her secret with you. You heard how badly she wants a daughter."

"Michel..." Carrie began hesitantly.

"I know you haven't agreed to marry me, but I don't intend to give up. Not after you said you love me."

"I do love you, Michel, but I...I'm not ready to get married. Everything is happening too fast."

"I knew you were special from the minute I saw you," he said fondly. "But we don't have to get married right away. We can have an extended engagement, if you like. I just want it to be official. This would be a perfect time to make the announcement."

"No, you mustn't do that!" When he was surprised by her vehemence, Carrie said in a milder tone, "I have to tell my parents first. Think how they'd feel if they read about it in the newspaper before I had a chance to tell them."

"You're right, of course. I hadn't thought of that."

"Well, now you understand. Let's have some tea." She started to walk toward the tent.

"I'm looking forward to meeting your parents," Michel remarked.

"You'd like them," Carrie said wistfully.

"How could I help it? They brought *you* into the world." He gazed at her tenderly.

Why did Michel have to be so sweet and trusting? Carrie wondered hopelessly. She tried to think of how to change the subject—something she did a lot lately—but he didn't give her a chance.

"Why don't I go home with you when you leave here? I can meet your family and give them an opportunity to look me over."

"No, I... That wouldn't work out. I'm not going directly home from here."

He frowned slightly. "Where are you going?"

Carrie improvised wildly, mixing a little truth with a lot of fiction. "Actually I might be going to America. An old school friend asked me to stay with her in New York. I'm between jobs at the moment, so it seemed like a good time to take her up on her invitation."

"You were going to simply drop out of my life without telling me?"

"I wouldn't put it that way," she answered carefully.

"What part didn't I understand?"

"You're overreacting, Michel. I'm just talking about a vacation."

"Which you never mentioned until I asked to meet your parents." He looked at her speculatively. "You never talk about yourself. Is there something you don't want me to know?"

"Like what?" she countered.

"That's what I'm asking you." He gazed at her steadily. "All I really know is that you and Gabrielle were at school together. You never mention your family or other friends. It's as though you have no past."

Carrie picked her way through a minefield. "You're making my case for me. How can we consider marriage when we know so little about each other?"

"I'm willing to tell you anything you want to know."

He waved an arm at the numerous guests. "My family is here today, and a lot of my friends. I want you to be part of my life, but you won't let me into yours. Why not, Carrie?"

"You're imagining things," she mumbled.

"I don't think so. Have I just been believing what I wanted to believe? The truth is, you don't want me to meet your parents because you don't intend to see me again after you leave here. This is just a summer romance for you, isn't it?"

"No!" Carrie couldn't bear to have him remember her that way. "Whatever else you think about me, please believe I love you, Michel."

"I'd like to believe it," he said slowly. "But how can I? People who love each other want to be together. I have a terrible feeling I'll never see you again after you leave here."

"That would break my heart." Her eyes were bright with unshed tears as she told the truth.

"Darling Carrie!" He took both her hands in his and held them tightly. "I'll never let that happen. Wherever you go, I'll come after you. The only thing that will keep me away is if you tell me you don't love me." He smiled tenderly as he added, "And even then I'll try to change your mind."

They were joined by a young couple, friends of Michel's. "You two look awfully serious. Don't you know this is a party?" the man joked.

Michel made the introductions and they all chatted for a few moments. When the woman asked him about a mutual friend, Carrie made a vague excuse and went to find Megan.

The two women took one of the graveled paths to a private corner of the garden, shielded from view. When the voices of the guests were only an indistinguishable murmur,

Megan stared at her friend curiously. "Is something wrong? You look upset."

Carrie told her what had happened with Michel. "What am I going to do?" she groaned. "I know the week is almost over, but I don't know if I can get through the rest of it. How can I keep on letting him believe we have a future together?"

"Maybe you do." Megan's jaw set firmly. "After Nick and I leave on Saturday you're going to tell Michel the truth. Then it's up to him, but I don't think he'll disappoint you."

"Are you sure you want me to do that?" Carrie's face lit with a mixture of hope and caution. "What if you change your mind and decide not to tell Nick?"

"I won't. It's time King Claude stopped victimizing everybody to save face. He's already ruined *my* life. I refuse to let him do it to the rest of you."

"I wish there was some solution for you and Nick," Carrie said in a muted voice.

"The only one I can think of is if Grandalia suddenly abolishes the monarchy and becomes a democratic country." Megan tried to make a joke out of it, since they both knew her case was hopeless. "I can't see that happening in the foreseeable future, but at least one of us might as well get a husband out of this trip."

Megan's gown for the grand ball was an exquisite creation of white lace that could have doubled as a wedding gown. The bouffant skirt belled out from a tight bodice that had a sweetheart neckline. It was a perfect showcase for the magnificent ruby necklace and earrings Robert brought to her room.

Megan was unmoved by the priceless jewels. The borrowed finery was simply a reminder of what a fraud she was. But no more. She waited until her maid and hairdresser had left the room before telling Robert her plans.

"You can't do that!" he exclaimed with an aghast expression.

"Watch me," she answered grimly. "Why won't you admit the game is over and you lost?"

"That's not true. Gabrielle—"

"Is never going to marry Nick," Megan interrupted. "She went so deep underground that you can't even find her. What makes you think she'll ever change her mind?"

"King Claude has ways," Robert replied vaguely.

"You're all living in a fantasyland," Megan said impatiently. "How long did you expect me to put my life on hold so you could carry on your conscienceless deception?"

"The king is very grateful to you. I'm sure he'd be willing to compensate you handsomely."

"Don't add insult to injury! You'd better start dreaming up a story that won't make you look too foolish, because I intend to tell Nick everything tomorrow. What he'll do about it is up to him."

Robert argued and begged, but Megan was adamant. He followed her all the way to the ballroom, still pleading, and only gave up when Nick joined them.

"You look exquisite." Nick's eyes glowed as he gazed at her. "I must be the luckiest man in the world."

"You're certainly the most handsome," she answered lightly.

Nick was one of those men who looked completely at home in dinner clothes. His were tailored to perfection and the white jacket accentuated his deep tan.

Those few moments were all they had in private before a group gathered around them. They were never alone for very long, and especially not on that final night.

It was a gala evening. Two orchestras alternated, so there was continuous music for dancing. The ballroom was decorated with arching sprays of purple and white orchids, and a bevy of waiters circulated constantly with champagne and canapés.

The midnight supper was as lavish as might be expected. Every conceivable delicacy was displayed artfully on a long, lace-covered buffet table that glittered with silver serving dishes. While the guests were eating, waiters continued to pour wine and champagne, and the orchestra played on.

Megan and Nick preferred to dance. "This is the first time I've been able to get near you all night," he complained.

"You're making up for it." She laughed. He had both arms wrapped around her.

"Be thankful I'm practicing restraint." He drew her even closer.

"What happens when you indulge yourself?" she teased.

"You'll find out tomorrow," he answered in a smoky voice.

Megan didn't want to let herself think about how exciting it would be—if Nick forgave her. "You still haven't told me where we're going."

"Try to be patient for one more day."

"But if I don't know where we're going, how will I know what clothes to take?"

"You won't need any." His lips brushed across hers. "We might not get out of bed for days."

She laughed breathlessly. "It won't look very respectable to check into a hotel without luggage."

"Do you really care?"

"No," she answered softly, gazing at his beloved face. "You're all I care about."

Megan packed very little the next day—mainly her makeup and some lingerie. Nick had finally told her the place they were going to was very casual. People wore mostly jeans and bathing suits. When she said she hadn't brought either of those things to Grandalia, he said he would buy her whatever she needed.

Megan was filled with equal parts of anticipation and trepidation as they drove through the beautiful countryside. Her heart swelled with love as she gazed at Nick's patrician profile. He looked especially handsome with the wind blowing his dark hair. It would be cruel if he decided he couldn't forgive her. She tried unsuccessfully to hide her fear as he turned his head to smile at her.

"Don't look so worried, angel," he teased. "You're going to like where I'm taking you."

"I'm not so sure. You must have some reason for keeping it such a deep dark secret."

"Okay, we're almost there so I might as well tell you. It's a little fishing village on the edge of the Riviera—the unfashionable part. Havril sur Mer is the best-kept secret on the Continent. A select group of us have been going there for years, whenever we need to get away from the paparazzi, or from pointless public functions. Our parents don't know about it and neither do any of the other people who pester us for one thing or another. It's the only place I can guarantee nobody will bother us."

"That's hard to believe. We're both so recognizable."

"Tourists don't know about the place, and wouldn't come if they did. There's nothing to do but swim and take long walks along the beach—and make love." He gave her a slow, sensuous smile.

"How could you keep it such a secret? The gossip magazines and newspapers would pay handsomely to know where celebrities hang out."

"We take good care of the natives. If they tipped off the media, we'd stop coming and their regular source of income would dry up. They aren't very hospitable to strangers, and they pretend not to know anybody's real name." Nick turned off the highway. "Here we are."

Havril sur Mer was small and unpretentious. A few men

were working on the fishing boats bobbing along the waterfront, tinkering with motors or spreading nets out to dry.

The sleepy little village, a short distance from the water, had a grocery store, a restaurant or two, and a bistro, none of them very fancy. It was, indeed, the last place you'd expect to find celebrities.

Nick drove through the village to a one-story hotel surrounded by small bungalows. When he stopped the car in front of a bungalow facing the water, Megan was prepared for a picturesque view, but spartan lodgings.

When they went inside, she was amazed at the luxury of the furnishings. The room wasn't large, but the carpeting was plush, and the draperies and bedspread were made from the finest fabrics.

Nick laughed at the expression on her face. "Did you expect a cot and a bare bulb hanging from the ceiling?"

"Maybe not that austere, but I must admit I'm surprised. I don't know why, though. Your idea of roughing it is hanging up your own bathrobe."

"Look who's talking!" he teased. "I'm surprised you didn't insist on bringing your hairdresser and maid along."

"You might wish I had when you see what I look like when I do my own hair." She laughed.

He put his arms around her and kissed the top of her head. "You couldn't be anything but beautiful, my love."

Megan rested her head on his shoulder, savoring this moment of closeness. But when his hands caressed her back, she knew the day of reckoning couldn't be put off any longer.

Drawing back reluctantly, she said, "We have to talk, Nick."

"What could I have done wrong already?" he teased. "We just got here."

"You didn't do anything—I did. Although, in my own defense, I never expected it to turn out like this."

Nick didn't take her seriously. "We can't discuss anything earth-shattering until we buy you some jeans and T-shirts.'' He consulted his watch. ''And we'd better go now before the store closes.''

''This is really important,'' she insisted. ''There's something I have to tell you.''

''You can tell me on the way to the store. I have our agenda all mapped out. First we get you outfitted, then we come back here and make love for a couple of hours. After that we take a long walk on the beach—that's what you need the clothes for.''

Megan couldn't help smiling. ''It sounds like a strenuous program.''

''That's why we'll have to go back to bed after our walk.'' He grinned.

She was secretly relieved at the reprieve, although it only postponed the inevitable. She had *tried* to tell him, though, so her conscience was clear on that one point.

The general store in the village didn't have much of a selection, but Megan was able to get what she needed. After she'd completed her purchases, she and Nick strolled down the short main street, each with anticipations of a different sort.

What happened next was shocking and unexpected. A man and a woman came out of a bar and turned in their direction. For a moment Megan had the unsettling sensation that she was walking into a mirror. Except for their different outfits, the other woman was her exact double!

After the first instant of surprise, Megan realized the woman had to be Princess Gabrielle. So this was where the princess had been hiding out all this time. Suddenly Megan feared their chance meeting had ruined everything—Nick would never believe she had meant to tell him the truth. He was staring from her to Gabrielle with an amazed and bewildered look on his face.

The princess was initially as startled as they were, then she reacted angrily. ''What are *you* doing here?'' she asked

Nick. "I suppose you told my father where I am and ruined this place for everybody. You always were a jerk!"

"Neither of us knew you were here," Megan said, because Nick was speechless.

Gabrielle turned on her furiously. "You! I'm surprised you have the nerve to face me—either of you."

"I must be losing my mind," Nick muttered. "Who is this woman?" he asked Megan. "You two could be twins."

"Scarcely," Gabrielle said witheringly. "She's just a cheap little actress they dressed up to look like me. Don't pretend you didn't know. You must have been in on it."

"In on *what?* Will somebody please tell me what this is all about?"

Megan moistened her dry lips. "Let's go someplace where we can talk."

"You're not going anywhere until I tell you how I plan to get even for what you did to me," Gabrielle raged. "I'm going to expose you for the fraud you are. If it weren't for you, my father would have had to call off the wedding plans. He'll be sorry, though. When I get through talking he'll wish he had. I intend to tell the whole world that the engagement was a sham, and I don't care about the consequences!"

As her voice rose, the handsome young man beside her tried to quiet her. Glancing at him for the first time, Megan recognized him as Jacques Duvalle, the French tennis champion.

"Calm down, Gaby," he said. "We've been over all this. You know it's no solution. Your image would suffer, too."

"I don't care! She can't steal my identity and get away with it."

"She's done a good job so far," he said crisply. "Let's go inside and talk about it over a drink."

"No! I can't stand the sight of them," Gabrielle stormed.

"Stop acting like a child," Jacques ordered. "If we dis
cuss the situation rationally, maybe we can find some way
out of this mess that won't make us all look stupid." He
led her into the bar, glancing over his shoulder to be sure
the other two were following.

Megan gazed at Nick despairingly. He didn't know the
whole story, but he'd heard enough to know he'd been
massively deceived. The stony look on his face didn't
promise forgiveness.

When they were inside the bar, she put her hand on his
arm to prevent him from joining the other two at a table.
"I can explain," she said haltingly.

"I doubt it, but it will be interesting to hear you try."
He raised an eyebrow sardonically. "I'm especially looking
forward to the part where we made plans for a life together
after we were married."

"You have every right to be angry, but please believe
that none of us meant to hurt you."

"Is that supposed to make everything all right? You pre
tended to be Gabrielle, let me believe you were in love
with me, and you didn't think I'd mind when it all turned
out to be a joke I wasn't in on?"

Unshed tears made Megan's eyes as bright as stars, but
she willed herself not to cry. "I do love you, Nick, with
all my heart. I know you'll never believe that now, but it's
the truth. It wasn't anything I planned or could control. It
just happened."

"How gullible do you think I am?" he asked angrily.
"You love me and that's why you helped arrange my mar
riage to Gabrielle? Give me a break!"

"I'm not trying to shift the blame, but her father and
Henri said it was a perfect match, that you and Gabrielle
were both just skittish about giving up your freedom. By
the time I found out neither of you wanted to marry the
other, it was too late. Nobody could find her, and everyone
thought I was the princess. I didn't honestly care about

relations between your two countries, but I cared about *you*. It would have been horrible for you if the story had gotten out that she ran away rather than become engaged to you.''

"That would have been preferable to marrying her." Nick looked over to where Gabrielle was listening sullenly, while Jacques talked to her in a low voice. "How could you possibly think I wouldn't notice the difference if she returned and took over? You might look identical, but she's the same spoiled shrew I remember from the old days."

"*You've* changed," Megan insisted. "From everything I'd read and heard, you were pretty imperious yourself. But when I got to know you, I fell in love with the real you. I hoped Gabrielle would, too, and she'd change as well."

He stared at her intently. "You would have tried to make us fall in love?"

"I wanted you to be happy," Megan answered simply.

"I *was* happy—with you." His anger was diluted by a mixture of love and impatience.

She shook her head sadly. "There could never have been anything between us, even if things didn't work out between you and Gabrielle. You're a prince, the heir to the throne of Grandalia. You have to marry royalty. I realize that."

Nick's patrician face registered strong emotions. "I don't know of anyone nobler than you."

She tried to smile. "Unfortunately, good intentions don't count as a title. I just want you to know that I intended to tell you the truth. I tried to before we left the hotel."

As he reached for her, Gabrielle called out shrilly, "How long do you think I'm going to wait? Get over here this minute or I'm leaving!"

Taking Megan's hand, Nick sauntered over to the table. "You're not addressing your adoring subjects, Gabrielle. I'd advise you to knock it off before I tell you what I think of your part in this sorry mess."

"I had nothing to do with it," she said indignantly. "It's all *her* fault!"

"There's plenty of blame to go around—starting with us. We should both have told our fathers we're mature adults, capable of picking our own mates. The trouble is, we haven't always acted mature in the past."

"Speak for yourself!" Gabrielle ordered.

"Give it a rest, Gaby," Jacques said curtly. "Nick is right. I told you we should tell your father we intend to get married."

"Married!" Megan exclaimed. "How can you do that? Jacques is a commoner."

"Luckily, Gaby isn't in line for the throne. It's not the fact that I'm a commoner that's going to panic her father." Jacques grinned. "It's the thought of having a tennis bum for a son-in-law."

"A tennis *star*," Gabrielle corrected. Her expression softened and changed to pride when she looked at him.

"Congratulations," Nick said. "But I thought you two broke up—rather publicly, as I remember."

"Several times." Jacques laughed. "Both of us were used to being top dog in a relationship and neither of us would give an inch. When we discovered what cold comfort that was, we agreed to compromise."

"I'm the one who gives in most of the time," Gabrielle said in mock complaint.

"You're enjoying the novelty of it," Jacques teased. "You never did it before."

"I'm happy for both of you, but you've created quite a headache," Nick said. "How could you let Megan and me become engaged?" he asked Gabrielle.

"I never thought Father would go that far. I was furious when I heard he'd gotten somebody to impersonate me. I phoned and said I'd never marry you, so they'd better call off the deception. But Henri said it would be a diplomatic nightmare and everybody would blame me for running out on Nick.''

"That should tell you how much she's changed," Jacques remarked fondly. "The old Gaby wouldn't have given a hoot."

"I never wanted to make trouble," the princess said plaintively. "I only want to marry Jacques."

"I can understand that," Nick said. "But it wasn't a situation you could just ignore. How much longer were you prepared to let it go on?"

"I didn't know what to do. If I came back and assumed my own identity, how could I break the engagement? The papers were full of your storybook romance," Gabrielle said with a tinge of bitterness. "The longer I stayed away, the harder it got. I still don't know what to do."

"You're going to tell your father we're getting married," Jacques said forcefully. "He and his ministers are the ones who planned the charade. They can put their spin doctors to work and figure some way out of it."

"We've been over and over it and there just isn't any way," she said hopelessly. "How can I expose my own father?"

"Do you want to let Megan marry Nick, while you spend the rest of your life as a nonperson?" Jacques demanded.

"I'm sure you realize none of us would ever have carried the masquerade that far." Megan spoke up for the first time. "I wanted this last weekend with Nick and then I was going home. I *am* going home," she corrected herself.

Gabrielle looked at her curiously. "Who are you? Where did my father find you?"

Megan explained how the whole deception had started. She finished by looking wistfully at Nick. "I know you can't forgive me now, but maybe in time you won't think so badly of me."

"I'll never forgive you—if you leave me," he added, taking her hands and raising them to his lips. "You're the love of my life, no matter who you are or what your name is. I'll never let you go.''

"You're just making it harder, Nick," she groaned. "Please don't ask me to stay. This thing with Gabrielle will be resolved somehow, but sooner or later you'll have to get married and have children. There won't be any room in your life for me."

"I can't imagine life without you. You're going to be my wife and the mother of my children. If my father can't accept that, then he'll have to find another successor to the throne."

"I couldn't let you give up your birthright for me," she protested.

"You can't stop me, darling. What good is a kingdom if it costs me the woman I love?"

"That's really sweet, Nick." Gabrielle's expression was uncharacteristically gentle. "You're a pretty good guy after all."

"It's too late to change your mind." Jacques laughed, putting his arm around her shoulders. "You're already committed to me."

"For a lifetime," she agreed softly. "But two fiancés are one too many. What reason can we give for calling off the engagement?"

"You could say you had an argument."

"That makes us sound irresponsible," Nick objected. "As if it was just a whim in the first place. Our subjects would be disgusted with us, and who could blame them? We need a good solid reason."

"Well, how about this? Nick has to produce an heir. What if I say I had a routine physical and found out I couldn't have children?" Gabrielle offered.

"Everybody would know it was a trumped-up excuse," Jacques said. "We want a lot of children, the sooner the better."

"I guess you're right. Our baby's birth wouldn't be cel-

ebrated the way it should be, and it would just postpone
the criticism. Does anybody else have any ideas? We
haven't heard your input,'' Gabrielle told Megan.

Megan had been so dazzled by the possibility of marrying Nick that she'd hardly been listening. "I'm afraid I
wasn't paying much attention," she admitted.

"You have a stake in this, too. Start thinking."

Gabrielle's half-heard proposal had triggered something
n Megan's subconscious. "I believe you were on the right
track," she said slowly. "There has to be a compelling
reason why you and Nick can't marry. Perhaps something
in your backgrounds that would make you incompatible."

"You mean, like insanity?" Nick grinned. "I'm crazy
about *you*. Does that count?"

Megan's face lit up. "No, but what if you had a common
ancestor? Royalty used to intermarry closely in the old
days. What if you found out you were related somehow?"

After a moment of surprise, the other three were jubilant.
"By George, I think she's got it!" Jacques exclaimed.

"Of course!" Gabrielle said excitedly. "Our blood types
could preclude our having healthy children together, or
some such thing. Both our fathers will issue statements of
deep regret, and Nick and I are off the hook!"

Nick lifted Megan off her chair and swung her around.
"You're brilliant! You've solved all our problems. What
would I do without you?"

"I hate to be the one to bring it up, but we still have
one small problem," Gabrielle said. "Megan and I could
be identical twins. It's bound to cause talk, especially when
Nick starts to be seen with her."

"So what?" Jacques shrugged. "People will just think
he fell in love with her because she looks like you."

"Fair enough, but some nosy reporter is sure to dig
around and find out everything there is to know about her,
like, where did she suddenly emerge from? The paparazzi
know everything else about me—why didn't they know I

had an exact double? One who just happened to be in Beaumarre when Nick and I supposedly became engaged. Won't somebody ask why no one ever saw us in the same vicinity? She told all her friends she was coming especially for the festivities.''

Megan smiled. "It's no problem because the substitute princess is about to vanish without a trace."

Nick's jaw set. "I won't let you go. If you leave I'll come after you."

"That's something we need to discuss, but it wasn't what I meant." She turned to Gabrielle. "This isn't my normal hair color or style, and I don't usually use this much makeup. I don't wear designer clothes or fabulous jewels, either. You'd be surprised at what an attention getter they are. If we passed each other on the street when I looked like my old self, someone might notice a resemblance, but nothing more. I'm really quite ordinary looking."

"I'll take exception to that," Nick said fondly. "You'd turn heads anywhere."

"I'll have to agree," Jacques said. When Gabrielle raised an eyebrow in his direction he laughed. "You can't be jealous. She looks like *you*."

Gabrielle turned to stare at Megan. "I'm afraid you're being too modest. I can't imagine hair color and the rest making that much difference."

"I can't, either," Nick said. "Your personalities are poles apart, but that's about all. You'd be instantly recognizable, no matter what you were wearing."

"Oh, really?" Megan grinned. "Do you remember being in a little bistro the night before your official visit to Beaumarre? You were alone and grouchy."

He frowned in remembrance. "How do you know that?"

"You spent the evening with a girl, telling her about the bridges you'd like to build in South America. You called her Angélique and told her your name was Philippe. She thought you looked familiar, but she never dreamed you could be Prince Nicholas, because you were just another guy in jeans and a T-shirt.''

He was staring at her in amazement. ''*You* were Angélique? I don't believe it.''

''Would you like me to tell you about the walk we took on the beach after the bistro closed?''

''I knew you were special even then,'' he said softly. ''It took a lot of willpower to put you in that taxi.''

''Isn't it fantastic?'' Gabrielle said exultantly. ''A bottle of hair dye is the solution to everything—no pun intended. Let's go back to the palace and start your transformation, Megan. It's spooky having an identical twin.''

''No. You two can go home. We're staying for the weekend.'' Nick exchanged a meaningful glance with Megan and held out his hand.

They walked back to the cottage with mounting anticipation. Megan knew their future was uncertain—in spite of Nick's confidence. If his father was adamantly opposed to their marriage, she couldn't let Nick renounce his title.

But when they were inside their room and he took her in his arms and kissed her tenderly, nothing else mattered for this short, enchanted period of time.

''My darling love, I've waited for this moment for such a long time,'' he said huskily.

''I was afraid it would never happen,'' she whispered.

''We've had a stormy courtship,'' he smilingly agreed, kissing the tip of her nose. ''But that's all over with. From now on I'm going to devote myself to making you happy.''

''Just love me, darling,'' she said yearningly.

''Yes, angel. Now and forever.''

Taking her hand, he led her to the side of the bed. While they gazed into each other's eyes, he began to unbutton her blouse. Megan shivered slightly as his fingers brushed her bare skin. When her blouse gaped and he dipped his head to kiss the valley between her breasts, a thrill of anticipation raced through her.

Nick tugged the blouse out of her waistband and slipped it off her shoulders. Then he unhooked her bra and tossed that aside, also. When she was nude to the waist, he cupped both breasts in his palms.

"You're so exquisite," he said in a thickened voice. "I want to know every inch of your beautiful body."

Megan drew in her breath sharply as his warm mouth tantalized each nipple with a circle of erotic kisses. And when his lips closed around one taut little rosette, suckling greedily, she uttered a cry of delight.

He lifted his head to stare at her with blazing eyes. "It makes me so happy to know you want me."

"You'll never know how much." She wound her arms around his neck and pulled his head down to hers.

He parted her lips for a deep, sensual kiss that made her legs tremble. While his tongue explored the moist recess of her mouth, she unbuttoned his shirt and swayed against him. The tips of her breasts moving over his bare chest was incredibly erotic.

"You don't know what you're doing to me, sweetheart," he gasped. "I wanted our first time to be slow and special, but you're driving me close to the edge."

It was a heady feeling to have such power over this experienced man. Megan smiled seductively as she unfastened his slacks. "I've never seen you lose control."

"I've never had such provocation."

He groaned when she slid her hands inside his waistband and kneaded his taut buttocks. But when she eased his slacks over his hips and caressed his rampant manhood, Nick uttered a hoarse cry and crushed her in his arms.

The hard proof of his passion threatened her own control. She arched her body into his, needing him urgently.

He removed the rest of her clothes and kicked off his own. Their passion flamed out of control after they were completely nude. Uttering little cries of delight, they touched each other everywhere.

When the tension was too much to bear, he cupped his hands around her bottom and lifted her off the floor. Megan wound her legs around his waist, inviting his fiery entry.

Nick's driving force filled her with joy. She met each thrust eagerly, surging toward him again and again. Their union was tempestuous, accelerating as their taut bodies sought release. They finally achieved it in a burst of sensation that rocketed through them both at the same time.

Total satisfaction left them relaxed in each other's arms. Nick cradled her close and eased her down onto the bed where they were quiet for long moments, awed by the depth of their love.

Finally he kissed her closed eyelids. "I didn't mean for it to be that fast," he said ruefully. "I'll do better next time."

She smiled blissfully. "I don't think you could."

"Wait and see. I intend to make love to you a hundred different ways."

"That's an ambitious promise."

"I didn't say I'd show them all to you tonight." He chuckled. "I have to save some surprises for the years ahead. We're going to be together a long time."

Megan's smile faltered. "I hope so. But even if things don't work out for us, I'll always be glad we had this time together."

"If you think I plan to let you go, you're very much mistaken."

"You have to be realistic, Nick. You're a prince. A lot is expected of you."

"Duty to my country doesn't include letting someone else pick my bride. You're going to be my princess, or they'll have to get somebody else to fill my job. That's what I intend to tell my father tomorrow."

"But you can't just—"

"I can think of better things to do than argue about it." His mouth took possession of hers, stopping her protest effectively.

Megan's sated desire was reawakened instantly, proving more urgent than any discussion. She moved voluptuously as he caressed her body and strung a line of kisses down to her navel.

After dipping his tongue into the small depression, he moved lower. Her breathing quickened as he raised her leg and kissed the soft skin of her inner thigh.

"Your skin is like velvet," he said huskily. "I've never known such perfection."

Megan's passion rose as his mouth moved to the juncture of her thighs. She cried out when he kissed her intimately.

Nick raised his head to gaze at her with glowing eyes. "Do you know how it makes me feel to hear you call my name while I give you pleasure? I do make you happy, don't I, sweetheart?"

"I didn't even know it could be like this!" she gasped.

"For me, either. I've never felt like this about anyone before. I can't get enough of you."

His renewed intimate kisses were building a storm inside Megan. She twisted restlessly and held out her arms to him.

"Not yet, darling," he said. "Let me do this for you."

The storm grew stronger, sending shock waves through her. As they built toward a thunderous crest that made her muscles taut, Nick entered her. They rode the waves together until the storm broke, releasing all tension and replacing it with complete fulfillment.

They were too replete to stir for long minutes. Then Nick smoothed the damp hair off her forehead, gazing at her tenderly. "What did I ever do to deserve you?"

"I'm the lucky one," Megan said softly. "I wouldn't have missed this time with you for anything."

Nick frowned. "That sounds as if you think it's coming to an end."

"No one can predict the future," she said evasively. "But the past is something we'll always have."

"I can tell mere words aren't going to convince you, so I won't bother to try anymore." He curled his body around hers and kissed the nape of her neck. "Go to sleep, darling. We have a big day coming up tomorrow."

Megan nestled in his arms, hoping this wouldn't be for the last time. She wanted to share Nick's confidence in the future, but the deck was stacked heavily against them. The monarchy, with its long history of tradition, would use all of its power to separate them.

She shivered and pulled Nick's arms more closely around her.

Chapter Eleven

Nick was still asleep when Megan awoke the next morning. She got out of bed quietly in order not to wake him. After dressing swiftly, she tiptoed out the door.

She wasn't gone long, but Nick was up and agitated when she returned a short time later.

Grabbing her by the shoulders he asked furiously, "Where the devil were you? When I woke up and you weren't here, I panicked!"

"What could happen to me in a sleepy little fishing village?" she teased.

"I was afraid you'd left me." He folded her in his arms, holding her so tightly that she could hardly breathe.

"I wouldn't do that," she said in a muffled voice. "Not without saying goodbye."

"There won't be any goodbyes," he stated. "And just to make sure of it, I don't intend to let you out of my sight."

"That presents a bit of a problem. I was going to ask you to leave me alone here for an hour or so."

"No way!" he answered promptly. "There isn't time, anyway. We have to start back to Grandalia."

"It's still early and we're not that far away. Please, Nick," she coaxed. "Go out and have breakfast. When you come back I'll have a surprise for you."

His expression changed and he blew softly in her ear. "Why don't I surprise you, instead? We still have ninety-eight ways to make love."

"Choose one while you're having breakfast." She laughed, pushing him gently toward the door.

"All right, but I'm taking the car," he called as he left protestingly.

"We'll have to do something about your lack of trust." She closed the door firmly.

Megan couldn't wait to use the bottle of hair dye she'd bought at the only drugstore in the village. It was time to take back her own identity.

After applying the dye, waiting the required amount of time for it to take effect, then washing her hair, Megan wrapped a towel around her head while she put on her makeup.

That didn't take long. She didn't bother with all the cosmetics that made Gabrielle look glamorous at any hour of the day or night. Megan used only a touch of mascara on her naturally long lashes, and applied lipstick lightly to the natural contours of her mouth.

After that she dried her hair without styling it. The result was a mass of light brown curls instead of the long, sleek style that was Gabrielle's signature. Megan lacked the expertise of a professional beautician, so her hair turned out lightly streaked with strands of blond. But her natural hair color had been streaked by the sun. She looked like her old self.

Megan stared into the mirror anxiously. Would Nick find

her as attractive? He was used to glamorous women. If he had second thoughts, it couldn't be helped. This was who she was.

In spite of her fatalistic viewpoint, Megan was nervous about seeing Nick. She came out of the bathroom slowly when she heard his key in the lock.

"I hope I stayed away long enough, because I'm not—" He stopped abruptly when he saw her, staring incredulously. "Angélique! You've come back."

"Do you really remember me?" she asked softly.

"I never forgot you." He trailed a finger down her cheek. "I hope you don't mind that I'm in love with two women."

"Which do you like the best?"

"Both of you are gorgeous, but I didn't fall in love with your lovely face," he said tenderly. "The warm, generous person inside you was what captivated me. That's the woman I want to spend the rest of my life with."

His kiss was gentle at first, but her response increased the tempo. He pulled her closer, moving against her suggestively.

"I thought you were in such a hurry to leave," she murmured.

"Not when I can make love to the new woman in my life."

"Men are so fickle."

"That's something you'll never have to worry about." He nibbled delicately on her ear. "Two women are all I can handle."

She wound her arms around his neck. "This one wants your undivided attention."

"You've had that since the day I met you." He swung her into his arms and carried her to the bed.

They made love slowly and sensuously, touching each other erotically. Megan wriggled with pleasure as Nick's hands and mouth explored her body intimately. She took equal pleasure in his groans of delight when she did the same to him. Giving mutual enjoyment was their goal and their reward.

When desire escalated into unbridled passion, Nick joined their bodies, making them one. The same molten sensations throbbed from one to the other in an ever-increasing tempo, building to an explosive conclusion.

They were bathed in a golden glow afterward. "It just keeps getting better and better," Nick said, stroking her body languidly.

"I know." She rubbed her cheek against his hard, muscled chest. "I wish we could stay here forever. This is a magic place."

"We make our own magic." He leaned down to kiss her one more time. "Let's go home and I'll prove it to you."

The atmosphere at the castle in Grandalia was forbidding. Megan could feel it as soon as they walked through the massive front doors. People were standing around in little clusters, speaking in low voices.

Michel came bounding down the stairs to greet Nick and Megan, having been informed of their arrival. "Where the devil have you been, Nick?" He looked harried. "Your father has been calling everywhere, trying to locate you."

"I had some urgent, unfinished business to take care of." Nick smiled at Megan. "I gather he heard my engagement to Gabrielle is off."

"He knows everything. You'd better go talk to him. He's angrier than a whole nestful of hornets."

"Is Carrie still here?" Megan was concerned about having left her friend to face the king's recriminations alone.

"No, she's staying at my parents' house," Michel said. "I thought it would be more comfortable for her, considering."

"She shouldn't be blamed for what I did," Megan protested. "It was all my fault."

"Carrie said she urged you to do it."

"I didn't need much coaxing. Don't be angry with her," Megan pleaded. "We wanted to tell both of you the truth, but things just got too involved."

"Don't worry. Carrie and I talked everything out." Michel gave her a big smile. "We're going to be married."

"Congratulations!" Nick clapped him on the shoulder. "So are Megan and I."

Michel's smile was replaced by a startled expression. "You can't do that!" he exclaimed.

"Does that mean you won't be my best man?" Nick joked.

"Be serious! I wish you *could* get married. Carrie told me how you feel about each other. It's a really rotten break that you're not free to do as you please, but you're different from other men."

"I'd like to think Megan would agree." Nick put his arm around her, smiling broadly.

She couldn't return his smile. If even Michel knew their union was impossible, what chance did they have?

A servant approached diffidently. "The king was told you had arrived. He would like to see you in his study, Your Highness."

"News travels fast," Nick said lightly. He took Megan's hand. "Okay, let's go invite him to a wedding."

Michel's face expressed his deep concern as he watched them leave.

The king was pacing the floor with a fierce scowl on his face. He confronted Nick angrily. "It's about time you came home. How could you just disappear like that when scandal is threatening the monarchy? What am I supposed to tell people?"

"The truth." Nick's eyes glinted with amusement. "That with deep regret and out of love for our countries, Gabrielle and I are forced to sever our engagement."

"That's utter rot! You could have perfectly healthy children."

"I hope to—a whole houseful of them, but not with Gabrielle."

The king suddenly noticed Megan. She had been lagging reluctantly behind Nick. "Who is that woman? Don't tell me you were off having a little fling while I've been left to deal with an out-of-control media. This is absolutely unforgivable, Nicholas!"

"Megan is not a passing fancy. She's your future daughter-in-law."

"What kind of nonsense is this? Is she the real reason you broke the engagement?"

"Actually, Megan is the woman I became so publicly engaged to."

"Impossible! That woman was an imposter brought in by Claude to deceive us."

"I'm truly sorry about that," Megan murmured.

A puzzled look replaced Damien's anger for a moment as he gazed at her face and hair. The jeans and T-shirt she was wearing added to his confusion.

"I don't understand. You don't look anything like Gabrielle," he said. "You couldn't have fooled us so completely."

"Makeup, clothes and hairstyle can work wonders," Rosamund remarked. She had been sitting quietly in the background. "I should have guessed. You weren't anything like the Gabrielle I remembered," she told Megan. "But you seemed so much in love with Nick that I just accepted our good fortune."

"I do love him, but I don't know if that's enough for you," Megan answered wistfully.

"It most certainly is not!" the king stated. "We don't even know your real name. Who are you? Where did you come from? What is your background?"

"My name is Megan Delaney. I'm an American and I work—" That was as far as she got.

"I don't need to hear any more," Damien interrupted. "Nicholas is a royal prince, in line for the throne of Grandalia. Surely you can see that an alliance between you two is impossible."

"I'm not making an alliance," Nick said. "I'm getting married."

"Not to her. I forbid it!"

"I'm sorry you feel that way, but it won't stop me."

"You would defy your king?" Damien thundered.

"Don't pull rank on me, Father. I let you use that excuse to pressure me into marrying Gabrielle, and look how that turned out. I should have stood up to you then, but obedience had been drilled into me from the time I was a child. I can't regret following your orders because otherwise I never would have met Megan, but from now on I'm making my own decisions about who I marry and what I do with my life."

If Nick had gotten angry and shouted, Damien would have known how to deal with him. They'd clashed often in the past. But the king was shaken by his son's calm statement of fact.

Damien tried reasoning with him. "I'll admit I was wrong to arrange a marriage for you. You have a right to choose your own bride, but she must be someone suitable to share your throne when the time comes. The people would never accept a commoner—and a foreigner at that!"

"The world is changing, Father. Royals are no longer regarded as gods. We're human beings who fall in love like everyone else. If the people want me as their king, they'll accept my wife as their queen."

"And I tell you they won't! Are you prepared to renounce the throne for this woman?" Damien demanded.

"If necessary," Nick answered firmly.

"No!" Megan said explosively. "I love you too much to let you do that. It's too high a price to pay."

"Listen to her," Damien urged. "She understands, even if you don't."

Nick ignored his father. "You mean more to me than any throne," he told Megan tenderly. "If I can't become king, I'll still serve my country. You and I together will work to make Grandalia and the world a better place to live in."

Rosamund rose and crossed the room to kiss her son. Then she beckoned to Megan. "Come with me. We have a wedding to plan."

"You support Nicholas in this insanity?" Damien asked his wife. But the fire had gone out of him.

"If I don't, he might not let me play with my grandchildren." She smiled. "A wise general calls retreat when he's lost the war, Damien."

Megan followed the queen out of the room in a daze. Would the king really give them his blessing—or at least, his permission to marry? She put the question to Rosamund when they were in the queen's sitting room.

"Damien isn't used to being challenged. It's one of the perks of being king," Rosamund said mischievously. "He'll be difficult to live with for a few days, but he'll come around. Especially if we can think of some way to make him believe he changed his own mind. That's what I do when he issues edicts I have no intention of following."

"Ordinary wives do that, too," Megan remarked wryly.

"Most happy marriages are the same."

"You and the king are very fortunate to have fallen in love with each other. I don't suppose every arranged marriage turns out that happily."

"Our marriage wasn't arranged. That's what makes Damien's indignation so foolish. We met at an embassy ball and fell madly in love. Admittedly, I was the daughter of a duke, but Damien's parents would have preferred a princess. I suppose a father never thinks anyone is good enough for his son.'' Rosamund laughed.

''In my country it's the mother of the son who's never satisfied with his choice. It's surprising that couples ever make it to the altar.''

''I hope you realize your wedding will be an international event.''

''Like the engagement?'' Megan asked.

''That doesn't begin to describe all the pomp and pageantry. We'd better start planning for it right away.''

Nick entered his mother's sitting room, smiling broadly. ''I told you everything would be all right,'' he said to Megan.

''Did your father agree to let you keep your present status?'' she asked cautiously.

''He said he had no other choice. I didn't remind him that he has a younger brother.''

''That was wise.'' Rosamund nodded. ''Damien only needed a good excuse.''

Megan looked at them both with dazzled eyes. ''I can hardly believe it! I expected to be on a plane for New York about now.''

''You're not going anywhere,'' Nick stated.

''Not permanently, but I'll have to get an apartment somewhere. We can't see each other for a while,'' she said reluctantly.

''Where did you get a silly notion like that?''

''We have to make sure the true story about you and Gabrielle doesn't get out. That means we can't be seen together. It wouldn't be credible for you to start dating someone else immediately. You're supposed to be heartbroken at having to call off your engagement.''

''Megan has a point,'' Rosamund mused.

''Not as far as I'm concerned,'' Nick stated. ''If you

think I'll agree to be separated for even a day, you're both badly mistaken.''

"You didn't let me finish," his mother chided. "I've been thinking about getting another social secretary. I can't seem to keep up with all my appointments. This time I believe I'll hire an outsider instead of choosing someone from the aristocracy," she said with an air of innocence.

"Someone like an American?" He grinned as her meaning became clear.

"Why, yes. I think that would be a good public-relations move. Would you be interested in the job, my dear?" she asked Megan. "It isn't very arduous except for all those parties you'd have to attend. And of course you'd have to live here at the castle so you'd be available if I needed you."

"Mother, you're a genius." Nick kissed the top of her head. "You can put her in the room next to mine."

"Don't push your luck too far," his mother admonished.

Megan had mixed feelings about living in the castle. She was thrilled to be with Nick, and she welcomed the chance to get to know Rosamund better. The older woman was delightful. In a very short time she and the queen developed a close relationship.

Unfortunately that wasn't the case with the king. Damien's attitude toward Megan was polite, but aloof. He might have been forced to accept her, but he didn't have to pretend to be happy about it. Megan was always conscious of him watching her with an enigmatic look on his face.

"He'll never accept me," she told Carrie despairingly, when they were spending an afternoon together.

Carrie was divinely happy and felt Megan should be, too. "Don't worry about it. Nick loves you. That's all that matters. There's nothing his father can do about it."

"I wouldn't be so sure," Megan answered slowly. "He's

not the kind of man who gives up easily. I have a feeling he's just biding his time, waiting for me to do something that will give him an excuse to break us up."

"Then play it safe. Be sweet and agree with everything he says. It will drive him nuts." Carrie laughed.

"I don't want to aggravate him. I want him to like me." Megan sighed.

"Be patient. I bet you'll see a dramatic change after you present him with his first grandchild."

"That's a long way off," Megan said soberly. "I hope Damien doesn't find the excuse he's looking for to call off our wedding."

When Megan and Nick weren't out for the evening, they usually spent it with Rosamund in the upstairs den. It was one of the cozier rooms—informal and comfortable.

Sometimes they watched a video on television, or played Scrabble. One night Nick remembered a card game he'd played as a child. It stressed speed over skill. All the players tried to put their card on the pack first.

There was much hilarity going on when Damien entered the room. He looked impassively at the three around the table. "I thought you were going to a party this evening," he said to his son.

"Megan didn't feel like it," Nick answered.

"I said I'd go if you wanted to," she protested.

"I wasn't keen on it, either. We've been out every night this week. It feels good just to lounge around in casual clothes."

"That reminds me, Megan, we'll need to do something about your wardrobe," Rosamund said. "With all the parties still to come, you'll need some new gowns."

"I have plenty of clothes."

"I don't think it's a good idea to appear in any of the things you wore as Gabrielle."

"That's a good point," Megan conceded. "I'll have to

see what I can do about changing them somewhat with scarves and different accessories.''

"Why bother? I'll have several of the designers send over a selection of gowns for you to choose from.''

"I'd rather you didn't. I've only worn some of my dresses once. It would be wasteful not to get more use out of them than that.''

Megan was being sincere, but there was another reason for refusing the queen's offer. She was hesitant to take any more from Nick's family, since the king felt the way he did about her. He was looking at her without comment, as usual.

Nothing brought a kind word from him. One night at the dinner table, Nick told his father about their plans for starting a charitable foundation after they were married.

"It was Megan's idea," Nick said proudly. "I was whining about being a figurehead with nothing meaningful to do, and she told me about all the options I had. My first choice would have been climbing around a construction site, but this will be exciting in a different way.''

The king turned his gaze on Megan. "This was your idea?''

"Everybody needs to do work that interests them," she answered defensively. "Nick is too young to sit around and vegetate.''

"I see," was Damien's only comment.

Eventually Megan resigned herself to the fact that she wasn't going to win his acceptance.

The press corps of both royal houses had shifted into high gear immediately after the broken engagement. Nick and Gabrielle had each issued a sorrowful statement and both kings expressed their regrets. Sympathy for the royal couple poured in. They'd never been more popular.

When Gabrielle renewed her friendship with Jacques a

short time later, her subjects approved. Their poor, sad princess needed something to distract her.

Gabrielle's rather speedy engagement to Jacques did raise a few eyebrows. Some observers said he caught her on the rebound and perhaps she should think about it before . taking such a big step. But the stunning couple seemed very much in love, and the prospect of a royal wedding after all, was enough to silence any serious criticism.

Carrie's marriage to Michel was the warm-up event for the royal set, putting everybody in a festive mood. There was a constant round of parties before the wedding, and Nick began to show up with Megan.

This union wasn't looked on with as much favor. He was obviously in love with her; she was by his side constantly. When their relationship appeared to be serious, people began to ask questions. Who was this Megan Delaney? Could the prince possibly be contemplating marriage to her? It would be unprecedented!

The groundswell of interest sparked articles, and letters to the editors of newspapers all over. The romantics wanted them to marry, while the conservatives declared Nick had to pick a mate who was his equal in status. Megan was uneasy at all the attention.

"Get used to it, angel," Nick advised. "Unfortunately you're a public figure now and people are interested in everything about you."

"I don't mind their interest. It's their disapproval that bothers me."

"You can't win 'em all." He grinned.

"I'm serious, Nick. What if your people won't accept me?"

"How could anybody not fall in love with you?" he asked in a deep velvet voice, taking her in his arms and stroking her sensuously.

When they made love, Megan always entered a private world where nothing bad could ever happen. Nick was so certain they would always be together, and she wanted to believe him.

It became difficult when the criticism of her came from the king's ministers. There were only rumblings at first, then one of the ministers expressed his opposition publicly. He called on the king to assure the people that Prince Nicholas wouldn't break with tradition by marrying a commoner.

That provoked fierce arguments among the king's advisers that spilled over into the media. Should the prince be allowed to marry for love became the main topic of conversation in the country.

Nick was angry, and Megan was desolate. She braced herself for the worst, even though he refused to admit it could happen.

At the height of the fury Rosamund said to her husband, "This thing is getting dangerously out of hand. You have to do something."

"I intend to. I'm going to put an end to this disgraceful situation once and for all." Damien's jaw set grimly. "The television people are setting up their cameras in my office at this moment. They've also been broadcasting announcements, telling the people I will address them at seven o'clock."

Rosamund slanted a glance at him. "What are you going to say?"

Before he could answer, his press secretary knocked briefly and entered, requesting an urgent conference with the king. The two men went into Damien's office.

Megan's stomach was churning as she sat in the queen's sitting room with Rosamund and Nick that night, waiting like audiences in many parts of the world for the king's announcement. The news had spread quickly and was picked up by the foreign media.

Megan knew what Damien was going to say—and what

she would have to do. Nick would argue, but there was no other solution. The fairy tale was coming to an end.

She could tell Rosamund was nervous, too, even though the queen tried to hide it. Nick's expression was serious but not concerned, which was like him. He was probably putting on an act for her benefit, Megan decided.

Damien looked even more forbidding than usual as he stared straight into the camera. After a few words of greeting he got right to the point.

"I wish to take this occasion to announce the engagement of my son, Prince Nicholas Philippe de Valmontine, to Miss Megan Delaney."

Megan was sure the tension had finally been too much for her. She must be delirious. The king couldn't be giving them his consent!

Nick sprang out of his chair, whooping with joy. "I knew we could count on Father!"

"Hush," Rosamund said, turning up the volume. "Let's listen to the rest."

"I know you will all accord this fine young woman the respect she deserves as your future queen," the king continued.

"That's telling the ministers!" Nick crowed.

Damien's imperious manner intensified. "I would take it as a personal affront if anyone questioned my son's choice, or his rightful claim to the throne. This union has my complete approval and that of Queen Rosamund, and I trust it will have yours, as well."

"Superbly done." Rosamund smiled.

"Therefore, I am sure you will all rejoice with us on this very happy occasion," the king stated.

There were a few more remarks, but the three people most intimately concerned had heard everything they needed to. They were all talking excitedly when Damien joined them.

His wife and son crowded around him. "I don't have to

tell you what this means to me," Nick said, pumping his father's hand.

"I'm proud of you, darling," Rosamund told her husband. "I knew you'd do the right thing."

He looked at her with a twinkle in his eyes. "I couldn't face the silent treatment I'd get if I didn't."

Megan approached diffidently. "I'd like to express my appreciation, too. I know you did it for Nick, not me, but I'll try to see that you never regret your decision."

"You're mistaken if you think I compromised because of Nicholas," Damien said quietly. "When you know me better you'll realize I never settle for less than the best."

"I don't have any of the qualifications you were looking for," Megan said uncertainly.

"You have everything but a title. I'll admit that was important to me when Nick first said he wanted to marry you. My opposition was automatic. Monarchs have always married royalty. But there was another reason for my disapproval. The prospect of marrying a prince can be very alluring—the glittering life-style, great wealth and privilege."

"Are you saying no woman would want me for myself?" Nick chuckled.

He was joking, but Damien answered seriously. "The things you take for granted can seem irresistible to someone who's never experienced them. Who could blame a woman for being dazzled by the luxury of unlimited servants, the wardrobe of expensive gowns to wear at endless parties?"

"Those things are certainly nice, I won't deny it. But they're frills I could just as easily do without," Megan protested.

"I discovered that when you preferred staying home to going out to yet another club. It was also revealing that you rejected Rosamund's offer of a new wardrobe."

Megan suddenly realized that Damien hadn't been

brooding over her unsuitability. A king was like any other father when his son's happiness was at stake.

She gave him a radiant smile. "I wish I'd been born a princess for your sake. But if it's any consolation, I'd love Nick if he pumped gas for a living, or flipped hamburgers at a burger joint."

"It's not something I can picture." Rosamund's smile was misty-eyed. "You'll both be far more effective running a charitable foundation."

"That was the thing that convinced me you were a jewel," Damien told Megan with a chuckle. "Perhaps now he won't pester *me* for a job."

"He'll be far too busy preparing for the wedding," Rosamund said happily. "We must start making lists first thing in the morning, Megan."

Damien gazed at the queen indulgently. "Nick's mother has been looking forward to this event for a long time. I'm sure she has grandiose plans. You might be sorry you agreed to marry a prince when you find out what you have to go through," he said to Megan.

"It can't compare to what I suffered when I thought I'd lost him," she answered softly.

Nick raised her hand to his lips and gazed tenderly at her. "That could never have happened. I would have searched the whole world until I found you again. That's how much I love you." Megan's heart swelled with joy at this fairy-tale ending. The prince had found his princess and they would live happily ever after.

Epilogue

The wedding of Prince Nicholas Philippe de Valmontine to Megan Elizabeth Delaney was an international affair. Diplomats and heads of state came from all over the world to join in the festivities. Luminaries from every field mingled with ordinary citizens of Grandalia to celebrate the happy occasion. The parties were nonstop, some lasting until dawn.

"I'll be glad when this is over and I can have you all to myself," Nick growled, when he and Megan shared a stolen moment together in her suite.

"It's your fault," she teased. "If you weren't a prince we could have gone down to city hall and gotten married without all this fuss."

"Do you mind, darling?" He looked at her searchingly. "I know this isn't the kind of wedding you expected."

"Nobody expects to be married in front of thousands of guests, but how can I mind?" She smiled enchantingly. "It's the price one has to pay for marrying a prince."

"I'll see that you never regret it, my love," Nick said tenderly. "I promise to make you very happy."

"You always have," she answered softly.

Newspapers and magazines all over the world filled columns and pages with every possible detail of the nuptials. They showed pictures of Megan's large canary-diamond engagement ring, and reported that her wedding gown was being designed by a famous French couturier.

On the day of the wedding an army of photographers and reporters lined the route to the beautiful, historic church where the ceremony would take place. Excitement rippled through the crowd as they waited for the glass carriage that would carry the soon-to-be princess to her prince.

Megan's suite was crowded with people helping her to get ready for the big event. Her hair had been styled and her face made up. Rosamund had briefed her one last time on proper protocol. Now all that remained was to put on her wedding gown.

It was an exquisite creation of satin and lace with a long, graceful train. The rosettes of lace on the bodice were outlined with seed pearls and the design was repeated on the full satin skirt.

When every hidden hook had been fastened, the queen placed a circlet of orange blossoms on Megan's head and arranged the attached tulle veil so her face would be visible to the spectators.

"You look absolutely exquisite, my dear," Rosamund told her.

"If I do, it's thanks to you." Megan smoothed her skirt gently. "You've done so much for me."

"You make my son happy. That's thanks enough for me." Rosamund kissed her cheek.

People cheered as Megan's coach traveled slowly to the church. When she stepped out in front of the venerable building, hundreds of flashbulbs flared, capturing for posterity the beautiful young woman who would someday be a queen.

The church was filled with candles and fragrant bouquets of flowers. A hush fell as Megan started down the satin-ribbon-swagged aisle. The distance to the altar seemed endless. She clutched her bouquet of white roses and lilies of the valley, feeling her legs begin to tremble. Could she fulfill the expectations of the people who had such faith in her? All she was bringing to this marriage was love. Would it be enough?

And then she was close enough to see Nick's face clearly, and her doubts vanished. He held out his hand to her and she took her place beside him where she belonged.

The service was very moving. When she was asked at the conclusion if she took Prince Nicholas Philippe de Valmontine to be her husband, Megan answered in a clear, confident voice, "I do."

At the end of the ceremony Nick took her in his arms and kissed her tenderly. That was when Megan realized this wasn't the end of the fairy tale—it was the beginning.

* * * * *

Share in the joy of yuletide romance with brand-new
stories by two of the genre's most beloved writers

DIANA PALMER

and

JOAN JOHNSTON

in

LONE STAR CHRISTMAS

Diana Palmer and Joan Johnston share their favorite
Christmas anecdotes and personal stories in this
special hardbound edition.

Diana Palmer delivers an irresistible spin-off of her
LONG, TALL TEXANS series and Joan Johnston crafts an
unforgettable new chapter to **HAWK'S WAY** in this wonderful
keepsake edition celebrating the holiday season. So
perfect for gift giving, you'll want one for yourself...and
one to give to a special friend!

Available in November at your favorite retail outlet!

Only from

™ *Silhouette*®

Silhouette

SPECIAL EDITION ™®

That SPECIAL *Woman!*

**These delightful titles are coming soon to
THAT SPECIAL WOMAN!—only from
Silhouette Special Edition!**

**September 1997   THE SECRET WIFE
                   by Susan Mallery (SE#1123)**

Five years ago Elissa's dreams came true when she married
her true love—but their honeymoon was short-lived. Could
she and Cole Stephenson get a second shot at happiness?

**November 1997   WHITE WOLF
                  by Lindsay McKenna (SE#1135)**

Hard-core cynic Dain Phillips turned to mystical medicine
woman Erin Wolf for a "miracle" cure. But he never suspected
that Erin's spiritual healing would alter him—body and soul!

**January 1998   TENDERLY
                 by Cheryl Reavis (SE#1147)**

Socialite Eden Trevoy was powerfully drawn to Navajo
policeman Ben Toomey when he helped her uncover her half-
Navajo roots. Could her journey of self-discovery lead to full-
fledged love?

**IT TAKES A VERY SPECIAL MAN TO WIN THAT
SPECIAL WOMAN....** Don't miss THAT SPECIAL WOMAN!
every other month from some of your favorite authors!

SHARON SALA

Continues the twelve-book series—36 HOURS— in October 1997 with Book Four

FOR HER EYES ONLY

The storm was over. The mayor was dead. Jessica Hanson had an aching head...and sinister visions of murder. And only one man was willing to take her seriously— Detective Stone Richardson. He knew that unlocking Jessica's secrets would put him in danger, but the rugged cop had never expected to fall for her, too. Danger he could handle. But love...?

For Stone and Jessica and *all* the residents of Grand Springs, Colorado, the storm-induced blackout was just the beginning of 36 Hours that changed *everything!* You won't want to miss a single book.

Silhouette®

SPECIAL EDITION®

COMING NEXT MONTH

#1135 WHITE WOLF—Lindsay McKenna
That Special Woman!
Hardened corporate raider Dain Phillips turned to mystical medicine woman Erin Wolf for a "miracle" cure. But he never expected to care so deeply for Erin—or that her spiritual healing would forever alter him body and soul!

#1136 THE RANCHER AND THE SCHOOLMARM—
Penny Richards
Switched at Birth
Schoolteacher Georgia Williams was stunned when her fiancé passed her in the airport, got attacked and suffered amnesia. How would she handle the revelation that this riveting man who stole her heart was *not* her groom-to-be—but instead his long-lost identical twin?

#1137 A COWBOY'S TEARS—Anne McAllister
Code of the West
Mace and Jenny Nichols had the *perfect* marriage—until Mace discovered some sad news. Jenny was determined to convince her brooding cowboy of her unfaltering love—and that there was more than one way to capture their dreams....

#1138 THE PATERNITY TEST—Pamela Toth
Powerful Nick Kincaid could handle anything—except his mischievous twins. His new nanny, Cassie Wainright, could handle everything—except her attraction to Nick. Now Cassie was pregnant, and Nick was being put to the *ultimate* test.

#1139 HUSBAND: BOUGHT AND PAID FOR—Laurie Paige
Fearing for her life, heiress Jessica Lockhart hired P.I. Brody Smith—and then proposed marriage. Her aloof bodyguard agreed to a platonic union, but that didn't mean the lovely lady had the right to wiggle her way into his heart.

#1140 MOUNTAIN MAN—Doris Rangel
Gloria Pellman was a single mom, raising her young son, Jamey—alone, thank you very much! She didn't need a husband! But when Hank Mason rescued them from his rugged mountain, Jamey discovered a friend...and Gloria discovered her heart was in danger!

Daniel MacGregor is at it again...

New York Times bestselling author

NORA ROBERTS

introduces us to a new generation of MacGregors
as the lovable patriarch of the illustrious MacGregor
clan plays matchmaker again, this time to his three
gorgeous granddaughters in

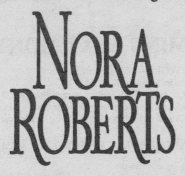

THE MACGREGOR BRIDES

From Silhouette Books

Don't miss this brand-new continuation of Nora Roberts's
enormously popular *MacGregor* miniseries.

Available November 1997 at your favorite retail outlet.

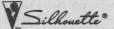